I0645063

My life was happy and contented for the first time in a long time—until I walked into the women's center...

"What's going on here?" I demanded.

There was a man, with a knife in his hand, threatening Beverly. He had her backed into a corner when I walked in the door.

"I'm going to cut up this bitch if someone doesn't tell me where my woman is."

"No, you're not!"

"What did you say to me?"

"I said, 'no, you're not!'" I repeated and started walking toward him. "You're going to leave her alone and get your useless ass out of here before I call the police."

"Gabby, get out of here."

"Don't worry, Beverly. In the army, I used to eat punks like this for breakfast."

He responded as expected. I had already sized him up and knew I could disarm him. He was all mouth behind that knife and only about twenty-five pound heavier than me. I was trained to fight in the service and spent weeks practicing self-defense when I took this job, just for moments like this.

"Are you dissing me, you bitch?"

"You're a lowlife punk, pulling a knife on a woman. Come here—" I motioned with my hand. "—and I'll take that knife away from you and castrate your little pecker." Yes, my anger had returned and I wanted to kill this bastard. Yes, I was stupid for taunting him, but I had my reasons. He shoved Beverly against the wall and growled at me.

In the moments she has remaining, as her battered body surrenders to Death's cold fingers, US Army Private First Class Gabriel Sumpter's life flashes before her, and her heartbeat slows. Beaten, raped, and left for dead in Afghanistan by a ruthless gang of fellow soldiers who think she's gay, she knows her chances of survival are slim. Even after she's rescued by a friend in the nick of time, the future holds little hope. If she recovers, which seems unlikely, she knows her life will never be the same. Her dream of making the army a career is definitely over, and what kind of life will she have while carrying the scars of her brutal attack, both inside and out? Three years later, still suffering PTSD, Gabriel's working for a battered women's shelter in her hometown of Pittsburgh, when she runs into the friend who saved her life, a man who'd stolen her heart in Afghanistan, and whom she hasn't seen since her rescue. But their budding romance is hampered, not only by Gabriel's PTSD, but she's also the target of a vicious killer and, this time, Death may win…

KUDOS for *Gabriel's Genesis*

In *Gabriel's Genesis* by E. Lessly Taylor, Gabriel Sumpter is a private in the army in Afghanistan. Chubby, self-conscious, and not a raving beauty, she tries to fit in by being as manly as possible, even to the point of carrying an unlit cigar in her month a lot of the time, so that most people think she's gay. Her best friend is a black corporal, Danny Washington, the only guy who sees through her façade. But their unlikely friendship angers some fellow soldiers, who cowardly attack, rape, and beat her, then leave her for dead. Danny finds her and saves her life, but Gabriel's career in the army is over. Once she heals from her injuries and returns home to the States, she goes to work for a women's shelter in Pittsburgh, where she runs into Danny, who's now a cop. Gabriel has changed a great deal. She is no longer chubby or unattractive and Danny falls hard. But as much as Gabriel would like to explore the relationship and where it might go, the PTSD she still suffers from her brutal attack make that a difficult path to follow. Although quite different from Taylor's first book *The Messiah Drug*, this story is heartbreaking, heartwarming, and filled with wonderful characters that you can't help but root for. ~ *Taylor Jones, The Review Team of Taylor Jones & Regan Murphy*

Gabriel's Genesis by E. Lessly Taylor is the story of a young woman who grows up in a home where she feels there are expectations that she can't meet. Our heroine, Gabriel Sumpter, has two beautiful older sisters and never quite measures up, at least in her own mind. To compensate, she becomes a tomboy, even joining the army, where most everyone thinks she gay, except the man who steals her heart. But when she is brutally attacked and left for dead in Afghanistan, everything changes. Suffering from PTSD from her rape by fellow soldiers, Gabby is unable to date or be intimate with a man, mistrusting them all. While working for a women's shelter in Pittsburgh, she discovers that Danny, the man who captured her heart in Afghanistan, is now a cop working two buildings down from where she works. The two try to pick up where they left off in the army, but Gabriel's fears of intimacy threatens to destroy their fragile romance, as her fears resurface. *Gabriel's Genesis* is a poignant and heartbreaking story of the struggle to overcome the effects of a brutal rape, something too many women have had to face. Well written and told with both compassion and sensitivity, it's a very worthwhile and thought-provoking read. ~ *Regan Murphy, The Review Team of Taylor Jones & Regan Murphy*

ACKNOWLEDGMENTS

Thank you, to all those who purchased and read my first novel *The Messiah Drug*. Like the first of anything, it meant something special to me. I'm very elated and encouraged to have received such wonderful reviews from everyone.

Gabriel's Genesis

E. Lessly Taylor

A Black Opal Books Publication

DEDICATION

*First to God, for the grace given me to share my stories.
To my wife, Carol, the one person I trust with my soul.
And to my kids, who have delighted me from the first
moment our eyes met. And my sisters-in-law,
God-sent to keep me on my toes.*

PROLOGUE

Gabriel

Hold your fire, Gabby," Danny shouted above the loud mayhem of weapons firing as we worked our way back toward our pinned-down platoon. "If we kill any more, our position will be exposed. The remaining Taliban don't know we're here yet."

Deadly bullets were raining down on our patrol, and all Danny could say was *don't shoot?* "Screw that, Danny," I told him as I took aim at the nearest enemy soldier. "They need our help."

"No, Gabby. The two of us are outnumbered and cut off from our platoon. If we continue returning fire, they'll know our position. I have a better idea."

The sounds of war were both frightening and captivating. There were screams, as bodies received terrible wounds from their flesh being ripped open by rifle rounds or shrapnel from exploding mortars. Nothing quickened you to the importance of life until you realized it could be snuffed out like a stepped-on bug—forever.

In this wild madness, people died on both sides, as

whistling rifle rounds pierced the air and each soul questioned as they fought, was the next bullet headed directly for that vulnerable spot between the eyes? The surviving combatants would later swear the thought of catching that fatal piece of metal never crossed their minds in the heat of battle. It was the warrior's code to claim nothing less.

"Okay, what's this plan of yours, Danny?" I asked after I took aim at the head of a Taliban gunman pursuing our platoon and then lowered my rifle. I was never one to rationalize a battle situation with a weapon in my hands. My solution—kill the enemy.

"Instead of holding their position and fighting, I think the cowardly lion has ordered the platoon to retreat, leaving us here alone. If we circle around that hill on our right, I think we can get in position to help them without getting ourselves cut off and becoming a target."

Danny's words did have a ring of truth to them. We were a platoon, but not a close one. Certain branches of the army swore to never leave a man behind. Those were trained to rely on their brother soldiers. But your basic army grunt was only looking out for his own ass, not that of a friend, like Danny was trying to do for me. So I followed him as we circled around a hill to our right until we were in position.

"Okay, Gabby, it worked. Look," he whispered and pointed to a hill across from us.

From the bushes we were hiding under, I spotted at least twenty of the Taliban soldiers that had ambushed the platoon when our rookie lieutenant, the cowardly lion as Danny called him, disregarded Danny's warning and led us into this suicide valley. The Taliban troops were moving to encircle our platoon, preventing what they called "infidel American troops" from escaping.

Earlier, we were approaching this strange valley that wasn't on our normal patrol route and, when Danny noticed, he made a point of informing our green lieutenant. "Sir?"

"What, Corporal?"

"I believe we missed our assigned waypoint and are approaching the wrong map position."

"Waypoints? What the hell is that? You sound like you were the one that graduated West Point—boy. Did you also attend West Point, ah…Corporal Washington?"

Ignoring that slight from the lieutenant, given to the delight of some of the other soldiers listening, Danny tried again. "Surely anyone who squeaked by graduating that illustrious academy can see that valley ahead isn't on the map coordinates that we were given—sir."

I watched as the WP grad's face became flushed at that put down. Danny had a way with words without being obviously defiant. And then stupid me let slip a chuckle.

"I tell you what, map reader, why don't you, and Private First Class Chuckles over there, take point and lead us through that valley ahead, since you are so sharp at knowing…ah…waypoints."

Danny stood there, shaking his head at the freckled-faced lieutenant, before nodding at me and picking up his weapon. Private First Class Chuckles grabbed her rifle and reluctantly joined him.

"You…boys…be careful out there now, and don't get your peckers shot off," that jerk the platoon had nicknamed Rockhound, because he has bad teeth like that always-horny actor in the movie *Armageddon*, shouted for all to hear. "Especially your big one—Private First Class Chuckles…ah…Sumpter."

I turned to curse him out when Danny stepped between us. The laughter from Rockhound and some of his buddies made our useless rookie platoon leader stick his skinny chest out. The fact escaped him that Rockhound was just sucking up and trying to get Danny's corporal stripes. Danny had earned them in a fair competition, proving he was the best soldier in the platoon before this green lieutenant was assigned as our leader.

Most of rural Afghanistan was a collection of steep hills and deep valleys. Many of the hills were bare of foliage and others had patches of forest. Those were the most dangerous, offering hidden positions for an ambush. That required Danny and me to risk life and limb, dutifully scouting each one, to prevent the platoon following us from being ambushed. Little did we know our rookie lieutenant had committed another grievous mistake. He allowed too much distance between Danny and me, scouting this valley, and the platoon. A large force of Taliban gunmen, hiding behind one of the many hills, waited until they had them trapped in that valley before opening fire. When the shooting started behind us, by the time we raced back, there were dead men from both sides lying in pools of blood on the ground.

From our position behind the ambushing Taliban troops, and in the loud madness of soldiers firing at each other, we were able to kill a half dozen of the enemy before we were exposed, giving our platoon time to reorganize and put the enemy in a possibly deadly crossfire. What we didn't expect was for our platoon to, instead, haphazardly retreat, leaving us exposed. That was when Danny pushed me under some bushes and ordered me to stop shooting. "What now, Danny?"

He took a deep breath before speaking, and I could tell his mind was racing. But this was when he was at his best—why he wore those two stipes on his sleeve.

"I think our subterfuge worked, and the Taliban doesn't know we're here. Let's work our way around them and see if we can save our comrade's asses. What do you think?"

"As an American hero once said, 'Let's roll!'"

Danny shook his head at my egotistic play on words, but he was right, as usual. We did catch up with what was left of our platoon and found them cornered behind some rocks with no way out and about to be overrun by about a dozen remaining Taliban troops firing down on their perilous position.

"Okay, this is where we decide who is the better shot."

"Oh, I thought the ribbon they gave me already answered that question," I said. He had caught me off-guard with that. Then I realized he must have seen my hands shaking and was trying to distract me.

"That was just target practice, and I let you win," he boasted as we took up position and got ready for…war.

"You let me? So, people are dying down there, and you want to have a competition?"

He just smiled and took aim. From our position, above and behind the enemy, we had them in a crossfire. As we were trained, we waited until one of Taliban would stand and fire from their hidden positions before we shot them. That helped shield the sound of our firing and kept us from being discovered until we had killed seven or eight of the enemy. The rest figured out their tenuous position and fled. Two of those died before the others disappeared behind a hill.

"Danny, Gabby, you guys saved our bacon," Tommy Jacks announced when we signaled the coast was clear to get out of here.

"Yeah, man, Tom's right. We radioed in our position and gunships are on their way, but we might have died by the time they got here," Jake admitted, voicing all of their opinions.

Not surprising, we were now welcomed as heroes by those who'd shunned us. The realization that came after seeing the Angel of Death close up, beckoning that dead boney finger at you, made close brothers of all—who survived. There were a few, including our lieutenant who was wounded, who later wanted to blame the death of those in the platoon who died on us. But the one question that none of them could answer, was why were we in the wrong location?

Lieutenant Cowardly Lion was still in charge of our platoon, but now most of the men put their confidence in the big brown man who was the last to board the helicopter for the ride back to camp. As the vehicle of our rescue winged its way south, others aboard plotted ways to break up the dynamic duo.

CHAPTER 1

Rockhound

US Army Charlie Company took up positions in section number seventeen, north of Kunar Province, Afghanistan. Their mission was to set up a base camp and outposts in the area and monitor Taliban movement from across the border in neighboring Pakistan. Stationed twenty miles south were helicopter gunships on alert awaiting orders to attack the enemy if spotted.

Like most of the country, this area was made up of high peaks and blind valleys that twisted between the hills, giving way to frequent ambushes from both combatants. For that reason, the rule was that two or more soldiers departed base camp together for a guard post in any Taliban suspected areas when relieving anyone on guard duty.

Outpost Baker was located high above the landscape about a mile from the temporary base camp, offering a panoramic view of anyone approaching but had a blind spot in its rear. Knowing this, the men lying in wait behind the outpost made sure they were out of the view of the guards there, so it was the perfect spot to grab this insubordinate soldier and teach her a much-needed lesson.

The full moon peeked between the hills, illuminating four angry men who waited impatiently as they hid along a heavily wooded path before spotting their prey. Watching the soldier nonchalantly climbing up the path, with weapon pointed at the ground, only augmented their belief that they would catch this bastard of a true soldier unawares. It was time to teach the arrogant dyke a thing or two.

This was a man's army, they preached while drinking in the barracks most of the day and coming up with this plan. There was no room for freaks in this battalion. It was bad enough there were too many spooks and wetbacks in this man's army. Now there was an increasing amount of gays and lesbos. This lesbo, in particular, pissed them off when she made a point of embarrassing them by sucking up to a spook in uniform. They were too friendly and acted like their shit didn't stink. No white woman should act like a whore. The bitch had no shame or respect for her kind, or the uniform, their alcohol-tainted reasoning concluded.

With her hair almost shaved off and the tattoos on her arms, she acted more like a man. They would show her what God made a woman for, they vowed.

With surprising swiftness, the intoxicated foursome leaped out from cover and quickly subdued their victim before she could raise her weapon and fire a shot. With her head covered in a pillowcase, the barrage of fists pounding her face quickly rendered her unconscious. Enraged, they dragged her off the trail, down into a small valley, and tossed her behind some bushes.

"I ought to piss on her and wake the bitch up first so she can enjoy this," the leader of this despicable band said as he removed her weapon belt, pulled down her pants, and took out a knife.

"Whoa, whoa, no need to stab the bitch."

"Shut up, Kyle." With a move that seemed practiced, Rockhound severed her army-issued camouflage pants and brown panties in half with one powerful stroke. He then placed the knife on her stomach and cut through her shirt, under shirt, and bra, exposing her breasts.

"Come on, just do her and get it over with," one of the men behind him said as the four stood staring down at the unconscious female soldier's nakedness in the moonlight.

"Shut up, Billy, we're going to spend all night teaching this bitch a lesson. When word gets out, those other bitches will fall in line. It's time we man up in this man's army, right?"

In the shadows someone grunted, seconding that.

During the assault, she regained consciousness and started fighting her rapist.

"Grab her hands," he commanded as she landed a few powerful punches to the face of her attacker. His cowardly companions reluctantly grabbed her and placed the weight of their bodies on her arms causing her to cry out in agony.

"Aaaaah! Get off me, you cowardly punks!" she screamed, ignoring the pain.

"Hell, no." Her rapist laughed. "We're not done with you yet, you—"

Twisting and fighting her assailants, but unable to see them with the pillowcase over her head, she struggled until she was able to slip her right hand free from one of the punks holding her down and she silenced her attacker in mid-sentence with a punch to the face, drawing blood.

"Hold her, dammit!"

Grabbing her breasts, he twisted them until she screamed. First she had to endure the shame of being attacked by fellow American soldiers, but then her enraged rapist started punching her in the face after he mistook her groaning for mocking laugher, when one of the cowards holding her arm twisted it.

"Is this funny now, bitch? Huh? Here, laugh this off." He then repeatedly punched the face underneath the bloody pillowcase. "What? What do you think of being with a real man, you lesbian freak? You like it, don't play coy." He laughed. "You like it."

The victim of his onslaught could no longer hear him after blacking out from his rain of punches.

"That's enough, man, you're going to kill her," one of his comrades in crime yelled at the repeated pounding he was administering.

"He's right," another added as he grabbed him. "That's enough. Come on, you taught the dyke a lesson. Let's get out of here before someone comes."

"Don't you boys want a taste?"

"Not after you nearly killed her. Look at her, she's a bloody mess."

"I don't give a damn if she dies. She's just a gay freak," he answered flippantly and slapped the bloodied pillowcase one last time. Then he got an idea to further humiliate her. "Help me turn her over."

"Why? Let's get out of here. Haven't you done enough?"

"Just do it. Let's try it this way. You're going to love this, you weird freak!" he screamed at the unconscious woman.

The other three, who'd soiled and denigrated the proud uniform they were wearing, let go of her and backed off, shaking their heads at what he was planning on doing to the dyke. From the sick smirk on his face, it was obvious he enjoyed degrading her.

Hell, they didn't care about that. Getting caught outside camp was their chief concern.

Standing and zippering up his pants afterward, he then kicked her in the ribs a few times until his accomplices had to pull him away.

"Enough, already. Come on, let's get out of here before we're missed back at camp."

"Okay, okay, Kyle. Damn! You know what? You guys are more of a dyke than that dyke."

When she groaned, as they walked away, he ran back, spit on her, and then savagely kicked the pillow-case. "Bitch!"

His three accomplices grabbed him by the shirt and dragged him up the hill and out of the small valley. Only the silent moon above, after witnessing their brutal assault, watched as the quartet slinked back into camp.

US Army Private First Class Gabriel Sumpter lay in the weeds, alone, partially nude, and nearly lifeless.

CHAPTER 2

Sergeant Rains

Having just finished writing the last of seven soldier evaluations, the sergeant's thoughts drifted to his family back home just starting their day, when his tactical communication phone rang. "Hello, Sergeant Rains here."

"Sarge, this is Donaldson, at Outpost Baker," the voice on the other end claimed.

"What do you want, Donaldson. Do you have to pee and want someone to find it for you?"

The man, on the other end of that put down, thought of something else his sergeant could do with it. "What—ah, no, Sarge. I was just wondering where the hell Sumpter is."

"What are you talking about?"

"It's Sumpter, Sergeant Rains, she was supposed to relieve me an hour ago," Private First Class Eric Donaldson claimed.

"Damn." Three of his men had suddenly claimed to have come down with the flu, and that negated sending the usual two men to relieve that guard station. Sumpter had taken it in stride, he recalled, when he explained she would be alone at that particular outpost tonight and laughed about being able to get some sleep.

"She checked in with me before she departed for your guard post, Donaldson. Dammit, I'll have to send out a patrol. Where's Watkins?"

"He's here, Sarge."

"Okay, one of you reconnoiter the area around your outpost."

"Okay, Sarge."

⁓⁓⁓

Danny

Twenty-five minutes later, an impatient Private First Class Donaldson spotted the heat signature of two soldiers in his night-vision goggles. They were heading toward his location. "It's about time those dickheads relieved us," he mumbled under his breath. He signaled them in code with his flashlight and hurried to join up with them.

"Hey, Danny, hey, Al, glad to see you guys. We were getting tired, waiting on our relief."

"Hi, Eric, we aren't your relief, Gabe was," Corporal Danny Washington explained. He was accompanied by Private First Class Al Burch. "Sarge walked into the barracks and ordered us out on patrol to find Gabe. I was last in the shower so I was elected."

"Hey, Danny, don't forget I was—"

"I know, I know, Al, you had a hot date. You keep reminding me about that. Have you seen her anywhere, Eric?" Danny asked, ignoring his complaining comrade.

"No, guys, and I've looked around the outpost but I

haven't spotted her. And with these lousy working night-vision goggles of mine, it's kind of tough to walk around in these thick woods in the dark without walking into something. And using a flashlight can attract the wrong people. You don't think the Taliban grabbed her?"

Neither man answered that question. It was something every soldier on guard duty feared. One never knew when or where the Taliban would attack. They could be male, female, or even a child. Both friendlies and the Taliban dressed alike. It seemed like, after every operation, someone was found either with their throat cut or not found at all. It was shoot first and ask questions later in the Afghanistan outback.

"Have you seen anyone moving around your outpost?"

"Only the two of you, Danny. What are we going to do?"

Danny just shrugged his shoulders. This wasn't like Gabe to wander off or neglect an assignment. With that huge chip on her shoulder—that thought provoked a snicker—she always needed to prove that she didn't need anyone's help.

"We didn't see her along the trail on our climb up here," Al Burch added, finally joining in the conversation, although still ticked off about missing his date.

"But we weren't actually looking off the trail either," Danny admitted. "Let's double back and check."

"What about my outpost?" Donaldson asked as they searched the areas on both sides of the trail leading up to the outpost. "That green rookie Watkins is there alone."

It was after Donaldson's question that they heard someone groan.

"Did you hear that?" Al whispered?

Danny nodded and risked pointing his flashlight to the right. There, the woods seemed the thickest, and with the bright moon overhead, each man realized it was a great place for a Taliban ambush. Danny motioned for each of them to spread out. If it was a setup, spreading out might guarantee one of them survived. The other two followed his lead as they carefully fanned out and then moved forward in the same direction. Had it been daylight, they would have quickly discovered her location. But in the dark, suspecting a possible ambush, it took them over ten minutes of carefully searching behind and under each bush and tree. With large boulders in the area, even with their thermal goggles, they were still susceptible to an ambush.

But the goggles did reveal a heat source farther ahead.

"Over here," Private First Class Burch whispered. He had to repeat it a little louder to get the others' attention. "There's something down in that gulley," he directed when they got close.

The three soldiers found her—bloodied, beaten, and unresponsive.

"Damn," Eric said when the pillowcase was removed and their flashlights illuminated the battered and bloodied face of the young woman. "She's a mess."

Danny checked for a pulse. "It's very weak, but she's still alive." He pulled up her severed pants and tugged her shirt over her exposed breasts. It was obvious to the three what had happened to her. "Give me a hand lifting her."

"No, Danny, we should leave her here and go get help. Moving her might do her more harm."

"Look, Eric, her pulse is so weak she may be dead by then. Either help me or I'll do it by myself. Either way I'm taking Gabe back to camp."

"What about my post?" Eric demanded. They each knew the question was directed at Danny, being the higher-ranking soldier. Eric sighed. "I can't leave a rookie alone there all night. He'll be scared shitless."

"Screw the post. We have a man down. Once we get her help, we'll come back and cover the post. On second thought, Al, you help cover the post until I can send someone to relieve you."

"Okay, Danny. I'm not getting laid now, anyway, why not?" Al whispered as he stood up and walked away.

"Help me pick her up, Eric," Danny ordered. Then, when she was in his arms, he nodded. "Okay, run ahead and let them know we're coming."

It was later decided his quick actions did save her life. She had swelling of the brain from a blow to her head and wouldn't have lasted more than a few minutes longer without emergency surgery.

ↄ✑ↄ

"The captain will see you now, Corporal Washington," Private First Class Jeanne Sturtevant announced to the handsome soldier who had been sitting across from her desk for the last twenty minutes. He had smiled and nodded at her when he first entered, and she told him to take a seat to wait on his review with the captain.

Only someone with previous knowledge of their past would have read beyond the innocent smirks and glances they traded. It wasn't a love affair, but definitely an affair. It was after the last of three parting shots of vodka in a bar that started it, but the memories they created together over the next two days cemented it. Now it was the aspirin they took for a headache that appeared once or twice a month at their, or worse yet, the army's expediency.

Their haphazard relationship was one of the many inconveniences soldiers experienced in a country where the lines of ownership were altered daily, producing sudden and unannounced shifting of locations. One could see the object of their affections daily or, in the shifting tide of this war, not for months. Thus, producing a tendency for one-nighters from even the most conservative with their futures so uncertain.

Danny looked into her eyes—avoiding the other secretary at another desk typing at her computer—winked when they reflected the same message, and then walked into the captain's office.

"Corporal Washington reporting as ordered, sir." Danny had expected to be called into his office when he turned in his report on what happened the night Private First Class Sumpter was attacked.

"At ease, Corporal, I have read your report. Normally what you did is frowned upon by medical people, you know that, right? You are never to move a critically wounded man."

"Yes, sir, Captain York, that's true. It is also known that you risk injuring someone giving them CPR, but it is worth the risk because, at that point, they are so close to death, it doesn't really apply."

The captain nodded at the young soldier. Like he'd told the colonel, he would have done the same thing. "Sit down, son," he said to the soldier standing at attention. The other news he had for him he knew would take him by surprise. "Son, you know we have been getting some very bad press back home about some of our female soldiers crying rape. I don't like this, but it has come down to me from high command that we label this as an attack by the Taliban." It didn't surprise him when the young corporal's face hardened and he just stared at him. But the captain knew the soldier had enough sense not to disobey orders, even though it was obvious, from the way he turned and shook his head, that he was pissed off.

"Sir, we both know that's not true. The pillowcase

used was army issue. I even have a hunch who it could have been."

"I read that allegation in your report, but you didn't name any names. Do you have any evidence? If you have hard evidence, I would love to hang this guy by his balls. If not, the report stands as is."

Danny just stared at the twenty-year army veteran. How could he allow them to railroad Gabby? If he had less time to go in the service, he might have asked him just that. But the thought of being suddenly transferred to some frozen and lonely outpost in no-man's land froze his tongue.

"You're dismissed, Corporal."

"Yes, sir." Danny stood up and saluted. He stared at stone face of his CO but, after deciding it would be a waste of time, he turned to leave.

"Wait, son."

Danny took a deep breath, turned, and faced his commanding officer.

"Listen, I understand you being pissed, I do." Captain York alluded as he walked around his desk and up to the soldier. "I understand she's a friend of yours. But it's the young lady who should be upset if she recovers, and, unfortunately, that's very up in the air I'm told. She will be shipped out to Landstuhl, that big military hospital in Germany, ASAP. This all came down from the old man. The general has a bug up his ass about women fighting in a battle zone. Actually, it's better this way than him using what regrettably happened to her as another reason to keep woman where they belong, according to him, at home."

"Yes, sir," was all Danny could think to say to his line of bullshit.

Captain York watched the young soldier walking out his office. From all reports, he was a credit to his unit, his other commanding officers all documented in his files, and was credited with saving the lives of his fellow soldiers on a few occasions, and this unfortunate soldier after she was attacked. He didn't know it yet, the captain thought as he sat down, but the corporal would be going home ASAP, as well as the others suspected of possibly being involved. Each to a different base at home to dissolve any potential confrontations.

Danny walked out of the captain's office an angry man. One of the secretaries was about to hand him a note about a party this weekend when he stormed past. Had the rapist been black, Washington was certain they would have thrown the book at him. Rockhound. Danny wouldn't be surprised if that lowlife, or one of the lowlifes he hung with, had something to do with Gabe being raped. But the captain was right about one thing, Danny didn't have any evidence.

Checking around, he discovered there were plenty of guys who had the opportunity. In a night encampment, it was easy to slip in and out of camp. Anyway, for the higher ups to cover this up like they had, whoever did this must be connected to some big wigs somewhere, or lucky as hell.

Danny decided to keep quiet about his conversation with the captain, but keep his ears open, because sooner or later, someone would get drunk and spill the beans. When they did, he would get even, somehow, for Gabby.

Little did he know someone had already anticipated that possibility and had set in motion the departure of everyone possibly involved. That included the victim, all of those who discovered the victim, and any possible trouble makers already under suspicion for having a problem with women in combat.

CHAPTER 3

Gabriel

I wasn't sure if I'd remember any of this later. Maybe that was why no one knew if comatose people were conscious of their surroundings—because they didn't remember anything about what it was like when they woke up. I could testify that a person in a coma did hear everything going on around them. What I wouldn't know until I woke up was if I'd also remember any of the things I felt and heard, possibly making that a moot point. Other than being unable to move a muscle or even raise my eyelids, I was awake. I was unconscious, but I was me.

Maybe if the doctors and nurses knew I was listening, they wouldn't talk so openly about my poor chances of ever completely recovering, about my vicious attack and battered face. *That's a bummer.* What great bed-side manners. They even complained about the smell of my crap when they had to clean me. The one doctor, he of the thick southern accent, apparently doubted if I would live much longer. If I could, I'd pee on his hand. He liked to slip it under my gown and check some unnecessary body parts when he was alone with me. *What? Am I a cadaver already? I guess there are some things I don't* want *to wake up and remember.*

I was in a military hospital. I knew that from hearing people called first by their rank and then their name. I knew my name was Gabriel Sumpter and I'd just turned twenty-one on…

Funny, I didn't know what day it was or how long I'd been lying here. I was unconscious, but I'd learned there were periods of deeper unconsciousness. I didn't know if it was actually sleep, but I blacked out completely for long periods…well, periods of time. I really didn't know how long, actually. It could be only for hours or days long, I just didn't know.

I probably should have started with why and how I got here. Painfully, all I remembered was walking to my scheduled outpost to relieve someone, I didn't remember who, and I was thinking about something funny one of my sisters said on her Facebook page. It was great being able to share things with them half the way around the world. I remembered smiling about that when I was hit from behind and knocked to my knees. Yes, I should have been playing attention, seeing it was getting dark out and nowhere, even miles behind our own lines, was completely safe.

I remembered being on my knees and groaning from the pain in my head. It was dark and became even darker when something was placed over my head. I was able to stagger to my feet, but when I tried to remove whatever was covering my head, fists started hitting me over and over. I tried to fight back, but they were coming from all directions. I remembered seeing stars, and hearing taunting laughter, before getting very weak and falling to the ground. Someone grabbed me, and I recalled being dragged along the ground. I tried to get up and fight back, but everything went black.

I couldn't imagine what my face must look like now, but if any of what I recalled was true…Lord help me. I was never the looker the other women in my family were, but hell, I must look like the elephant man lying here. I knew I was attacked and possibly raped. *By whom? you ask. I don't know. I see a face, faces, but they're blurry.* Whoever he or they were, he or they apparently nearly killed me. And according to that perverted southern doctor with the stink-finger, the jury was still out on that outcome.

I was a soldier in the US Fourth Infantry Division Charley Company stationed in Afghanistan. We were on patrol in Korangal Valley in what was Kunar Province. I was on my way to relieve soldiers on guard duty when I was attacked. Despite the trauma I'd suffered, I did remember one face. It was the handsome brown face of a good friend. I could see his face, and I knew we were close, but his name escaped me, for some reason.

When I recovered from this, and I believed I would, my dream to make the army a career was over. If I couldn't be safe with my brothers in arms, why stay? Sure, I'd read about other female soldiers molested by superior officers, and that was sick. But never one being nearly beaten to death. It didn't happen because I was a sex symbol. I grew up a fat, overweight, and average-looking redhead kid. And until my last year in high school, I had never even kissed a guy, much less gone out on a date.

The others in my household were the prototypical great-looking American family. My mom Cathy, even in her fifties, still had her looks and the taunt figure of a teenager and could pass for our older sister. A few times the grinning woman was asked just that when out with us girls. She was pretty, intelligent, and driven. John, my dad, whom I loved very much, could star in movies as the leading man he was so good looking, with his chiseled features and smiling eyes. He was a very successful attorney, loved the outdoors, and was the love of my life. I was a daddy's girl. Then there were my two older sisters Lea and Shay Sumpter. Well, they were Lea York and Shay Walsh now after getting married, a year apart. I thought it was because both of them were pregnant, but mother kept that a secret. Anyway, my sisters were so attractive, they had won almost every beauty contest they were in since they were teens. They were blonde, blue eyed, with centerfold good looks. And why did I love them so much? They were just as beautiful inside. Never once had they flaunted their perfect looks and off-the-rack figures at their rotund and mannish-looking, plain-Jane sister, but had been completely supportive of whatever I weird thing I'd done to myself—from coloring my hair bright colors to rebelliously wearing Dad's clothes sometimes.

My family was a beautiful foursome that could have decorated the cover of *People's Magazine*—and then I came along. I figured the gene pool was nearly empty when I was conceived. I would joke to myself that I was the oddball because they were trying some new position from the Kama Sutra when the little swimmers met the egg. *Should have stuck with the old Missionary position, Cathy and John.*

I wouldn't have been surprised to learn my father punched my mother in the mouth when he first saw me slip out from between her tanning-booth-brown, but pregnant, legs because there was no way I had any of their genes. I was a pudgy and a plain-looking child buried under freckles. All of the others in my family were tall and thin. My sisters had my mother's long thin neck, high cheek bones, long legs, sky blue eyes, and blonde hair. They had boys following them around like lost puppies since kindergarten. But me? I was a redhead like my father so maybe there *was* some of him deep in me. I sure as hell hoped so.

Growing up, I actually ate less than any of them, but still gained weight. The more my mother berated me about my weight, the more self-conscious I became. I would never be like her or her other daughters, I wanted to scream at her, but I didn't. Allowing someone as driven, but well-meaning as she was, to stifle my earlier expressions, became a detriment to my emotional growth. I knew she just wanted the best for me, but it caused me to eventually rebel and purposely gain weight…well, not purposely, but I did, because I no longer cared and ate whatever I wanted.

At fifteen, I cut my hair very short on one side and colored it a different wild color, sometimes every month. It would be much later before I got up the nerve to get a few of the many tattoos I wanted. Eventually, my mother gave up trying to craft me in the Sumpter image. No more diets placed on the refrigerator for all to see. I no longer had to attend the beauty contests and be envious watching one of my sisters walk away with the crown. Looking back, I thought my absence pleased my mom more than me, for obvious reasons.

That was when my dad stepped in, and we began to do everything together. He taught me how to shoot guns, and he was surprised that I was very good at it. We often went hunting and fishing together, and he laughed when I wasn't afraid to handle worms or bait my hook with squiggly minnows. We did all the things he loved but could never do with his petite wife and feminine daughters.

That's why I loved him so much. He accepted his fat,

talentless daughter, with the blue or green hair without the least bit of criticism. When I decided I wanted to join the army instead of college, it was the only time I remembered him telling my mother to shut up when she vigorously opposed it.

Now, should I recover or not, I was afraid it was something she might hold over that caring man's head and that bugged the shit out of me. Thinking about that hurtful period of my life pained me and I wanted to black out again for a while.

Chapter 4

Danny

Three years later:

Okay, guys, just like we practice all the time, let's be quick and thorough. We want to take him alive if possible, but he might be heavily armed. If we have to take him down, shoot to kill. Van one will enter from the front of the building. Van two will cover the rear, and van three will move up after we enter and cover the front," Pittsburgh Police SWAT Captain Jerry Handover commanded over their head phones. "Okay, let's roll."

A black van pulled up to an apartment building on Sturdivant Street. It differed little from the row of apartment buildings on the block, except for the six heavily armed SWAT officers charging toward the front door and up the steps in prefect formation. They entered the building and raced to the third floor apartment of one Victor Hugo. He was wanted for the murder of a store clerk during a simple robbery gone bad.

SWAT Officer One stopped and motioned for cover from SWAT Officer Two. One and Two stopped at door number thirty-six. Officers Three, Four, and Five moved up as Officer Six remained at the top of the stairs, covering the steps and protecting their egress.

"Go!"

Officer Three kicked in the door as the other officers rushed into the apartment.

"Pittsburgh Police! Hands over your heads," multiple voices commanded as they spread out in the apartment. After searching every room, they found the apartment empty.

"No sign of him, Captain. And no indication he came back here after the robbery attempt."

"Yeah, Wash. Maybe it was a bad tip that he was spotted here. But this is his place, all right. I'll get some plain clothes detectives to keep it under surveillance. He might come back later."

"If we don't catch him first, Captain."

"The apartment is clear, we missed him. Saddle up," the CO commanded over the SWAT head phones.

SWAT Officer Three walked down the steps, chatting with Captain Handover. "I hate it when a mission ends this way, sir. A whole day wasted."

"Yeah, I know, Wash, but your day's over, mine's just beginning. I've got to write all this shit up and try to explain how in the hell we missed him."

They had just reached the first floor when they bumped into a woman walking in the front door.

☙❧

Gabriel

When I pulled up to Rosa's apartment building, there

were cops everywhere. That gave me an ominous feeling because her abusive boyfriend had threatened to kill Rosa, and I feared he had done just that after I had promised we could keep her safe. My heart was pounding in my chest as I climbed out my car. Ignoring the obvious, I hurried up the steps to the building.

"Excuse me, miss." A SWAT officer stepped in front of me at the base of the front steps. "You can't enter this building."

Now I had visions of Rosa's blood splattered all around her apartment and her body cut up in pieces. *Yes, I have a very vivid imagination.* I was afraid to ask this huge lawman how it had happened. I wasn't sure if I wanted to know.

"Wait," he added just before my stomach ejected my lunch and after seeing the other Swat Team members exiting the building en mass. "I guess it's safe for you to enter now."

"Thank you, Officer."

Now that I was able, I wasn't sure if I wanted to enter, not knowing what was waiting for me in Rosa's apartment. I took a deep breath and, after three or four huge cops walked past me blocking out the sun, I reluctantly climbed the steps and walked into the building.

"Oh!" I was startled by the sudden appearance of two additional large police officers in heavy gear and with large weapons who stepped directly in front of me. Everything about these men seemed large. They smiled from under their raised face shields and stepped aside to let me enter. It was like walking between two obelisks.

"Officers." I decided to risk asking as they turned their backs and were leaving. "Can I trouble you to hang around a few minutes more? I work for a women's shelter." I read the disinterest in their body language but continued anyway. "I have to pick up this battered woman from an apartment on the second floor, and I'm afraid there might be some trouble."

I noticed the officers looking at each other and, from their lackadaisical attitude, I knew I would be going it alone. I sighed and started to walk away.

"Sure, miss," one of the cops said, stopping me in my tracks. "Officer Wash here would love to assist you. Wouldn't you, Officer? We *are* here to protect and serve. Right, Officer Wash?"

I stood there, stunned, as if my panties had fallen around my ankles.

"Ah, sure Captain Handover," the other officer said in a voice devoid of enthusiasm. "Oh." He'd taken a reluctant step toward me, when he stopped and turned toward the retreating officer. "You are going to leave me a vehicle, right?"

I watched the cop he called captain laugh as he ignored the other officer and walked out of the building. Officer…whatever his name was…just turned and stared at me. That was the first time I ever regretted asking the police for help. "I can give you a lift back to your station," I volunteered, hoping to mend fences.

"Thanks," he said but, even shielded by the dark sunglasses he was wearing, I could tell he obviously didn't mean it.

I didn't care if he did or not, as long as he was there. Then he smiled at me.

During the next half hour, I was so glad he was there. Rosa's boyfriend Hector, and another man, arrived at the apartment about fifteen minutes later and just walked in without knocking. Her loser boyfriend ignored the officer, got into a shouting match with Rosa, and then became very hostile when she tried to leave.

"Where do you think you're going?" the boyfriend asked.

"I'm leaving you, that's where I'm going. You aren't going to hit me anymore."

"We can work this out, Rosa," Hector said, stepping in front of her. "Don't be a bitch."

"Who are you calling a bitch? Get out of my way, loser."

I was about to step in when the cop stuck his arm out preventing me.

The boyfriend got in her face. "Don't you dare disrespect me in front of these strangers!" he shouted, trying his old pattern of intimidation. "They won't stop me from kicking your ass, girl." He knocked a lamp off the end table that shattered when it hit the floor. It seemed to encourage him. That, and the dude with him, laughing. "Just because this woman is here interfering in something that is none of her business, or this cop," Hector said. "I'll kick your ass and his, even if I go to jail. No one disrespects me, bitch!" he yelled and raised a fist at Rosa.

"That's enough," I heard this gruff and commanding voice order in the mayhem.

When the officer stepped in to intervene, I was surprised when both men jumped him. Before I could help, he punched out the friend and kicked the boyfriend's ass all over the apartment. I had to move quickly out the way when that loser Hector was tossed over the couch and bounced off the floor near my feet, almost knocking me down. I received a *"Sorry,"* from the tosser. He only stopped stomping Hector's ass when a begging Rosa stepped between them and pleaded. The other guy was still in dreamland on the floor.

Bad ass cop, I was thinking. *Bad ass.*

The apartment was quickly full of cops and the losers were arrested for assaulting a police officer. Truth was, they were the ones being assaulted. They threw some punches, but I didn't think a single one landed. Plenty of his sure did. I just stood there, mesmerized by the ease in which he quickly dispensed of them—without losing his sunglasses. Wow. I felt like I was back in the army, kicking ass, for a moment. Wow.

After things calmed down and the apartment emptied, I wasn't sure exactly when it dawned on me that something about Officer Wash or Walsh...or something...seemed very familiar. When the two idiots were arrested and taken away, I asked if he was leaving? He smiled at me and then said no. He was sticking around for his ride.

Rosa was in her bedroom collecting some jewelry she had almost forgotten, and we were alone in the living room. I had noticed him watching me when he thought I wasn't looking. He wasn't my type, but I had to admit there was something appealing about him. Maybe it was just his being there when I needed him or...or, being ex-army, maybe I was just impressed with the way he handled himself. I didn't know, I wasn't sure, but I felt a little uncomfortable being alone with him now. Why? Any man that...physical...stirred my blood...a little. He was on the other side of the room, standing at the door as our protector, and had little to say, but there was just—

"Ah, thank you for being here," I said when I got up from the couch, turned, and looked over at him. I shouldn't have, because he smiled and then walked over to where I was standing.

"At least the trip here wasn't a complete waste."

"What?" I looked up, pretending not to be affected by this man standing over me, blocking out the light.

"We came here to get one asshole," he said to my confused question, "and ended up with two. And what's the chance of finding a beautiful red rose in this outhouse."

The smile on his face behind those glasses, and that

smooth deep base voice saying that, took me back to—
No! I had covered my mouth and then dropped my hand
so as not to seem obviously shaken.

"What's wrong?" he asked with this smirk on his
face.

"Nothing. Excuse me," I said and went looking for
Rosa. "I just remembered something," I whispered to myself as I backed away from him. And then the next sound
was Ms. Play-it-Cool tripping over something on the
floor and ending up falling down on her butt.

"Oh, my, are you okay?" I sat there wondering how I
was going to play this off when he stepped around the
couch, leaned down, and offered me his hand. "Let me
help you, miss."

I meant to say thank you or something, but, when he
was lifting me up, I was so close I could smell his cologne. I could feel the heat from his body. Our lips were
close for a moment. Thank God, he didn't release me
right away, or he would be picking me up off the floor
again. "Ah—thank you, Officer—ah, thank you."

"No problem. Are you sure you're okay?"

"I'm fine."

"Believe it."

It was him. My body could sense it from the way my
knees went weak. I walked in and had to sit down on Rosa's bed. If that was him, why—

"…and I can't find my mother's rings," Rosa was
saying.

I was so shocked I wasn't paying attention.

"Let's go, he probably stole them, the punk," she
confessed angrily.

*Thank God those eyes are hidden behind his sun-
glasses,* I thought as Rosa grabbed my arm and was tugging at me for some reason. At one time, those eyes almost made me reveal to him just how I felt, back then,

and I still remembered how those tantalizing eyes kept me awake nights, tossing in my army bunk—and doing other things. *But that was a long time ago*, I told myself, and today I was sure he was a different Danny Washington. I knew for damn sure, I was a very different Gabriel Sumpter.

"Shall we go?"

I quickly turned. "What?" I asked her.

"I'm ready to go."

"Okay, okay, Rosa. Are you ready—oh, never mind." I followed her out of the bedroom and right into—

"Are you ladies ready?" he asked, standing right in front of me—us.

I had to peel my eyes away from him. One, so I could breathe again before I fainted, and, two, Rosa was standing there with her suitcase and seemed anxious to get out of here, fearing her boyfriend might return.

"Oh, okay. Let's go then," I caught myself mumbling nervously.

When Rosa started to climb in the back seat of my car, I almost stopped her. After unlocking my car, when Danny turned his head for a moment looking around, I had motioned to her to get up front with me. The teasing hussy grinned at me and then purposely climbed in the back seat. What I feared, happened. That large man rubbing shoulders with me in my small car was a distraction. I almost pulled over and asked him to get in the back, but he was still wearing all that SWAT equipment and looked very intimidating. Add to that, the manly scent emanating from the guy seated beside me was like pollen to this bee. I'd always loved his choice of colognes. They were never eye watering like some, or you could smell them coming for miles. No, one had to almost be in his arms to notice, and when you were that close, it seemed to hint of even more exciting things.

Okay, stop it, Gabby. He is probably married with kids. Or, or dating someone. Or with your luck, now he's gay.

"Nice!

"What?" I stopped trying to get my key into that stubborn ignition slot that seemed to purposely move, thwarting my effort. Funny, it never was that hard to do before.

"I said, nice car."

"Where can I drop you off, ah…Officer…ah, Wash?"

"The Zone Two, West End Police Station, if that's not too far out of your way."

Shocked, I stopped trying to start the car and looked over at him. *Okay, what's going on here? That station is two doors down from the WARV—Women Against Rape and Violence—office. That can't just be a coincidence.*

"Is that too far out of your way?" he asked, noting my hesitation.

"What? Ah…no. Actually, our building is on the same block a few buildings away. We like to be close to police stations, when we can, to help protect our clients. But, to be in honest, we have only been in that building a few weeks." I smiled at him and he seemed okay with my answer.

All the way over there, I noticed him repeatedly staring at me as I drove. I was praying he wouldn't ask me a certain question and make me lie. I almost made it, but when I parked my car he sat there, scrutinizing me. He had chatted with that traitor in the back seat, who was making eyes and sticking her tongue out at me in my mirror, about living here and about the best places to eat and party. I had nothing to say to either of them as I drove, just nodded or shook my head.

He took off his glasses when I parked and turned to

both of us. "Thank you for the ride and pleasant company, ladies."

I finally got the chance to stare into those eyes. If it was possible, they were even more seductive, and, even in his work gear and a day's beard, he was better looking than I remembered.

"My name is Danny Washington. Can I ask you yours?"

I looked at him and opened my mouth, but nothing came out.

"Her name is Gabriel Sumpter, and mine is Rosa Hernandez. Miss—Rosa Hernandez," the hussy emphasized.

I spun around and looked back at the traitorous, flirtatious woman in my back seat. She was grinning at me, clearly knowing what she was doing. Another woman could sense when there were naughty vibes between a man and woman.

I wasn't sure I wanted to look at him again after that. I sat with my head down, avoiding his. My appearance had changed a lot so, if he didn't recognize me, that was understandable. None of my friends had. But forgetting my name—no! Surely, he remembered my name. If he didn't, I would really be disappointed. For a moment, no one spoke. The silence could mean one of two things. I was afraid to see one of those two things on his face, and afraid to admit I was hoping for the better of the two.

I heard a door opening and quickly looked to my right. He was still sitting there staring at me. It was that traitorous Rosa who had given up waiting and decided two was company and three…

I watched her walk around the front of my car, grinning at me from ear to ear. We were expected, so I knew she would be buzzed in and taken care of when she entered our building.

"Gabriel."

Just the way he said my name made my knees weak. It had been three long years, and when I heard him say my name I knew that, after all this time, and all I'd been through, I still had feelings for him. That surprised me. I had labeled all men with the same pen. *A-holes!* And, after all this time of building up a wall, how could he so easily kick it down with one word?

"Gabriel?"

Three years of emotional and physical abstinence, and after dealing with the terrible after effects of my assault, just hearing my name—and now I was thinking— But who could blame me. Other than those times when I couldn't sleep and had to take something out of my sock drawer and relieve my built-up tension, I had reconciled all my energies to my job. It wasn't a planned celibacy, but after the trauma of growing up a withdrawn child, of being brutally attacked and nearly killed in the army, of the radical changes in my appearance and personality, I had just put that important part of life on hold. As inexperienced as I was with men, anyway, I couldn't know what I was missing because I had yet to taste that life. You could only imagine the taste of that beautiful cake pictured in the magazine that your taste buds never savored and could only envision what it must be like.

I had reluctantly accepted a few dates, after recovering and returning home, sometimes just to get out the house and to stop feeling sorry for myself. The truth was, I recoiled whenever a man touched me, and, in my pitiful case, that could be from a simple kiss on the cheek for a nice evening. The nightmares would return and throw, not just cold, but iced, water on any plans he or I might have had.

I needed therapy and that had helped—a little. But now, after looking in those dancing brown eyes and hearing my name spoken from those full lips, I realized maybe I was the one missing out.

In my panic, I started to get out the car when he grabbed my arm. I gritted my teeth and had to look away until he finally released me.

"Wait. It is you. I can't believe how much you've changed. Girl, you're beautiful."

Those words drew my eyes to his like flies to sh— no, ah…like bees to honey. I wanted to say something but—

"Well, I can see the last few years have been great to you. Wow. I kept telling myself I was imagining things in that apartment. That beautiful redhead couldn't be my Gabby."

His Gabby? Say something, girl. Right! My body was trembling, not to mention that my stomach was in my throat. *But this is your Danny*, I tried telling myself.

We had spent a lot of time alone in Afghanistan on patrol and guard duty. Everyone believed I was a lesbian then, so the guys kind of avoided me, but not Danny. We would talk about everything. He would tell me about the women he was with, and there were plenty, and we would discuss everything like two guys or two close friends would. Coming from Pittsburgh, we were both rabid Steeler fans and would debate if we hated the Ravens or the Cowboys the worse.

And he was the only one who eventually saw through my masquerade and told me…

CHAPTER 5

Three years earlier:

Danny and I were sitting at our guard post north of one of the quick-response camps we set up in the region. There was a report that the Taliban was trying to infiltrate the main base at night again to get close enough to launch a mortar attack, killing our boys, and then sneak back across the border. We finally got tired of that…crap…and set up quick-response camps. At our guard post, we were set up with a long distance thermal scope to scan our appointed area after dark. Intelligence reported the valley below us was often used by the Taliban, and our orders were to call in any movement. There were the usual squadron of copters waiting in the rear to attack anyone we spotted before they could get close. But it was like Danny always said, we couldn't rely on them to protect our asses. We had to be prepared to defend ourselves, if necessary, or be overrun.

Everything looked quiet the first four hours. If we made it through the next eight hours, we had a week of leave waiting on us. That started the usual conversation about our plans for R and R. Danny was talking about Susie, a nurse he was seeing, and how passionate she was. I didn't realize until it was too late that it was a lie to catch me in one.

"How much time do you have before rotating back home, Gabby?"

"Three months. Seems like three years.

"I know, right?"

"I want to—"

"Don't thank me, Gabby, if that's where you're headed. You would do the same for me. I know that," he added.

"Well, I owe you."

"See? No, you don't. I thought you knew that, girl. Before we leave here, you may save my life, that's how it works. Or you may save someone else and that person saves mine. That's how it works in a combat zone, so no more of that I-owe-you crap."

It was what I expected him to say. Most guys would have made a disgusting suggestion about how we could settle that debt that had something to do with my kneeling in front of him, but not Danny. Was he thinking things like that? Oh, yes, no doubt, because he was a man. Hell, women thought the same thing about men and so was I but, like him, I never would have teased him about it.

When he moved forward from where we were sitting and scanned the valley below our lookout post with the thermal scope, I had a moment to reflect on my friend Danny Washington. He was tall at about six three or six four, and a solid, muscular man at around 230 pounds. Physically, he was a muscular brute, with the personality of a boy scout and the smile of a con man. He was a ruggedly handsome brown man. You didn't have to like him, or him you, to get along with Danny, but the few who messed with him got a wild man and their butts kicked.

Word was out—just leave him alone. And with him being my friend, I noticed they also made less fat dyke or lesbian jokes around me.

I didn't know why, but we became good friends. He was such a flirt and seething with confidence, and that was a quick turn off for me when we first met. Maybe it was because we were both different. I was butch-looking with my short hair and tattoos, and he was the only black soldier in our group. We had quite a few southern boys, but only a few were bigoted assholes toward either of us.

Even more surprising, I started having feelings for him. Not surprising for a female, because he was a great-looking guy with an endearing personality, but surprising for this woman, pretending not to like men. But the women he fooled around with were all petite and pretty. I was heavy but a toned 160 pounds and masculine looking with my normally auburn hair buzzed cut close and dyed black. But that playboy never let another woman interfere with our friendship, and I admired him for that. If we were doing something or just sitting at a table eating, any woman who came on to him or that he wanted to talk to, he always put it off until he was alone. Maybe that's why we became—

"What?"

He snickered after disturbing my trance. "I said the valley looks clear. No bodies in the thermal scope."

I was so busy imagining being in his strong arms, I hadn't noticed when Danny turned and spoke to me.

"Good," I said. "Maybe we can take turns getting some sleep tonight. You can be first."

"See, Gabby? I knew you wanted me to go first just to get me in a vulnerable position and asleep so you can do weird things to my body."

"Yes," I said when he sat back and tried to look serious, "that's what I dream about, you turkey."

He laughed, but little did the grinning turkey realize lately that was just what I was dreaming about. There were those few days, just after that wonderful time each month, when I craved him—Damn!

After another scan of the valley below for any Taliban, we started talking again about the week off we have coming up in a couple of days.

"Do you have any plans for the week, Gabby?"

"To be honest, I just want to get away from all this and sleep for a few days."

"Same here."

"What? You getting sleep? I heard you talking about all the hot nooky you wanted to get." I knew quoting him the way he talked in front of the guys, when he thought I wasn't around, would make him uncomfortable. It did. He gave me that look he got when tongue tied. Poor guy, I wanted to laugh. *You're not the ladies' man everyone thinks you are, are you?*

"I do have another date with that nurse at the air base at Jalalabad." He removed his helmet. "I'm not sure if I can get a pass, but I hope so because she is amazing in bed."

It didn't surprise me anymore when he talked frankly about sex with the women in his life. I sensed he wasn't bragging like men did. He was that comfortable around me was how I took it.

"She just loves oral, giving and getting."

"What?"

"Susie, the nurse I was telling you about, she loves oral. Do the women you date love oral? Duh! I guess they would have to woman to woman, right?"

Studying that picture in my mind caught me off-guard. "I don't know, I guess," I said.

Then he got real quiet. It never occurred to me that two women making love to each other would be licking…everything. My only sexual experience was laying there and having my boyfriend Harold spending sixty painful seconds taking my virginity, during my senior year in high school, and risking getting pregnant during two other even quicker unscheduled attempts. I'd never even seen a man naked, other than in mags, movies, or online.

I knew it was my crazy outward appearance that underlined everyone's judgment about my sexual preferences. Hell, that started back in high school. I knew that, and I acted the part around the guys here, but I only pretended to hit on the women in uniform, even though a few had hinted they were interested. By giving out high fives to the guys, and adding F-bombs to the end of every other sentence I spoke, it sold my ruse and prevented me from getting fondled or worse, like some of the other women tearfully complained about when we were all alone.

"Why so quiet?" I asked him after a while. It was obvious something was on his mind.

"Gabby?" he asked, giving me a look I had never seen before. "You consider us good friends, right?"

I sensed he was about to say something I didn't want to hear, so I ignored him, moved over to the tripod holding our thermal scope, and scanned the valley again. Like the other times, thankfully, I saw no movement in the scope. "Yes, Danny, I consider us good friends," I answered when I sat back with him.

"Then why keep it a secret from me?"

He didn't say what "it' was, and that was another reason why I liked him. I knew the gig was up, so I took a deep breath, leaned back, and closed my eyes. I even thought about confessing everything and then kissing him.

"Gabby, we don't have to talk about it."

"Look, Danny." I took off my helmet and turned toward him. "I've never claimed to be anything but what I am. People just looked at me and assumed I'm gay, and, yeah, I have never refuted them, I guess."

"Well, if I offended you by talking about screwing other women I've dated, I apologize."

I could have taken that the wrong way. Was it okay to be frank with gay women but not with straight? "No, no, Danny, I loved listening to you boast," I teased.

"Boast," he said, laughing. "What boast? I'm the real deal, girlfriend. And now that we've cleared that up, I'll try and leave some time for you in the back of my date book."

"Oh, you will, huh?" I answered, admittedly amused by his bullshit.

"You are my best buddy, of course I will. Hell, you also deserve a piece of heaven." He spread his arms. "But I have to warn you, with my long waiting list, it may take a few months for your turn."

"A few months, huh? I'm sure your list is as short as—"

"Don't go there. I'm sorry, but you'll have to work your way to the front."

"You're a dickhead."

"It's a good thing that thermal scope is pointing the other way."

"What? Why? Oh, you *are* a dickhead."

"Your hot body would burn out the lens from sitting this close to me."

That was how easily we played with each other when we were alone. He was the first person I could talk openly about…well, just about any subject, and we did. Unknowingly, he taught me more about sex, when talking about some of his exploits with women, than anyone had while I was growing up, including Harold's few minutes total humping on me. Sometimes, I thought Danny forgot I was a woman and talked to me like one of the guys. I enjoyed listening to a man's view of things.

I never let on, but I was often shocked by what he, and some of the other women in my barracks, admitted actually doing with their lovers. I knew this wasn't the '50s or '60s, and what could be shocking anymore, right? But I grew up somewhat shielded because I wasn't popular, being the butchy fat girl. Some of the women here admitted to having new partners almost every week. Elaina, a little thing weighing about a hundred pounds, admitted she like doing more than one guy at a time, and some of the others agreed that was on their Bucket List. *Their Bucket List, really?* I sat there on my bunk speechless, and I figured they accepted that, thinking it was because I wasn't into men.

Danny and I maintained that great friendship, but I believed he started looking at me a little differently after that night. I looked at him in a different light now that he knew.

Looking back, he rarely talked about being with other women after I admitted my masquerade. I took that as a complement, rather than his now being embarrassed. We joked about everything else—but sex.

I always had one type of conversation when alone around him, and another when others were present, if I spoke at all, which was usually not the case. I had included the F-bombs in every sentence I spoke, when I spoke, to underline the toughness and masculinity that people perceived I had, and it worked.

Also, never wearing any makeup on this pale white skin that redheads were born with helped, as did dressing only in loose fitting army-issued clothes all the time.

I carried a cigar in my mouth on occasions, but never lit the nasty-tasting thing. I would just bite off the end and no one seemed to notice or call me on that. Why maintain the deception? I didn't know why at the time. I came to realize that all of the people I met, who acted tough, were hiding an emotional weakness. Later, I discovered that included me.

And for the first time after that night, and my mother would love knowing this, I found myself wishing I was the skinny woman she craved for me to be. Because I started wanting Danny to look at me as a desirable woman and not just his army buddy. What were the words to that song? "Regrets…I've had a few. But then again, too few to mention…"

CHAPTER 6

A few of the empty army barracks on base were turned into various forms of recreational abodes. Some were for sports, like pool, table tennis, and foosball. Others became meeting places for drinking and socializing. There was a barracks on base with a black and gold door for soldiers from Steeler country in western Pennsylvania. That barracks was full of people drinking and having a party when I walked in. Most weren't from the area, but that mattered little because the barracks was known for having a good time.

There was music playing and a few couples trying to dance around others standing around shooting the breeze. There was what passed for a bar on one side, serving whatever booze we could garner. Usually only beer was served. The walls were adorned in Steeler football posters from Swann to Big Ben. Terrible Towels were hung from the light fixtures. Six tables were in the back of the barracks and were packed.

Most of the women were dressed for the occasion, from shorts to miniskirts but, like the men, I wore army fatigues. Everyone seemed to be having fun. Through the merriment, I spotted Doris and Janet at one of the tables on the far side with Danny and a soldier I only knew as Joe.

As I squeezed through the revelers, I saw a real "dick" named Dick, or actually Richard, at the table next to theirs with some of his country boys. Dick was also from the Pittsburgh area, but there were always some southern country boys who followed him around. He was usually making some stupid gay joke around me or a black joke when Danny wasn't around. Funny thing was that changed when a certain handsome guy was here.

The regulars hung out here when we were able to get some special food to eat, booze, or sometimes to smoke some grass. None of us did the heavy drugs…well, none but that dick and his hicks at the next table.

"Hey! There he is. My man," Dick said, high-fiving the other losers and mocking me.

I heard Dick shout above the usual drinking clamor and music. It became clear who it was as I approached the tables. That same asshole stood up and made a scene of repeating it. The group at Danny's table ignored that idiot, turned, and greeted me.

"My man—Gabby!"

I shot that dick at the other table the finger. He just gave me that stupid grin of his.

"Hey, girl," a slightly inebriated Doris said, greeting me.

"Hey, Doris." I did notice she was sitting next to Danny with only one hand on the table. He told me where she liked to keep the other one and, being a man, he didn't seem to be complaining. That had never bothered me—until lately.

"Come grab a seat, Gabby," Danny suggested. "Joe here came up with a case of cold beer. We smuggled some in here. There's three left if you want one."

I was about say, "Heck yeah," when that poor excuse for a soldier behind me opened his big mouth again.

"Yeah, Gab," that dick-head at the adjoining table said, injecting himself into our conversation. "The great thing is when you finish with a bottle of beer you can take it back to your barracks and pretend it's a black dude humping you. Opps," the drunk idiot added. "Make that a brown dude, like big Danny here. After all, the bottles are—"

"We know, asshole, the bottles are brown."

"Who are you calling an asshole, you bitch?" he asked threateningly. Spit flew from his mouth, and he made a fist, as if he intended to hit me. "Or should I say—butch?"

"Say whatever you want," I said when he walked around to where I was standing. "One thing we both know." I got right in his face. "How does it go in Rent? Oh yeah, I'm more man than you are now, and I'm more woman than you will ever get—little pencil—Dick! And we all know where you like to place brown bottles don't we—" Bending over, I pointed at my ass. "—little Dickey?"

The cat-calls and laughter exploded, in a barracks that had quieted down when we started arguing. I figured that was what prompted him to slap me. I fell backward into some guys at another table.

Danny disengaged himself from a petite hand holding him under the table and jumped between Dick and me.

Danny shoved him. "Back off!"

"Screw you, Washington."

I had regained my feet and was about to return the slap with a punch or a kick in the balls, when Danny, inadvertently pushed me back into the same table of guys, trying to get at Dick. "What did you say to me?" Danny asked. He had been about to apologize for pushing me when he heard that punk talking smack.

"You heard me!"

Those were the last words "Dick" was able to say as Danny snatched and tossed him across one of the tables. Someone from that table grabbed Danny from behind. Mistake. Danny elbowed him in the head and then back-kicked him across his table. Two others took a step toward him, but changed their minds when he motioned for them to keep coming. They had all seen him kick butt before but the alcohol, or whatever they were smoking, had dulled their memory.

"Black bastard!"

Danny turned to face a renewed loudmouth coming at him with a chair raised over his head. A front kick sent the chair and the holder flying across the floor and out cold. The fight had only lasted a minute, but by then Dick, was a limp dick.

Danny, to the displeasure of a frowning Doris, hustled an angry woman who wanted revenge, back to my barracks before the MPs arrived. I was a little pissed at him for interfering.

"I want to fight my own battles."

"I know that, Gabby. I kicked his ass not because of a little slap, but because he called me out in front of everyone. I know you can handle yourself, but I can't have guys thinking I'm a punk."

When I looked up at him, he seemed very serious about that. It made me feel good, and I had to admit having him fight for me felt even better. Maybe now was a good time to tell him how I felt, and—then I chickened out when I remembered what he was enjoying when I first walked into that barracks.

Two days later, we were on patrol in the Korangal

Valley in Kunar Province. We made a quick-response base camp there, and I drew one of the guard duties. True, along with Danny, I was one of the best sharp shooters in our platoon, but I would have sworn I got that guard duty because word got out about the fight. It was while walking alone to Outpost Baker, to relieve two soldiers, when something hit me on the head and I…

CHAPTER 7

Present Day:

It took a couple of hours to get Rosa straightened out. In our lingo, that meant her ride arrived and she would be driven to another town and then flown or driven to another state to start over again. Thankfully, she didn't have any kids. That made it tough on everyone.

In the years I'd worked at the shelter, we'd had to remove twenty women from western Pennsylvania, most with kids, to another location for their safety. When I first started, I thought that was severe, making people drop everything—family, and friends—but after two women were beaten to death and the third shot dead, it didn't seem severe now at all. What was even scarier was some of those same cowardly men, who drove their women to flee, came around threatening us.

I'd had to pull my gun out on a couple of occasions. Little did those cowards know I could shoot off the tip of their dicks at fifty yards.

I waited around before leaving work today until Beverly Davis, the head of WARV, locked up, and then I walked her to our cars. I was armed and licensed to use it, but Beverly was against violence, period. That sounded great, I told her, until some punk punched her in the mouth and raped her.

The real reason I waited around for her to close up was in a building a few doors down. I was hoping he was gone by the time we left. The feelings he stirred up were totally foreign to me lately. I didn't get the hots anymore for guys—girls or guys—not me. The possibility of those intimate feelings awakening in me was buried in the dirt and blood one terrible night in Afghanistan. I spent the last few years in therapy getting over my hatred of men. My energies were now directed at preventing that from happening to other women. That changed earlier in the day when that man, sitting in my car, said, "Gabby," his masculine voice bringing me back to the present. "I never got the chance to say how sorry I was for what happened to you."

Okay, it was out there. But I felt this pain in my chest I thought I had gotten over. I stared forward, less the tears that took me a long time to control, returned. Dammit!

He kept talking. "I visited you each day at the hospital until they suddenly shipped me home. If I knew who really did that to you, I would have killed the SOB."

I couldn't look at him. I was struggling to hold back the tears because one of the few things I remembered from that terrible time was his talking to me and saying pretty much the same thing. Even in my coma, listening to him, my heart was breaking.

"I should have been there and—"

"Danny, it was meant to be." I bit my lip, still refusing to look at him. "Believe it or not, I'm better after it. I decided to stop playing Gabe and become Gabriel. For the last three years, I've been Gabriel."

"Well, I'd like to also be friends with Gabriel—if she'll let me."

Damn—damn—I wanted to—but I couldn't look at him. What I was starting to feel was so strange and frightening, that I climbed out the car and quickly walked into the building leaving my door open and him in my car watching me.

I became Gabe, the dyke, as that asshole Dick used to call me, to avoid what I was now feeling. Growing up, my emotional growth was stunted by unreasonable demands. Since I could never be the beauty the other women in my family were, I shut down. In my teens, boys meant nothing to me—with the exception of my father.

I decided to take a boyfriend because it was convenient during my senior year. He took me wherever I wanted to go, bought me things I wanted, and it only cost me a painful few minutes leading up to my prom. Now this hunk of a man was resurrecting those virgin feelings again, and I didn't know how to handle them, so I ran. I believed that was the best thing because he didn't deserve to see the dark side of me. Not this sweet man.

When I entered the lobby, I hurried past Elaine at the front desk, past Beverly talking to Rosa in her office, and straight to the bathroom. It took ten minutes of sobbing to get myself together. That was a first for me. I didn't cry. Not at my sister's beautiful weddings, or being in the room at the miracle of the birth of three of their five kids. I had learned to shut down any deep emotions because I didn't like being out of control. There was always a wild rage in me wanting to get out. I could go months without feeling it climbing up my chest and wanting to rip someone's head off for something they said or did to me. Thank God, I worked for and with women during those early years. I would have gone postal on some guy at work grabbing my ass or making some chauvinistic or ignorant remark. But with subduing my rage, I also chained down my passion and became numb. And now years later, out of the blue, by a man in blue, they were…resurrected.

I wasn't crying because I was in love with Danny. It was because the emotions, I had spent my life hiding from, had burst free, and now I was open to those strong feelings. Inadvertently, I had smothered that passionate side of my personality in my attempt to survive my supposed short-comings when compared to my stunning sisters. It worked. But at what cost?

There was a part of me as Gabe that was very aggressive, very opinionated, and didn't give a damn who knew it.

As Gabriel, I struggled to keep that side of me hidden. Why? Because I was very afraid I couldn't control what I might do or say if it was unleashed. In therapy, I learned how to deal with these strong emotions I felt sometimes. My therapist bore the verbal scars from that struggle.

It was like there was a part of me…ah, inside…that was wild and impulsive. That wanted to search out my limits, like screaming once at the top of my voice in a quiet library, driving my car a hundred miles an hour in a school zone, or to slap silly the next woman who gave me a condescending glance because I decided to go braless in a tight shirt for no other reason than because I wanted to. And with my large breasts and long nipples, I would draw plenty of attention. When somebody really pissed me off, I wanted to walk up to them and punch their lights out. That frightened me, and I had kept those strong emotions hidden deep in my soul the last three years until—Danny!

I applied some makeup to my face and walked out the bathroom like my actions were because I had to pee really bad. No one appeared the wiser. All women knew what that was like.

Thankfully, Danny allowed me to hide in the bathroom. When I peeked out, my car door was closed, and he was gone. Each time I walked to the lobby, I half expected to see him standing by my car waiting for me.

"Thanks for walking me to my car," Beverly said now as we neared the parking lot on the side of the building at the end of our day.

"No problem, sweetie. Hey, I probably won't be in until after lunch tomorrow."

"That Williams woman?"

"Yes, I'll have to sit outside and wait until her man leaves before I can talk to her."

"You be careful, Gabriel."

I smiled at her and patted my purse. That prompted the usual scowl from Beverly and a chuckle from me. At just over five feet tall, the petite brunette was always concerned about my safety. With her fiery verbiage, she seemed a lot bigger.

"What's that on your window?" she pointed out as we approached our vehicles.

"What?" I asked before I spotted what she was pointing at. When I walked over to my car, I saw a white piece of folded paper under the wiper. Just in case, I opened my purse, put my hand in, and touched something metal as I walked around my car. Everything looked okay. The parking lot was empty and I didn't see anyone lurking nearby.

"Is everything all right?" Beverly asked.

I looked around again before answering. "Yes, just making sure." When I unfolded the note it read: *412-555-6069 Danny. Call me tonight. Please!*

I could feel the apprehension rising up in my chest. I knew he just wanted to be friends, and he was, a great friend, but—*ah, that was with a different woman,* I told myself.

"Deal with it, Gabby," I whispered, trying to ignore the anxiety I was feeling.

I had attended rape-counseling classes. I knew, for some women, it took a long time to find some normality. Each case was different and had to be treated…differently. But it wasn't being raped, that I was afraid of with the note writer. Danny would never do that to me or anyone else. He never had to, with his looks and personality. He was so confident it boarded on cocky—the type of man that got more out of seducing than taking. I was more afraid of me.

Sometimes, I had nightmares that were so real I woke up feeling like I just screwed the whole Steelers football team, and it wasn't enough to tame my demons. I wanted to screw the coaches also. In those dreams, I took pleasure in giving myself to men. That was not me, or the me before I felt degraded by whoever assaulted and nearly killed me.

Did all women fight the urge to become a whore? I wondered after those nightmares. Then I thought, were they only nightmares to me because, in them, I completely lost control and acted like a—

But it wasn't because I craved sex. The sick part, and I didn't tell my therapist, but I thought I was punishing myself for all those years of pretending to be what I wasn't.

"Are you all right, Gabby? You look like you've seen a ghost?"

"What? Yes, no. See, this is just a phone number from an old friend from the army," I explained as I gave it to her to read.

"Is he a problem?" she asked, her face showing concern.

"Danny, no, he's one of the nicest men I've ever known."

"Does he want a date?"

I looked at Beverly and realized that was the first time I even considered that.

"Look, Gabby, from the counseling we've had, I know you have sworn off relationships. But unfortunately, that has also included friendships. If this Danny is a nice guy, like you've said, give him a call and let him be a—friend."

I just looked at the older woman, as she smiled at me and left it at that. What made working for her enjoyable was her ability to state her opinion and then leave it alone—right or wrong. As I watched her drive off, I considered what she said. I had made so many changes in my life, maybe there was room for one more. I got into my car and hesitated before turning the ignition key. I had made plenty of transformations in my life, starting with my appearance.

I was in Landstuhl Army Hospital in Germany for almost a week before coming out of the coma. When I opened my eyes, my entire family was standing around my bed. Even my mother had tears in her eyes and, at that moment I forgave the matriarch of the family for not knowing she had crushed the spirit of who I really was. What was very special—and I didn't deserve it—they all stayed the two weeks I was there before being transferred to a VA hospital in Pittsburgh.

Thank goodness for them, because I was freaking out every time a male came near me. Even my wonderful dad, when he noticed, cautiously kept his distance and that bothered both of us, but he understood—I hoped.

"Private First Class Sumpter, ma'am," the male nurse or orderly said when he walked in my hospital room after I became sentient—the same man who probably was in my room every day I was in that coma. "I have to take some blood."

"The hell you will. You touch me and I'll castrate your punk ass!" I screamed at him.

"Ma'am, I—"

"I—you had better get the hell out of my room." I tossed my water bottle at him. It was the third man I had cussed out today.

"Ma'am, I have orders to take your blood sample."

"You can kiss my ass, blood man. Now get the hell out of here!" I screamed.

The poor man was going to say something else but wisely exited my room. The word was out, I didn't want any man near me, doctor, nurse, food server, or anyone else.

I knew I was being a brat, but every time I saw a man, the image of what happened to me fired up my anger anew. I pictured myself face down in the dirt while some filthy pig violated me like I was a…pig…and no one was there to help me. And then I became angrier after learning the official report stated I had been assaulted by the Taliban before being rescued by American soldiers. I didn't see who it was that attacked me, but whoever did spoke English like a native. The Taliban would have either killed me there, or taken me hostage and then raped and killed me later. It was my own countrymen. My country was hiding the truth for political reasons, and that angered the hell out of me. I felt like I was being raped and violated again.

Another reason I was thankful my family was there with me in Germany was that my dad went to the commanding officer of the hospital and had him issue orders that no male was to enter my room or have anything to do with me while I was there. I was sure that being a pain in their ass sped up the orders to ship me stateside. I thought both the CO and the hospital had something to do with getting rid of the screaming asshole in room number 334.

"Gabriel, you can't go through life avoiding men," Brenda Hall explained.

Those obvious words were spoken by my counselor at the veteran's hospital after I arrived in Pittsburgh. That was on day one, so I was guessing my bad reputation preceded me. I only got to cuss out the male food server and, for that display of blue words, I didn't get any breakfast or lunch.

"I want you to try a little more to tolerate the men here," Mrs. Hall recommended "I understand your anger, I do. But as you get out of this room and move around, you will find there are others here who have suffered and are suffering much worse than you."

"I don't give a shit about what others are suffering." Standing up, I limped over to the window and stared out at the rainy day. *That figures.*

"And that's the point, isn't it?"

Turning around, I crossed my arms and swallowed the worse of the words bubbling up in my chest. "Go to hell, Mrs. Hall."

She walked out on me that day, but during the daily sessions I was required to attend, I began to listen to reason. A week later, I tolerated the presence of males, but I wouldn't make eye contact or talk to any of them and saved my cursing for any who came too close to me.

It was in that hospital, where I got the best counseling, but it came from another patient who befriended the crazy woman everyone was afraid to sit near. Delores Johnson, a former soldier who lost her lower left leg below the knee in Iraq from an exploding roadside IED, got to the heart of my pain.

"Do you mind some company?" the woman standing over me asked.

I had spotted her walking over toward me and probably the only available empty chair at a table in what was loosely called a lunch room here. I took a deep breath and then nodded when she asked if she could sit down.

"Good. My name's Delores," she said and reached across to shake hands as she sat.

Ms. Moody frowned but retaliated. "My name's Gabriel."

All during our meal, Delores talked incessantly. I found myself enjoying listening to her. Some of the stories she told about the hardships of being a woman in the military were both funny and sadly true. I figured that was what bonded our friendship. I said little, but after that day, I was the one who sought her out.

We were sitting outside in the sun on a cool day, but it was better than spending another hour with the smells of a VA hospital.

"So, Gabriel, I hear you are leaving in a few weeks."

"Yeah, my broken ribs are still a little sore, but I feel good. The doctors just want to keep me here longer to monitor my head injury. They try and hide it, but I think they're worried I'm still so pissed off I might shoot some swinging dick that looks at me the wrong way when I do leave here."

Delores laughed and then high fived me.

"I've got another month until my leg infection is healed sufficiently for that fake leg they want to give me," she explained. "Just my bad luck of course, that I got that infection or I would have been out of here months ago. There I was—" She then took a long drag of her cigarette and respectfully blew it out in the wind away from me. The pain of her loss floated up with the smoke. "With my leg half ripped off and bleeding, tossed into the dirty sand from that explosion, and I get that infection in this supposedly sterile hospital, of all places."

"Yeah, I hear that happens a lot," I said, speaking to her obvious frustration. The story she told was all too common here.

"What are your plans when you do get out?" she asked.

"Well, I was taking on-line counseling courses while in the army, so I would like to finish that. I figure six months of applying myself and I could graduate. School has always been easy for me. I just was never properly motivated to work hard at anything other than the army."

"Did your rape motivate you?"

I looked at her in shock. I had never told anyone here about that, but things do get around.

"Don't look surprised, girl," she said, while tossing the butt on the ground, rubbing it out with her shoe, taking another cigarette out the pack, and lighting it up. "You had little outward serious injuries, other than walking with a limp and facial bruising, so it had to be something else that put you in here. And after hearing you cuss out the men…well, two plus two. And from the look on your face, I guessed right, huh?"

"Yes, you did."

"Oh, don't fret. It also happened to me."

My surprise turned to empathy as I watched her take a deep drag on her cigarette. *Memories, the gift that keeps on giving.*

"It has happened to many women in the services, they just cover it up." Delores blew out a cloud of smoke and we watched it rise about our heads before she continued. "I went to the higher ups, and all I got out of it was a transfer to a service battalion, driving a truck. The same truck that blew up and cost me my leg. The rat who transferred me probably slept like a baby after he found out what happened to me, thinking that's what I get for not keeping my mouth shut. Raped, maimed, and still full of fight. I guess I'm really Army Strong!"

"Be all you can be!"

We slapped hands after trading meaningless army slogans.

That terrible bad luck she had to physically carry around with her would have made me a basket case, but in the short time I'd known Delores, she was always upbeat and positive. She would come over, sit with me, and try and cheer me up when I was feeling sorry for myself. Something that usually occurred after a visit from my family. I took the blame for that. One or more of my family visited me almost every day and were always upbeat and completely supportive. But they always looked like they just stepped out of a beauty parlor. Even my dad. Watching them turn heads, when they entered and left my floor was…

Even more depressing were the blank stares I got afterward, as if I had to be an adopted Sumpter. Funny thing was, I could have accepted that. And now to hear all the shit she was carrying, I was impressed that this kind woman always tried to help me, to lift my spirits.

"Let me leave you with this, honey," she said, after taking another long drag of her cigarette and blowing out the smoke. "Don't let anyone pee on your flowers. They need watering, but not that kind."

"You're not bitter?"

"What good does that do me? All that does is ruin my today. He did that to my yesterday, why would I let him rape my today and tomorrow? The hands of fate will pay him back somewhere down the line. I believe in that shit. And you know what? I was raped at knife point and I lived. That's important to remember, I lived. Here at home, women are raped and killed. I lived. Hell, I'd feel worse giving it up free to some loser and then finding out he's married with a bunch of kids. Know what I'm saying? Shit. So, I'm going to get fit for that leg and move on with my life. Look, girl, all guys want is to spread them anyway, so missing part of my leg won't matter, right? Besides, with my shapely ass, I could cut off the other one and they won't even notice."

We both laughed at that truism about most men, and she did have an ass that drew stares and whistles from the disgusting men in the building.

"Don't let what happened to you turn you off to men. That is, unless you prefer women?"

I shook my head no. *Damn, I'm letting my hair grow out and I'm still being mistaken for being gay.*

"Okay then," she said. "See, I met this guy in Iraq who made such wonderful love to me. We weren't in love, or anything, but the sex was just amazing. He rocked my world, girl, and was fun to be with, ya know? He didn't get what he wanted and then move on the next girl. Hey, don't judge." She laughed. "I'm guilty of doing the same thing. But I want that again."

"Nothing more? I mean the family and all that stuff."

"Maybe. He did come to see me in the field hospital after he heard what happened."

"He did, huh? He seems like a great guy." That caused me to remember another great guy who came to see me when I was in bad shape.

She nodded. "Yeah, he is. He was being shipped back to the states, the lucky hunk, and said to drop him a line when I'm able, and we can continue where we left off."

"Oh, really?"

"Hell, yeah. Don't look at me like that. The truth is, I really put a sexual whipping on that boy," she said and then stood up and rotated her hips in an obnoxious manner.

I looked around, laughing, but no one was out to notice her, and I was sure she didn't care either way.

"Don't block out that part of your life because of some loser," Delores said and sat down. "It's too good to let him steal that from you also, the pig."

What? I thought. *Is this crippled woman psychic?* I didn't want to delve into my bitter feelings on the subject, even with this sweet woman, so I was about to get up and walk back into the hospital building when she grabbed my arm.

"Gabriel, when I look at you…well, I should explain." She tossed her cigarette on the ground and stepped it out. "I watched you a few times when your family visited. I don't mean this to be cruel, but it was like watching the atypical ugly duckling among beautiful swans. You seemed so out of place. I can only imagine the pressures that put on you growing up with those…swans. Don't say anything—" She put up her hand up. "—let me finish. I don't care about that shit. I believe in being who you are, don't compromise, fight it."

"Fight it?"

"Yes. It's much easier to conform than to be yourself. Fight for who you really are. That was why I joined the army."

That moment was the first time I had seen real emotion on the face of this interesting woman.

"My family was very driven, and I wasn't," she continued. "I was happy to just get married to a man I loved and had fun with, and have his kids. I always thought laughter was the best medicine. In a way, I was like you. I was…different. But that's all I wanted out of life, except that wasn't good enough for my family. The Johnsons are doctors and lawyers and such, and insisted I do the same, instead of just allowing me to be me. Did I have the grades, yes? I was a straight A student and disinterested in school. I could have bested all of them, if I put my mind to it, but that's not what I wanted, so I joined the army to teach them they can't run my life. Now look where I am," she said and spread her arms. "The worst part is I know they are shaking their brilliant heads and saying, 'See? We tried to tell her.' But I've decided my goals are still within reach and so is my happiness, and so is yours. I'm not going to be a doctor or lawyer, regardless of what they want for me. I'm going to put on some tight pants, when I get out of this place, and capture Mister Right For Me."

That was how our conversations went after that day. And every time I would get ticked off about something, she would give me that look and later ream me out. After a few days of that, I made an effort to find myself. As long as no male, other than my doctor, touched me, I was able to converse with men. But if one tried to hit on me, he caught a verbal cursing whirlwind.

As I yielded to the idea of just being me, something else was happening. I started losing weight. Not because of my injuries, or a desire to improve myself, but from my total dislike of what they called food here.

Delores was the first to notice. "Are you losing weight?"

"I guess. I hate the food here, and I'm not a picky eater."

"Well, if you're doing it, anyway, why not work at it and get in great shape?"

"I was never—"

"Sweetie, every time you talk negative about anything, I'm going to get in your shit. Remember, I told you we aren't going to live in yesterday anymore. You aren't a swan, I get that. Neither am I, when compared to your gorgeous sisters. Damn, I would give my other leg to look like them. But I'm not an ugly duckling, and neither are you. If you ever make it back to…Germany…was it? Find your plastic surgeon and give him a great blow job."

My head whipped around. "What?"

"Yes. From what you told me, he or she worked a miracle on your face. Other than a little bruising, your face looks great. No scars that I can see."

"Good point, but how about I just give him a hand shake and maybe chocolates."

"Okay, virgin Mary. But forget about being raped. I need a leg and you need to try hard to become the best you can while stuck in here. I'm trying, and, girl, you need to get on board with this."

Delores was able to motivate me with common words and sometimes naughty examples. For some reason, she was the first person that I wanted to be better for and not disappoint. The next two weeks there, I worked out feverishly every day in the gym. I was nearly one hundred and seventy pounds when I was transferred here and, in two months, I had lost almost forty pounds and replaced it with a toned body.

"Look at you, girl," she said as I stood in my room in just my underwear. "Your stomach is firm and flat. You have a shapely ass a black woman would be jealous of, girl."

I chuckled and shook my head at her. She then walked up to me with her crutches, and let them and her pants drop to her ankles.

"Delores?" I laughed and hurried over to lock the door to my room.

"See, this is what you call an ass," claimed the sassy woman, posing on one leg in a thong.

It was. The shapely lady missing a left leg from the knee down had everything else. I walked over to her. "I will never have your butt, Delores."

"Yes, and I don't have your firm boobs. I would

trade my butt for breasts that stand up like yours in a heartbeat, girl," she said, placing her hands under hers and lifting them up. "Yours look even better than ten-thousand-dollar-each fake ones."

"Delores, you are too much."

"Seriously," she said as we got dressed. "I was fifteen the last time my nipples looked up at me."

We laughed. Thankfully, no one walked into my room and caught the strippers posing.

"I bet those skinny swans in your family don't have your curves."

"They don't want them."

"Oh, yes, they do. Tall, skinny women look great in their clothes, but they don't make men salivate when they take them off. Most models look like flat chested little boys naked, with their tiny little butts."

I just chuckled at that picture and didn't argue the point. Yes, my sisters didn't have my curves, but plenty of their own. They were the complete package.

"Girl, you are no longer that fat kid. I don't know when you will allow a man to see you naked. That's probably a long, long way off—" I noticed she corrected herself when I frowned. "—and don't worry about when, but it will happen. And when it does, you will love the look or pure lust in his eyes as he feasts on your firm body."

Her kind words had helped me get in great physical shape, but it was my piss-poor attitude that was most affected by Delores. She was continually telling me I wasn't and would never be a swan, but I was by no means an ugly duckling. Proving that, she taught me how to wear makeup that would accentuate my facial features. My hair had grown out—it always did grow fast—and she styled it for me. I had lost so much weight that, one day, Delores, and some of the other female patients and staff, found, traded, purchased, and donated clothes, making that terrible place into a boutique for me. I was humbled by their kindness.

But again, it wasn't just the change in my appearance that I took away from that place when I departed, after hugging everyone and allowing my family to take me home. It was also the fact that I had climbed out of that bitter shell of mine and, for the first time, I had some idea who I was. I wasn't the fat girl in high school hiding in the baggy clothes. It wasn't the butch façade I allowed to permeate that truly identified who I was. I had lived a lie, but it held everyone at arm's length, protecting my fragile persona.

The woman who rose up from the shame she felt—after first being cruelly violated in the filthy dirt by my fellow soldiers and left for dead, or later by the leaders of the army—finally broke free from my anger and hate. Or more honestly, I found a place in my soul to hide it.

What those terrible months of my life had accomplished was to break the shell I was hiding in and expose the chick inside. Now I had to find shelter for protection, and food to grow on. Beverly, hiring me on the spot, before I finished my education, offered me the protection I needed and counseling other women was food for my soul.

As I pulled out of the parking lot today, I had thought my life was complete. Almost three years, of being the robot I had become gave me safety and a life where I mattered. I wasn't necessarily happy, but very content. But I thought that was the next best thing. I was also improving the life of other women. I wasn't a doctor, but I was providing a source of healing to other women. I wasn't a lawyer, but I kept other women from committing murder or being murdered. And, finally, I was now attractive enough to make my mother proud.

CHAPTER 8

Two things prompted me to call Danny. One was that, while driving out of the parking lot at work, I spotted who I believed was Rosa's crazy boyfriend Hector standing on the corner watching me drive past. Thankfully, if that *was* him, she was gone before he made bail. The second reason was the same as the first, only it was another loser I saw in his car, watching me drive past.

It took a while to learn that they—these losers who beat up women and children—reasoned that an organization like ours, that helped women disappear and start over somewhere, was to blame for their troubles. So, they congregated here, hoping to learn something about how we operated or maybe where we took people. That was a good reason why we had to act quickly before they could *re*act. Having our clients spotted leaving their homes or our building, and having that escalate into a deadly confrontation, was everyone's fear.

Needing a distraction from those concerns, I pulled over, parked, and dialed my cell phone.

"Hello…hello?"

"Ah…Hi, Danny."

"This is a recording. If your number is between twenty-six and fifty, please call back tomorrow. He is presently pleasing the first twenty-five women who called today."

I tried not to smile at his silliness. But it was just what my nerves needed to calm down. "After all this time, I see you are still a self-centered dickhead."

"Oh, hello, Gabby. That was my answering machine. I'm so sorry if it inconvenienced you."

"Yeah, right. Very funny."

"If it made the lovely woman I saw today finally smile, it was worth it."

Listening to his bull, I remembered why he endeared himself to me in Afghanistan. Danny had this way of making everything amusing. Not obnoxiously so, but pleasantly amusing. He knew, and somehow would let you know, he didn't take himself seriously.

"Did that make me smile? No. Vomit? Yes. Well, I'm number—" I almost said sixty-nine for some reason. Maybe it was his phone number in my head, I didn't know, but I caught myself. No telling how much bull that would have generated. "—seventy-five, is there a chance of seeing you today?"

"Well, actually, Gabby, I'm on a stake out now, but I'm relieved in an hour. How about my stopping by your place around eight? That would give me time to get home and shower, then I'll pick you up and we can go out for a meal and maybe a movie or something?"

It was always the auspicious way he said things that convinced me to agree with most of his suggestions. The only one I turned down in Afghanistan was swimming in one of the rivers there…was it the Helmand?…I didn't recall. I remembered it was a very isolated section in a bend of the river and there was no one was around—that we could see, anyway. Maybe it was because we were returning from an outpost and starting to relax as we neared our base camp that prompted Danny to suggest something so outrageous.

"Gabby, I have a great idea," he said when we cleared a hill and stared down at the river. He then turned and looked at me with this silly grin on his face. "We're both hot and sweaty from the long hike. Why don't we jump in the river for a quick swim before reaching base?"

"You are kidding, right?" I asked him as he looked around. And from the stupid grin on his face I had a hunch he had more in mind.

"Nope, come on. We made good time and aren't expected back for another hour."

"Go swimming in what? No! You're kidding, right?" I knew from the smirk on his face that he wasn't.

"I'll close my eyes when you get in and out if you're shy."

"Are you nuts? Wait! That's exactly what will happen. Some Taliban sniper will shoot off your nuts."

"Well, then you have nothing to worry about, now do you? Come on, Gabby, live a little."

"No thank you. What if someone comes along? It will ruin my reputation and only enhance yours."

"Okay, okay, scaredy cat. Will you be offended if I do?"

I just shook my head at him, thinking there was no way he was going to do this.

"Great, hold my weapon for me. What are you looking at? Not that one, you dirty girl, my rifle."

"You wish."

He then grinned and disrobed right in front of the "quote" lesbian. And he didn't stop at his underwear, like I thought he might, or I would have. No, he stripped naked, shook his much-larger-than-I-expected pecker at me, and then ran, laughing, down the hill and dove into the river. I had stood there watching him disrobe, figuring that might embarrass him into thinking clearly. Not a chance. When I realized he was serious, I nervously looked around, hoping we were alone.

One thing I did notice, despite my frustration with stupid swimming naked in the river, was that this careless, irresponsible man had the body of an Adonis. I had to admit I was impressed with his muscular legs and thighs, six pack abs, broad shoulders, muscular arms, and I'd already noticed where else he was very blessed.

Thankfully, his ill-advised skinny dipping lasted only a few minutes, as I nervously scanned both sides of the river, half expecting a hoard of savage Taliban gunmen to descend on us, until the very cold water shrank his motivation and apparently, and from an eyewitness report, something else…

I tried erasing that naughty picture from my mind as I sat in my car, chatting with Danny.

"Great, Gabby," he said, startling me from those thoughts, "I'll see you around eight. I have to get back to work before my partner Gloria wakes up."

I overheard someone mumbling something in the background and Danny laughing.

"Anyway," he continued, "text me your address. I'll call you if I have a problem finding your place."

Before I could answer, he was gone. My next thought, as any woman on a date would know, should have been what to wear. It wasn't. I was more concerned about whether or not I could handle being alone with him.

He would be a gentleman. That was just who he was. But would my phobia turn a nice evening into hell. It had happened on the few dates I convinced myself to go out on, leaving the poor guy sorry he asked. How did I know that? Because they never called again and avoided me the next time they saw me—and, actually, I couldn't blame them.

The only reason I let myself think I could be normal around a man again was because of who it was asking. At no time did Danny ever say or do anything to hurt me. He stood up for me without hesitation, even when I didn't want him to. He had risked his life to save mine. How then could I deny him something as simple as a date? But, on the other hand, did he deserve to be saddled with a raving lunatic for just trying to hold my hand or kiss me?

Okay, back to the important things, what to wear. Now if it was up to me, I would wear one of the conservative outfits I'd purchased since losing the weight. True, they all resembled what I was wearing now. A blouse that fit nice, but didn't reveal any of my girls, and a skirt that fit my body's curves but not to the point of highlighting any particular part. The hem was just above the knees, offering a nice view of my legs, and none of my skirts or pants hugged my ass. And like most business women these days, I was usually wearing slacks, jeans, or a pants suit. Enter my two sisters Lea and Shay who determined it was time for me to update my staid wardrobe.

What had surprised me about those two sassy ladies was I figured they had five kids between them, Lea two and Shay three, because they wanted kids. Wanted to be moms. They did, but the last three births were good-Catholic-girl surprises. Apparently, my sisters were more interested in getting laid than procreation. In a word, my sisters loved sex.

They both said that, being good Catholics, using the rhythm method of birth control, and going two weeks without sex during their fertile cycle, was hell. At first, they agreed to make their husbands wear condoms only during that fertile period, defying the church's teaching for a few weeks. Then they changed their minds, after missing the joys of spontaneity, and decided they would use birth control pills and just go regularly to confession. Happy life was a happy wife, they laughingly told me. And if the constant grins on their husband's faces were any indication it worked.

But back to my dilemma. My sisters highjacked me into going to the mall and purchasing new clothes that better advertised my "ass-sets," as they teasingly stated.

"Okay, Gabby," Lea informed me, when the three of us arrived at the North Hills Mall, "we are going to pick out a few outfits that are men getters for you."

"Lea, I don't need any help getting men."

"In those vanilla work clothes you normally wear, yes, you do."

With that said, Lea, like Shay, who also still had the figure of a runway model after having her kids, picked out two outfits for me that barely reached mid-thigh and had very revealing tops. With their lean figures, clothes like those fit their tall frames. With my figure, they only highlighted my curves to the point I thought it appeared I was clearly advertising.

"Aren't these a little too revealing?"

"Baby girl," Shay added. "It's time for you to be more revealing. Unlike our flat asses, you have the kind of shape men drool over. Now that you are in great shape—look—look how the material of this dress would hug your body."

"She's right, honey," Lea concurred as she took an even shorter black silk dress off its hanger and held it up, "I wish I had your perky tits and ass so I could wear this. I told the father of my children, that if I catch him staring at your shapely butt one more time I'm going to punch his lights out."

I didn't let on, but hearing my sisters claim, even if they were bullshitting, that they envied anything about me, felt wonderful. I was never in their class in anything I did growing up. Not that they looked down on me. They were great sisters, just in a class by themselves. Few, if any, in our school could complete with my sisters for beauty.

"See, Gabby, with this silk number—" Lea held up the little silk dress. "—you don't wear anything underneath."

"No underwear?"

"No, it fits like a second skin. And with your tits, you don't need a bra."

"No bra, are you kidding? With a cool breeze, I might put someone's eyes out."

My sister's laughed, both knowing why.

"Good point, Gabby," Shay admitted and continued their searched for the perfect outfits for me.

"Would you guys actually wear something out on a date without underwear?" I asked as we looked at other dresses.

"Girl, I do it all the time," Lea said, surprising only me. "There is nothing worse than having bra and panty lines ruining the lines of a beautiful and expensive dress." She smiled. "And when we're out on the town, dancing or having dinner and I tell hubby that, he gets all hot and bothered. Sometimes it's not true, but I like the response I get from him."

We both looked at Shay and she nodded.

So, I hadn't decided, as I walked into my house, did I choose something to impress his eyes or his heart? I'd struggled with being around men, so I never dressed to impress. Not in high school, the army, or even now, years afterward. I dressed less to look good but more to be comfortable. Sometimes the outfit might not have matched the season, the weather, or the place, but if it was what I wanted to wear, I didn't care what others thought. After spending more time with my sisters since I'd returned, I'd mellowed somewhat and dressed less conservatively and more appropriately for an occasion.

The outward me had conformed somewhat, but the inner me was struggling to keep up. I needed therapy when I first returned to the states. When my father learned about my phobia of men, he wouldn't visit, for fear I wouldn't allow him near me. Surprisingly, I was okay with that because I knew threating him like a pariah would break his heart, and I couldn't promise I wouldn't react that way, not yet.

My outpatient therapist, Judy Lang, was amazing. She dared to take me back to those painful days and, instead of reliving the bad ones, had me remember the good days in the service. Funny, almost every time a man was part of those good times, it was usually the same man. In fact, it was always the same man, she helped me to realize.

The same man who—when the other guys covering our backs as we were leading a patrol in Kunar Province, Afghanistan ran—saved my life by shoving me to the ground when we walked into another ambush…

⁂

I lay there with my face in the dirt thinking, *This can't be happening again.*

"Gabby, keep down!"

I heard Danny's panicky shout from…somewhere. I had my head down, spitting dirt out my mouth and trying to survive, and could hear bullets whizzing past, too close for comfort. Looking to my right, I realized he was close and just shouting to be heard above the clamor.

"I don't have a choice," I shouted across at him as bullets ripped the air over my head. "Every time I raise my head, they try and shoot it off."

We were hunkered down behind some rocks and firing blindly trying and keep them at bay, but running low on ammo. Every time we tried to move, a hail of gunfire erupted. They were getting into position to cut off any possible retreat on our part before moving in and engaging us in a fire fight to the death. We were waiting on the rest of our patrol to cover our exit, but they had apparently fled the ambush probably believing, and rightly so from the hail of bullets we all walked into, that we were already dead.

"Gabby, they have us, unless I divert them away," Danny claimed.

"How? You'll just get yourself killed. Let's just hunker down. The others will notice we're missing and come back for us."

"Maybe, but by then we'll be dead if they have mortars. Even if they don't use them, we're outmanned."

"I think we should—" I stopped arguing when I looked over and noticed that look of determination on his face. I trusted this man.

"Listen, Gabby," he said, as I watched him take off everything that might slow him down. "Now when I run to our right and draw their fire, you slip back down the hill, circle around, and climb that hill behind us. From that position, when they come down on me, you can pick them off one by one. Hopefully, they'll realize they're in a cross fire and retreat. Then I can crawl away unseen and meet you there."

"I don't know if we should split up, Danny," I shouted across to him.

"You're the best shot. You've told me that ad nauseam." Even pinned down and being shot at, he was firing insults. Later, I figured out why. He grinned. "I'll save your fat ass and you can save mine by shooting those bastards. Oh, shit!"

The distinct sound of a mortar round in the air prompted both of us to risk getting shot and quickly move from that location—miraculously, just in time, because that round landed in the same spot we had just vacated. Danny took off running, and he was correct. They started shooting in his direction. I kept my head down and crawled as fast as I could down the hill. That first explosion, however, tossed me in the air and even farther down the hill. My ears were ringing as the dust settled, but I was able to find my rifle and get in position to cover his exit.

At first, I panicked after climbing that hill. I didn't see him in the section of the wooded valley where he ran. My spirits dropped. I did see some Taliban soldiers moving down the hill in the direction of his body. Pissed off, I took aim and fired off a six-round clip. When I shot the first three in the head, the others ran for cover back in the opposite direction. That's when my heart leaped. I saw Danny appear and start carefully working his way toward me. *Hurry*, I thought when I lost track of where the Taliban soldiers were. Thankfully, Danny was about twenty feet away when he dropped to one knee and aimed his rifle at me. Stunned, I dove for cover just in time as two Taliban soldiers fell dead five feet behind me.

Twice that day his quick actions had saved my life. As darkness fell, we were still miles from camp but, luckily, we found a small cave-like indentation in this hillside, covered the opening with bushes, and spent the night. It was chilly so I didn't mind his holding me close for warmth. Truthfully, that was the best part of the night.

We decided to take turns sleeping as the other stood guard. With my eyes closed and my face buried in his neck, I caught an occasional scent of his cologne. Being held like that, I felt the growing urge to kiss him. A couple of times, my lips brushed his neck, and if he noticed he didn't…respond. Frustrated, I was about to turn his face toward mine and kiss him when I realized he was sleeping. I relaxed back into his arms and stood watch until the exhausted man woke up.

At dawn, we were able to sneak away and meet up with a patrol sent out to find us. Or more likely, our bodies. That day sealed my affection for that man. Had I any past experience with intimacy, I would have offered him my body behind those bushes. Not to scratch any itch I had, because then my embers were cold, but to thank him in a special way I'd never done with anyone. I wasn't a virgin, but in offering myself I was. Would he have turned down my "Thank You" sex? Hell no, after all, he was just a man. And everyone knew which head they listen to.

That desire for intimacy I kept hidden, no buried, after my brutal attack. Anger and retaliation were the emotions that lay just beyond hearing a wrong word or action from…anyone. Yes, I still cared deeply for Danny, but after what I had endured, he was now part of a classification that I rejected en masse, with no exceptions.

The letters he wrote to me, those first few weeks while I was recuperating, I never opened and tossed in the garbage. Maybe it was because they were post marked from home that hurt so much. Who can reason correctly when angry? And I seemed to be angry all the time when in the hospital.

I didn't know if everyone could sense that there were two goliaths deep inside all of us battling for freedom, first, and then dominance. One was an angry beast that boldly confronted things with no respect of person. The other was more loving, but also could consume anyone who got too close. Keeping both subdued was my goal.

Maybe, it was just how I saw things, I didn't know. But after I came out of my coma, I started acting like the bitch people thought I was. Despite my prayers at night to be able to forgive, I woke up each day angry. I wanted to go back to Afghanistan and kill the bastards who cowardly attacked me in the night. Each time I moved, the pain would remind me just how brutal my assault was, how little they, or he, cared about the helpless female lying in the dirt, bleeding to death. In the army, I never backed away from any man who challenged me. Giving away a height, reach, and weight advantage, I lost more than I won against men, but I took the physical punishment, and no opponent escaped me unblemished. The daydreamer, walking to the guard post as ordered that night, never had a chance to defend myself. I think that hurt my pride the worst.

In the hospital, as I recuperated, all men became those men. If I'd had a gun in there, I probably would have shot a few smartass doctors right between their condescending eyes without a bit of remorse. My therapist helped save my soul. I wasn't completely healed inside or out, but I no longer lived in hate. I still couldn't stand to be touched by males, but now I wasn't going to kill them because they did—wound them, or maybe shoot off a finger, but not kill them. A man could live a good life with nine fingers.

Getting the opportunity to rescue other women, from cowardly men beating and raping them, became my life's work. It energized me. Gave me direction. It was very rewarding after I saw the fear in their eyes and then the relief when they were whisked out of danger, and we were able to place them someplace where they could start fresh without being afraid at every knock at the door or sound in the night.

"It would be much more efficient," I once told Beverly, "if I just shot the bastards in the head. It would save a lot of needless paper work for everyone. No one would have to leave their town and family or get a useless restraining order before they got murdered. A man *hits* a woman, I shoot his ass right between the eyes. A man *rapes* a woman, I shoot him in the dick first, wait until the pain makes him very sorry, and *then* shoot him right between those suddenly remorseful and repentant eyes."

Thankfully, with the help of therapy, that demon was subdued now, because I was licensed to carry a weapon. I carried a gun and Taser in my purse, at all times, when working. I'd had to pull both out on a few occasions, but hadn't had to use either—yet.

CHAPTER 9

Danny arrived at a quarter to eight. Sneaking a peek out my window, I watched him getting out of a beautiful silver gray Lexus. He was dressed in tan slacks and an open, white, short-sleeved shirt with a matching tan T-shirt underneath. He looked amazing. He was half the way up my driveway, and I was both nervous and—from the moisture I felt—something else. Admittedly, I was excited like a kid at Christmas. Santa wasn't coming down the chimney, but walking up my…I had to stop peeking out the window. He was getting close and my thought were getting naughty.

After fighting with myself for the last hour, I was wearing one of the outfits my sisters purchased for me and made me vow to wear on my next date. It wasn't that little black silk number Lea liked that I'd wear commando, with my ass almost hanging out. I had yet to get up enough nerve to wear that. But, admittedly, it did fit perfectly and looked hot. Still, I was in a dress I worried might be a little too short to sit down comfortably in and that revealed more of my breasts than I normally would have. And I had to admit that I looked great in this dress.

It was coral colored with a deep V-cut bodice and layers from my waist down. It fit comfortably, and outlined my figure. But I was more concerned with what it might convey.

I took my small white evening purse—with my weapons taken out—and headed for the door to meet him. That was a first. I always carried one or both wherever I went, but tonight, I didn't think I would need them. The tan man wearing tan, I knew, would take good care of me.

Yes, that dirty thought also crossed my mind. I blamed my bad sisters.

"Oh my, you look amazing, Ms. Sumpter," said the handsome man walking up to my door. Looking at those dancing eyes, I smiled, and then he said something that was poetic justice. "You look so good, I should have brought my gun to keep the guys away. May I?" he asked, offering me his arm.

I tried to hide my trepidation with a smile, as I nervously took his arm and allowed him to walk me to his car. I didn't realize until later that I never said a word.

Danny opened my car door for me. I would have rather he had not, because I didn't want to accidently shoot him my…ah…Brittney. I did manage to demurely sit down in my little dress and swing my legs in. After he closed my door and walked around the car, I was able to pull my dress down from my cooter. For some reason, maybe nerves, I recalled why my chaste mother always carried a scarf around her neck when going out in something short—that maybe her daughters talked her into wearing.

"Okay," Danny said as he put on his seat belt. "I have reservations for this quiet and quaint restaurant in the Shadyside section of town that I like to go to sometimes. It's a little dark, but they serve great food and don't hassle you. And the best part is you can hear yourself talk."

"That's fine with me, Danny," I said, finally joining in the conversation. The small talk about our day helped me relax as he drove. I needed that because my leg was trembling and I couldn't stop it. Finally, the hot guy seated beside me started to resemble the knucklehead that took off his clothes and dove into—*No! Picture something else*, I berated myself. Too late, my leg started trembling again.

The restaurant was called Stoney's. It was everything Danny promised. I actually liked the eclectic environment. We had a booth in a corner and that enabled me to sit without flashing anyone.

"Try their surf and turf, it's delicious."

"I was thinking about just a tossed salad with ranch dressing, but I'll try it."

The meal was as great as advertised. I think that made Danny very happy. We ate and talked about some of the crazy times we had in the service and the nutty people we knew in uniform, wondering how they survived over there and what were they doing now. Thankfully, he avoided mentioning what happened to me. I knew he would never ask, and I certainly wasn't going to bring it up. *No, enough about that!* I was having more fun than I could remember, and the looks we were getting as a couple made my day. Never being the center of attention before, I was actually enjoying being stared at. My date didn't seem to notice or, if he did, he played it off beautifully.

We were sipping coffee, after that tasty meal, having both turned down dessert. They had this double chocolate cake that I wanted something awful, but the new me had to say "No thanks" when he did.

"How did you get into helping battered women, Gabriel?" he asked, peeking over the cup of coffee at his lips.

Fine, it was in the open, just wearing a different outfit. *Okay, Gabby, just relax.* "After what happened to me, I guess I just wanted to help others." Maybe it was a good thing he asked, I thought, because sitting here trying to avoid staring into his sexy brown eyes, I was starting to picture myself naked in his strong arms, and that was a very dangerous daydream. After a deep breath, the new me was now back in charge. "Why did you become a cop?" I asked, trying to hide my uneasiness on the subject

"I get to beat up crooks." He laughed. "No, basically for the same reason. Being a police officer is similar to being a soldier. You risk your life protecting others."

"You never married?" I asked, while gazing down at my coffee cup.

He didn't answer me so I looked up at him. When his eyes started searching mine, I worried he might think I was interested in the job.

"No," he said, just before his silence would have forced me to explain why I asked. "I haven't met anyone yet that I wanted to get that serious with. I'm not sure if my job scares people away."

"I would have thought—sorry."

"No, don't be." He shrugged. "Maybe I'm being too picky. That's what my mother says."

"You have your mom, a sister, and an older brother, right?"

"Yes, my dad was a soldier and was killed when I was a teen."

"Oh yes, I remember you telling me that."

"My older brother works construction in Cleveland, and my baby sister just got married a year ago and moved down to Miami. It's just Mom and me here."

"Are you living together?"

"No! Ah…I mean, no," he said, more calmly. "I have a place in the Mt. Lebanon area, and she lives in the opposite direction in Plum. She sold the big house in Bloomfield, finally, and moved to an apartment.

He seemed edgy about that so I let it slide. *Guys and their moms.*

"What about your family, Gabby?"

"My family…well, my mom and dad now live in North Hills. Both my sisters live near them with their families. Lea works in real-estate, and Shay is a happy stay-at-home mom."

"Why didn't—"

"Because." Nervous, I cut him off, fearing where he might be headed. "I wanted to be on my own. I like my location in Greentree. It's near everything. I'm less than thirty minutes from downtown, the airport, and most of the better malls in the area. Greentree is a nice quiet place. Traffic can be hell, but that's the same everywhere in Pittsburgh."

"That's true."

For a short time, silence dominated the conversation. We grinned at each other between sips of coffee, but nothing was said. I did take the liberty of wondering what it would be like to kiss him. He had what I'd heard other female soldiers once call kiss-able-looking lips. I knew that was as far this evening would go, *imagining* that kiss.

"Anyone special in your life now, Gabby?" he asked, catching me off-guard. Thankfully, he waited until I had swallowed my coffee before asking that, or he might have been bathed in it.

"Why? Do you want the job?" It slipped out before I could weigh his possible answer. Anyway, it made him smile and that helped me to relax and quit squeezing my legs tightly together before I got a cramp. It wasn't working, anyway.

"I'd probably have to get in a long line of men for the job, but I'm sure it would be worth the wait."

Now I was the one with the stupid grin on my face. I found myself crossing and recrossing my legs under the table but that…ah…*feeling* wouldn't go away. "Danny, I've had problems adjusting to men after what—"

"No, Gabby," he said, shaking his head.

"What?"

"Listen, you don't have to explain anything."

"No, with you, I do. Because I know you will understand, if anyone will."

"I do understand, and that's why it isn't necessary."

Again, those eyes. Why couldn't I love someone like him?

"Gabby, here's my card," he said, handing one over. "If you ever need me or the police for anything, please call me. I know the business you are in deals with some lowlifes."

"I do, Danny, but I'm armed. And we both know who the better shot is."

He smiled and shook his head at me. That seemed to replace the tension that had crept into our conversation. "I would stubbornly argue that fallacy—if I hadn't seen your amazing legs in that sexy little dress."

I winked at him. He always could make me feel glad to be a woman, even in sweaty army fatigues at a dusty outpost.

"Now, if you were wearing that ugly army brown, I would hotly disagree with your erroneous opinion of your marksmanship."

For the first time in forever, what he said made me feel so feminine I had to look away. Yes, I had garnered the attention of some of the men here when we entered, but just hearing Danny feeding me his line of bull felt wonderful.

"What would you like to do now, lovely lady, maybe a movie? Your call."

When I turned and looked at him, the voices in my head were offering a few very interesting suggestions. I was sure he misread the smirk on my face. It had more to do with my lack of experience performing any of those interesting suggestions. "To be honest," I lied, "I was enjoying just talking with you."

"So was I, but I'm trying to impress you this evening."

"You already did that in Afghanistan."

"You say the sweetest things. If I didn't know you liked girls, I swear you were trying to get into my pants."

Caught off-guard, I spit out the last sip of coffee in my cup—that I'd been planning to enjoy—and laughed out loud, causing more than a few customers to turn and look our way. Again. After patting the tears from my eyes, and the coffee from my chin, I noticed my date enjoyed that—too much. "You're right, again," I joked. "Haven't met a real man in *sooo* long. But I promise, when I tire of the ladies, I'll let you know."

"I'll be waiting," he said with that teasing smirk of his, those brown eyes dancing with mischief. "Until then, shall we go?"

I nodded. Where we were going, I wasn't sure, but the evening was fun so far. When he asked me to wait there for him and walked away to pay the check, I took that private moment to assess where this evening could be headed. Normally, a woman with a handsome stud like Danny would be figuring out how to seduce him without his knowing it was her idea to at least get to second base, and maybe get to touch home, if things worked out. But I wasn't normal. My thoughts were about what to do if *he* acted…normal.

I was startled when he appeared and then offered me

his hand. As I took it and stood, I thought maybe he just wanted another look at my legs. I smiled at him and led the way. At least I hoped that was on his mind. We were in his car before I realized I had allowed him to hold my arm and escort me this evening without once gritting my teeth and feeling like I wanted to punch his lights out for touching me.

Maybe, I mused as he drove, *maybe I can be close with him again*. Even if it was just as friends, I'd really missed that. I had forgotten how much until he made me laugh. Like sex, laughter was something often missing in my life. Riding next to Danny, I realized, for the first time, there was no one I trusted more than the guy driving, no one. Not because he had already proven he would die for me, and that should have been enough to strip naked in his car and do him while he was driving, but because he had always put me first. That carried over even to the women who offered him—hell, who freely gave him—far more than I did.

Growing up, I was rarely put first and deservedly so. There were those in my life who deserved it more than I did, and I had no problem with that. But that wasn't the case with Danny. Some of the women he dated in the army were real beauties but, with him, that manly looking, cigar-chewing butch was his close friend and came first. Women were jumping in and out his bed, and I wasn't, but he treated me as if I was special. If ever I had a true friend, it was the handsome brown man driving. Recognizing that, I smiled at him.

"Where to, my lady?" he asked cheerfully as he drove.

"Take me home, James." The inquisitive look on his face wasn't surprising. "Instead of a movie, I thought we could just chill and talk over a glass of wine, and I can change into something I'm more comfortable with, and it comes in army brown. Is that okay with you?" I teased.

The knucklehead suddenly swerved over on the highway and parked the car on the shoulder. "Out, Gabby! I've had enough of your shit! Get out!"

I was stunned. He looked so serious I started wondering what did I say and how I was going to get home.

"If you're going to take off that beautiful dress," the idiot added, "you'll have to walk home."

"You…you turkey." I turned and reached for the door handle. "I should get out and walk home."

"No! Please don't, Gabby." He laughed, reached over, and grabbed my arm. "I'll have to get out and walk with you. And in that beautiful dress," he added with a smirk, "there's a chance, with your legs, that you might get a ride first. Just a chance."

I just shook my head at the fool. But hearing him call me by my nickname, and the teasing, I was beginning to think things were getting back to normal between us. Feeling comfortable with him, I blatantly crossed my legs getting his attention as my dress rode up. "Boy, that is the first time a guy promised to kick me out of his car if I take my dress *off*."

"Ah…ah."

"Ah, what? Too late now, buddy," I said and gave him a finger snap.

But, like a famous fairy tale at midnight, things quickly started turning into pumpkins and mice. For some reason the closer we got to my house, the more nervous and frightened I became, as the memory of that powerfully built naked man, about to jump into that Afghani River, flashed in my mind. The more I remembered just how big he was, the more anxious I became. What if we—how would I—could I possibly? I couldn't handle—I began to have what I guessed was a panic attack. I was noticeably fidgeting in my seat and damp under my dress.

Danny looked over at me. "Are you okay?"

I took a deep breath but didn't answer him. I wasn't sure how to verbalize what I was feeling, or even if I could speak. He would look over at me at every chance while driving. When he pulled up in my driveway, I was getting dizzy and gasping for air. I bolted from his car and ran up to my house before he could park.

"Gabby, wait!"

I could hear him calling my name, as I struggled to get my key in the damn door, and then I ran in the house, closed, and locked the door. I stood there panting, as if I had just escaped from the cold hands of a serial killer, and not my Danny.

"What is wrong with you, girl? Stupid! Stupid! Why would you run from him of all people? You have faced down lunatics at work, and you run from Danny? You're nuts…" I found myself saying repeatedly as I pounded my fist against my front door.

Tiptoeing over, I peeked out the curtains. He was still parked in my driveway, sitting in his car looking at the house. "Go out and talked to him, girl. Go ahead and open the door before he leaves."

After talking myself into it three times, I opened my door and stepped outside. Instead of getting out the car he sat there staring at me. Ashamed, I looked down at the ground, shaking my head and hugging myself, before turning and walking back into my house. When I heard his car door close, I fought the strong urge to run and slam the door closed before he got to it. Instead, I left it open and backed into my house. My panic grew with the sound of his footfalls on my driveway. Somehow, dry mouthed and yet feeling a cold drop of sweat running the gauntlet down my spine and hiding between my butt cheeks, I was able to look up at the man whose face was full of concern.

"Gabby, are you all right?"

Too late, he was in. "I'm sorry, Danny. I started having a—a panic attack."

"Was it something I said or did?"

"No," I confessed as I paced the floor. "No, it's my phobia after that damn attack. Men make me very nervous sometimes."

"I can understand that."

I stopped pacing and looked at him. "Can you?"

"Hell, yes. And now that I know you are okay, I'll leave you some privacy."

"No, Danny, I have to get over this. If I can't trust you, who can I trust? Sit down, please, and I'll get us something to drink."

"No, Gabby." He walked up to me, raised his hands to hold me, and apparently thought better of it. "I think it's best you're alone now."

I wanted to beg him to stay. When that great-looking man turned and started walking toward my door, I was searching for the right words to convince him. When he stopped, I caught my breath as I stared at his back. My emotions were racing from panic to passion…and back again.

"One thing." He turned around at my door. "I'm off this weekend. Can I cook dinner for the two of us Friday night?"

I felt the fingers of fear tightening around my chest again. I knew I must have looked the part as I stared at him. I was about to say yes when my anxiety got the best of me. "That sounds nice, Danny. Can I think about it before giving you an answer?"

"Yes, if you promise to look this great the next time." He smiled, as his eyes painted a trail first down and then up my body, making his intentions obvious. "You take as long as you need."

Then I took a step backward when he walked across the room toward me. Thankfully, my feet froze before I embarrassed myself by backing into the wall behind me. He leaned down, kissed me on the cheek, turned, and walked out my house, closing the door behind him. I stood there rubbing my cheek like a school girl. I was scared to be alone here with this man, but I let him kiss me? I took a deep breath, the confusion of my affliction once again not making any sense.

Rushing to the window and peering out, this time, I watched him back down my driveway and wave as he drove off. Looking out at the empty night, I wondered how in the world I was going to deal with the man I knew I was falling in love with—again.

After sitting on my couch with a glass of wine, reviewing all the highs and lows of my life, I finally gave up and went to bed. After a long shower, putting on PJs, and lying in bed tonight, I realized my real enemy was fear. I grew up afraid to compete with my gorgeous sisters, afraid to compete with other girls in school, afraid I couldn't measure up to my mother's high standards she wanted for me, and tonight, what came between me and a wonderful man was fear. I made a decision while lying in bed. Only time would tell if I could—

The phone rang.

CHAPTER 10

Danny

Pittsburgh SWAT officers, Bilicki and Sellers, stood at attention in the captain's office.

"Okay, I'm going to say this for the last time. If I catch either one of you beating up another suspect again, you're fired."

"Did you say 'catch us,' captain?" Sellers inquired.

"That's what I said. If another officer reports you beating the hell out of another citizen of our fair city, and word reaches any of your commanding officers, you two are history. Some things are to be done in private, or not at all. Do I make myself clear on that issue?"

The two voiced agreement simultaneously.

"Okay then, get out of my office."

They walked into the locker room to the derision of three other officers.

"Did the captain ream you two assholes out for beating up that brother?"

"Yorkavitch, the captain understands it's all in the line of duty," Bilicki explained.

"So, beating up a guy who proved to be telling the truth was in the line of duty," Danny asked.

"Now listen, Washington, at the time, he was a suspect in raping that little black girl. We were just incensed that a person would do that to a child, regardless of their color, right, Bilicki?"

"That's right," he agreed as both men high fived each other.

"What's your problem anyway, Washington? Are you saying white officers are biased?"

"I'm saying you are," Danny answered and stood up from trying his shoes.

A pompous Sellers walked up to him and got in his face. "We just kick ass, regardless of the color of their skin. Do you have a problem when it's the dark skin ones we kick?"

"No." Danny looked around at the six or seven white faces gathered in the room, who were growing more interested in the conversation and where it was headed. "Only when it's just black faces and for reasons you know are bullshit excuses, just to get your little pecker hard."

Sellers took another step closer but Washington didn't back off, even though he was outnumbered. Instead, he blew Sellers a kiss. But even that insult couldn't motivate Sellers to risk another ass whipping like Washington had administered to him back in the army and again in hand-to-hand completion during police training exercises.

"You better watch your back, bro," Sellers threatened as he stepped back.

"Yeah, you *are* the cowardly kind who would sneak up from behind, you asshole."

Sellers conveniently waited until Bilicki grabbed him before putting on a show of anger, fooling no one but himself, and the similar rectum-orifice holding him back. The other officers knew he was all talk and, hiding behind his badge, got off trying to intimidate people.

"You'd better watch your back!" a red-faced Sellers shouted, spittle flying out of his mouth. "You'd better watch your back! Get off me, Bilicki!"

Washington turned his back to him and walked out of the locker room and past other cops in the office who were distracted by the shouting they heard coming from the locker room. Getting a glare from the captain standing in the doorway of his office, Danny headed out the door.

It was thinking about seeing Gabby later today that quickly cooled his temper. The vow to change departments was put off because he was running late and was more concerned about what he had time to cook. That problem was solved when he spotted a sign ahead. It wasn't what he planned for dinner but, being pressed for time, he pulled in the parking lot. He had envisioned two medium-rare steaks, simmering in caramelized onions and mushrooms, but time, or rather the lack of it, became the impetus behind his decision.

Danny rushed into his house, placed the food on the kitchen table, and then hurried into his bedroom. He quickly decided on what to wear and stepped into the bathroom to shave and shower. The surprising change in Gabby's appearance occupied his thoughts while the hot soapy water cleaned his skin.

When they first met, the huge chip on her shoulders was a big turn off. He couldn't have cared less if she was gay. He was more into petite females, anyway. And hell, her arms then were almost as big as his and her ass was bigger. With a helmet on and that cigar she chewed in her mouth—sexually, you couldn't tell if she was male or female.

But as a soldier, she more than carried her weight,

and he grew to respect her for that. Between the two of them, they won every shooting contest, with one or the other finishing second. And more times than he wanted to admit, he got the silver medal.

Being the odd couple, they were often paired together when out on patrol. And he came to rely on her quick responses to trouble that saved them when caught in one of many firefights or ambushes. While the others ran for cover, he and Gabby stayed in the open, covering for them and, in most cases, killing the ambushers with their uncanny accuracy before the bad guys could do any real damage. That was another reason the two of them were often buddied up together—few of the other soldiers in their platoon felt they measured up to their highly efficient comrades.

It would be very hard for anyone from their old platoon to recognize that tough-talking woman now, Danny thought as he washed. Gone was the extra weight—he was quick to notice that. She was a stocky-built woman. Add her very close-cut hairstyle, that also gave him the false impression she was butch. But that slowly changed when she started to relax around him, and he listened to her expressing her feelings about soldiering and life.

His sister Ariel once confessed to her very close brother that she was bi and preferred women more than and men. That confession didn't come as a surprise. He had sensed it in the way she looked and acted around other women. He and Ariel would break out laughing and tease each other when caught staring at the same girl's shapely ass. But when she met her Wayne, that changed. Now, when they chatted, she claimed to be happily married. Nothing about Gabby gave off those same vibes when around other female soldiers. Honoring their friendship, he'd kept that to himself until that night on guard duty together.

After spraying cologne in places men always hoped would be visited, Danny got dressed in comfortable black slacks and a matching form-fitting shirt. With his teeth brushed and nails cleaned, it was only a quick brushing of his hair to complete his preparation. And just as he looked in the bathroom mirror and announced he was finished, his doorbell rang.

∽∾∽∾

Gabriel

The flowered white summer dress I decided to wear combined the attributes I wanted to display. It was short enough to show off my legs and cut low enough in front to advertise, without revealing too much of my décolletage. The back was open down to my ass, but after working out in the gym the last few years, I didn't mind showing off my tanned back and toned shoulders. And the best part was it felt so light and comfortable on my body that, with the wedges on my feet, I was ready to dance. After walking under a few spritzes of some very expensive perfume that one of my naughty sisters hid in my shopping cart—expensive enough that I could have purchased four bottles of my usual—I was ready. I thought I looked good as I stood outside his front door.

Funny, after all my preparation, this was the hardest part. The man on the other side of the door was everything a girl could want. Handsome as hell, had a great sense of humor, and loved to laughed, and, from what I remembered some of the women whispering in our barracks, knew how to make a woman scream for the Maker—many times. *Okay, Gabby, knock, he's waiting.*

Danny had called when he got home, after the unfortunate ending of our first date, and we talked for hours as

I tried explaining the therapy I had taken and the anger I was dealing with. He was very understanding and compassionate, and my sad story didn't keep that turkey from saying silly things and making me laugh. I became so relaxed that I almost invited him back over for a late night drink and—but those wonderful, hopeful words froze in my mouth as my damn fear threatened a rematch the minute he would have walked in the door.

I'd thought about the man on the other side of this door all day and tried ignoring my anxiety that he might write off this troubled woman. I couldn't blame him. That guy was very popular with females—back in the army, anyway. I was dressed to leave a lasting impression on him like my sisters suggested, but my mental affliction might have already negated that. Damn.

After Danny left, I'd gotten a neck cramp, sitting on my couch and looking expectantly over at my phone all evening. Then, after I had given up hope and went upstairs to bed, the phone rang. It rang each night this week around bed time, and afterward the voice on the other end said goodnight to me. Was it planned that way so I could dream about him? I didn't know, but that was what happened. In those dreams, he was making amazing love to this passion virgin in some interesting places…and places. Oddly, I never dreamed about having sex with anyone that I knew before I met Danny.

Unlike many unfortunate victims of sexual assault, I never had nightmares of the event to remind me of that terrible moment when my humanity was debased. Something I never had the courage to reveal when in therapy was that, despite the terrible things that happened to me, it was the passionate woman of those dreams about Danny that I craved to be. She seemed so happy. I couldn't remember ever being that happy. Was that what a woman felt after getting her world rocked? Usually, after waking up the next morning after dreaming about him, I lay there warmed by the embers. But by the time I took my shower, I had erased those memories and yielded to my anger. But after talking with him on the phone, the next day I woke up happy and carried those illicit pictures from my dreams with me throughout my day.

"What are you grinning about?" Beverly had asked me—twice, actually—when I was at work the next day.

"Something funny I saw on TV last night," I answered.

She may have bought that the first time, but not the second, judging by the inquisitive smirk on her face as she walked back into her office.

Finally, on Thursday night, while sitting up on my bed and shaking my head for most of the conversation, I accepted his dinner date. I also got no sleep afterward from worrying, but here I was standing at his door like a nervous teenager.

And, yes, I thought about turning around and leaving before—

"Hello, Danny," I said to the warm look of elation on the face of the man opening his door.

Like the sun rising and chasing away the cold darkness, his glowing countenance did the same to my fears. And when he stepped back and started applauding after ogling the woman standing at his door…well.

"Wow, you look awesome, Ms. Sumpter."

"Why thank you, sir. May I add, you look handsome yourself?"

"You may, but it would be unnecessary. The mirror already told me that."

I chuckled as I stepped into his house. "Oh, it did, huh?"

"Why, yes. I'm sure yours told you the same thing when you stood there admiring perfection."

"It would be vain of me to admit you are correct, sir, so I shall remain mute and demure on that point."

"As you should, my lady. Speaking the obvious is a waste of your melodious voice."

"You are really full of it tonight, Danny, aren't you?"

"I am, but you do look amazing, Gabby, and—mmmm—smell even better."

"This is a very nice place you have," I said and walked around his living room, trying to change the subject.

Getting complements from anyone was new and exciting, but the way he was looking me over was a little uncomfortable. I knew that was the impression I wanted to see when I picked this dress to wear. But making men…randy…wasn't exactly my cup of tea. I did enjoy trading silly complements, however.

"Yeah, not too many neighbors here, but it's close enough to get to any place in the south hills, yet far enough away to avoid the noise and congestion. Can I give you the ten-cent tour?"

"Lead the way."

He seemed proud of his house and all the work he'd put into it the last two years, from the very clean and functional garage, to the nicely laid out back yard with a beautiful patio. At dusk, I couldn't fully appreciate the flowers he described in his garden. The kitchen was average size but had plenty of room for two, and all the appliances in the kitchen were stainless and appeared relativity new.

The living room was stylish, with a dark brown leather couch and love seat. Both items looked expensive and not those cheap-plastic-looking chairs. The room had the usual light brown carpeting. Decorative table lamps, a large flat screen TV on the wall over a warm-looking fireplace, and other accessories added to the room's style.

I was impressed with his taste—for a bachelor—and how neat everything looked. I would never pick leather for couches, especially during hot weather, but all-in-all the room was remarkable.

I had to smile when we completed the tour on the first floor and he looked up the stairs and then nervously at me. It was his home, but I sensed I was in charge.

"Is that the end of the tour," I asked?

His mischievous grin returned and, with his hand gesture, he offered me the lead. I was a little concerned, walking up the stairs in front of him with the little dress I was wearing, but I forged ahead, anyway. *Letting him see a little leg isn't a bad idea*, the devil in me whispered as I started up the stairs. I did sneak a peek back and, sure enough, his attention was centered—elsewhere. It would serve him right if he tripped and fell. Now that would be apropos.

The first two rooms on the second floor were nice sized. One was furnished as his spare bedroom and the other he used for his collection of exercising equipment. That would explain why he looked so buff. There was a clean four-piece bathroom between the rooms, decorated in seascape colors and ornaments, with an opaque glass shower door. Only what I figured was the master bedroom at the end of the hallway remained on the tour. It carried an unspoken significance that both of us, I was sure, understood.

It was the only room on this floor with the door closed, and I could just imagine why. I thought about sparing him any embarrassment if it was a mess, like I imagined most bachelor's bedrooms would be, but I was feeling cocky so I decided to hell with that and started walking in that direction. I was expecting him to make apologies before we reached his bedroom, but he remained quiet. *Oh well.*

"Nice room," I said when I opened the door and he turned on the light.

It really was. There was a huge bed with a thick comforter in alternating stripes of light blue with white and blue pillows. The furniture was tan and looked expensive. The carpet was the same light tan as in the rest of the house. At least there was none of those wild colored or crazy patterned carpeting some people liked.

There was a huge walk-in closet, open, on one side of the room with one of the doors a full-length mirror. The en suite bathroom looked large, was very clean and brightly colored, from what I could tell looking in the partially open door. When I glanced back at him, he winked.

I took that as a challenge. There were double glass doors, I noticed as I walked across the room, that led out to a porch or deck. I knew spending too much time in this room might give him unwarranted ideas, but my curiosity was peaked.

"Those lead to the deck."

I smiled at him and then walked over and looked out the doors.

"Open them," a voice said from behind me.

When I did, a beautiful redwood deck off his bedroom opened up to me in the light reflecting from his bedroom. It was partially covered with a roof but there was enough uncovered deck to lie out and have fun in the sun. There was a comfortable-looking glider with puffy pillows against the house, a coffee table in front of the glider, and a stainless steel grill in the far corner. Three or four recliners were folded up and stacked in another corner of the deck.

"I love it out here," Danny said and then walked past me to the end of the deck.

I watched him look around at the darkening woods

behind his house. Apparently, there were no houses behind his, offering complete privacy.

"We just missed it, but I love this view at sunset." He
spread his arms. "I sit out here after work with a cold
drink and watch the sun setting behind those tall ever-
green trees. And sometimes, on a night like tonight with
that bright moon overhead, I can catch deer prancing in
the woods over there. The best part is I have complete
seclusion, so I sleep out here on my glider when the
weather's right and there's a nice breeze. I've found
that's better than sleeping in my bed with the air on. This
kind of quiet is therapeutic after dealing with the nuts on
my job all day."

"I can believe that, Danny," I said as I walked up and
joined him.

Looking around, I saw he was right. I could just imagine how peaceful if must be out here. Everything about
his home relaxed me. All day, I'd worried about how I
would feel when I was here. Now I decided that it was
talking to him every night this week that had taken the
panicked thoughts from my mind. Even when we were on
patrol in the dangerous hills of Afghanistan, he could talk
away any apprehension I was feeling.

"Hungry?"

"Yes," I answered as I turned around and looked at
him.

When he reached out and held my hands in his, I
didn't panic. He almost did, I noticed, as he quickly let
go. "Good," he said and, obviously gaining courage after
realizing I wasn't going to bite his head off, kissed me
lightly on the forehead. "Let's eat. But I have to apologize for dinner."

"It's okay if you're a lousy cook. For this view, I
forgive you."

That was greeted with a shake of his head but those

dancing eyes gave him away. *Damn, he's good looking.*

"No, smart ass, I'm a very good cook. As luck would have it, I was running late from work today and didn't think I would have time to cook something special, so I decided to stop and pick up dinner."

"Whatever you picked up, I'm sure will be fine, okay?"

He reached for my hand. I let him take it and lead me back into the bedroom. After closing the deck doors, we walked out of the master bedroom and down the stairs.

"Pretty lady, please take a seat in the living room, and I'll get us something to drink while the food warms in the oven."

I did as suggested. Alone, it gave me a chance to adjust the hem of my skirt when I sat down. Maybe it was silly, but I was nervous wearing a few new skimpy items that my brazen sisters also included in my new wardrobe. The skimpy thong panties covered very little on either side. *Why did I wear them then?* Well, their vivid stories of how their men were stunned when they saw them was the catalyst I needed. What I didn't consider until now was that, if a man saw that much, what happened next was easily predictable and probably, by then, unpreventable. Anyway, I was a little uncomfortable showing that much skin. But that wasn't a stranger in the kitchen. It was a man who had saved my life—twice.

"Here we go," Danny said, walking into the room with two glasses of white wine. "I set everything on low so we have plenty of time to chat, if that's okay with you."

"That's fine with me, Danny." I crossed my legs and sat back with my wine. "I'm in no hurry."

"Great," he said and sat down beside me.

Curiously, he sat a little farther away from me than I thought he might. Knowing Danny, he was allowing me room to relax. Our last date was probably still fresh on his mind, I knew it was with me.

"Okay, girl, tell me more about what brought about this amazing physical change?"

I peered into those sexy brown eyes much too long before I realized it. "Ah…after I came out of the coma, I learned I was in a hospital in Germany. When I looked around, my entire family was there for me. My sisters left their kids at home for two weeks to be with me every day. I was deeply, deeply touched by their sacrifice. Growing up, I was so below-average looking, I never felt a part of my family of four centerfold-looking models."

"I doubt that."

"That's because you have never met the Sumpter women. Believe me, I love my family and they love me, but they are all tens. Ten plus, if that's possible. Trust me, Danny, they are all head turners. Wonderful, kind, and loving people, but head turners wherever they go." I took a sip of wine and then I remembered something crazy. I set my glass down and turned toward him. "Danny, when any man would walk in my hospital room my skin would crawl, and, usually, I would cuss them out until they left. I couldn't understand out why they kept coming back until I finally figured it out. They were willing to risk getting hit in the head with my bed pan for a chance to hit on my sisters."

I sighed. "Anyway, when growing up I realized I could never measure up, so I decided to be just the opposite. That worked out great for me because the pressure was off and it felt wonderful. Young girls are under so much peer pressure to look a certain way. Then when people started to think I looked gay, I let that image define who I was. It was like the final straw. No one could see the real me and, after a while, I lost sight of who I was or wanted to be."

I started feeling so nervous, sitting there on his couch with him looking at me, that I recrossed my legs and started chewing on a nail. Looking back, I wasn't sure if I did so demurely—the crossing legs thing. Adding my three years in the army, this was the third of fourth time I'd worn a dress, other than to work, in the last five years or so, and none this short. I had become a pants-and-jeans person.

"Seeing how much I meant to those wonderful people gave me the incentive to get back on my feet. Strangely, as I was recovering back in the states, I couldn't eat the lousy hospital food and started losing weight. That's when I decided to make an effort to lose weight. In the hospital, I met some wonderful people, both patients and workers. They encouraged me to—as they say in the service—be all that I could be. A friend of mine there taught me how to properly apply makeup and showed me some nice hair styles that accentuated my face. My sisters were shocked the next time they saw me and made a big deal about how good I looked, and that touched me so much. Those two are so beautiful, inside and out."

"That's amazing, Gabby. I have to admit when I visited you in the army hospital and saw the terrible condition you were in, I never thought you would ever look this good. Actually, I was more concerned you might never recover."

"From what my doctors said, Danny, it was that close."

The concern for me written on his sweet face started to unnerve me. From the way my body was reacting to him, I was beginning to think having dinner alone here might have been a bad idea. After years of celibacy, I began to realize there was a part of me that I wasn't as in control of as I thought.

"I was stunned when they shipped you off to Germany so quickly, but I was happy as hell when I received orders to be shipped home two days later," Danny revealed. "I think they did so because I made it plain to everyone I was going to kick somebody's ass if I found out who the pig was that hurt my friend."

I knew he meant it, and I was moved hearing that. I wasn't sure if I was in love with Danny, but I'd always liked him. He never asked anything out of line from our friendship and had accepted me at my worse. I had to admit, back then, I'd begun to wish he had, but now things were different. I was happy with the work I was doing for battered women and proud of the change in my outlook on things.

I'd come a long, long way and had some idea now what I wanted from life.

But the emotional part of my life, that I'd always ignored up to now, was causing me to recross my legs—I was learning that was what I did when nervous—the reason being this was the only man I allowed inside that circle. I'd dated the last three years, on a few rare occasions, but I never allowed them inside me or my emotional circle. The amazing guy sitting beside me, sipping wine, had the keys to open every door of mine. And what was making me nervous was that if he tried putting that key in my ah…door tonight, I wasn't sure if I could, or wanted to, stop him.

"What about you, Danny?" I took a sip of wine for my dry throat and, out the corner of my eye, watched him watching me. "What have you been doing since returning?"

Getting him talking about himself might help me relax, I hoped. He gave me this mischievous look so I was leery of whatever he was going to say next.

"No, there isn't anyone special, if that's what you're

asking. I've dated, but the women I've met seem so…so hollow."

"Hollow?"

"Yeah, they don't have a deep center. They seem to change directions every day."

"Like me?"

"Yeah, like you." He snorted. "Come on, Gabby. I admit this new you is strange to me, but I'm sure once you made up your mind, this is who you really are. I'm talking about people whose personality changes almost daily. I have a problem with people like that. It's as if they're afraid to be who they are, so you really can never get to know them. I'm looking for someone I can trust. Well, I guess everyone is looking for that."

I was speechless. He was speaking about me, tonight anyway.

"So, you haven't found Miss Right yet, and are settling for Miss Right Now?"

He raised his glass and looked over it at me as he drank the last of the wine. "Only time will tell."

Shit, he smoothly turned that around, I thought, looking away. What was funny, and I was struggling to hide that from him, was that he might be right.

"Ready to eat?"

"What? Oh, yes." The "ready" word was all I heard—at first. I was ready for something, but eating dinner was far down on the list. I decided it was time to take control of this evening. "I thought you would never ask," I said and then accepted his hand, stood up, and followed him into the kitchen.

"I hope you like KFC or I'm in trouble," he said, with a tinge of uncertainty in his voice.

I stopped, put my hands on my hips, and frowned as if I was really disappointed. The innocent hurt in his eyes was something I'd punish myself about for a long time.

"Just kidding, just kidding." I walked up to him and surprised myself when I kissed him on the cheek. That wasn't motivated by desire, but my guilt. "I love the colonel's chicken. I have an idea," I volunteered, trying to mend fences. "It's a warm night. Why don't we take our dinner outside?"

"Cool."

We made our plates of chicken, coleslaw, mash potatoes and gravy, a biscuit, and a fresh glass of white wine. When I looked up, he started walking toward the patio doors.

"No, Danny, the balcony deck. I like the privacy out there."

"Whatever you want, my lady."

He seemed pleased with my suggestion, as I knew he would. I was running the show now. I even started up the steps early, for obvious reasons. Okay, yes, I was enjoying this awakening side of me. It was new, exciting, and with a man I would give my life to protect—and I almost did on some of our patrols in Afghanistan, as had the man walking up the steps behind me.

I was thinking, as I climbed the stairs, that I might later regret not having more experience with men. But, in some ways, my inexperience might be to my advantage because I didn't have an established ego on how things should evolve. I stifled a laugh when I realized something, as I stopped and allowed him to enthusiastically open his bedroom door for me. This was the power all women possessed, especially when a male was interested in them. And this little white flowered dress would get any man interested. *Wow! I'm starting to think like a Sumpter female.*

But this was all new to me. With my only boyfriend in high school, he begged for so long, and was constantly trying to buy my favors, that after a while I kind of felt indebted to him. I later learned, and the results bore some truth, that two inexperienced people lost their virginity that night.

There was only one of those people sitting on the glider tonight, and it wasn't the man sitting across from me. I had overheard firsthand a group of women talking about him in my barracks. Two claimed they dated, were intimate, and that Danny was amazing in bed with his large…ah…talent. Some of the other women were laughing about wanting to do him because he was hot. And after seeing that talent firsthand, during his skinny dipping tomfoolery in Afghanistan, I knew from whence they spoke.

"This is better," I stated as I set my plate down on the coffee table. "Just enough light from your bedroom to eat with and still have some ambiance."

"Great food and a beautiful view."

He looked the other way to hide his grin when I turned to access the nature of that comment. *This dating thing is fun,* I thought. The food was tasty and—watching my good friend attempting to seduce me—I was having a great time. *Thank you, my sisters, for this little dress.*

We finished the meal while making small talk. As usual, the food was delicious and my third glass of wine gave me that warm feeling.

"Let me take these dishes downstairs and get us another glass of wine."

"I don't mind helping, Danny."

"No way, you're my guest. Just sit there looking beautiful, and I'll be right back."

Yes, this is fun, I thought as he hurried into the house with our plates. A few minutes later, as I questioned if I should drink any more, I heard music playing, and then Danny stepped out on the deck and placed the glasses of wine on the coffee table.

"May I have this dance?"

Damn. Dancing wasn't my cup of tea. "Danny, I'm not much of a dancer."

"That's okay, I'll make it easy."

I took a deep breath and stood up. I had lost control again, and the ease in which it occurred made certain parts of my body…moist. He took me into his arms, not too close, and moved slowly enough for me to follow him. As I relaxed, he pulled me in closer. I thought he was being a little forward, but it actually made following him, as he led, easier.

I felt like I was floating. I had never known dancing could be so intimate. The strength of his arms as he held me was impressive. His rough hand on the skin of my bare back had me dreaming. Not to mention how suggestive it was when our thighs rubbed as we moved.

I took my arms from around him when the song was over, but before I could sit down, another one started. He grabbed my arm and pulled me close. This time, we started dancing a lot faster with an upbeat tune. As he tossed me around, I started laughing and doing some wild dance steps that would have possibly been embarrassing with anyone else watching. Alone with him, I didn't care how odd I looked. I kicked off my wedges and had a great time barefoot, trying to keep up with the "dancing machine."

We finally sat down after a second fast song, and I caught my breath. Thank goodness for the cooling breeze blowing across his deck. It was such an enjoyable evening. I felt like the bell of the ball.

"Thank you, Gabby, for the dances."

"My pleasure." I said between breaths. "I guess I should practice more."

"You were light on your feet. That great army training, I'm guessing."

"Ha, ha, ha. Yeah, that's it."

I was laughing with him when he stopped smiling and just stared at me. The air suddenly became energized, and the intense expression on his face made intimate parts of my body react. When he moved closer to me on the glider, I gasped, and hoped he didn't notice. I knew I had to make a decision, and quickly. What I wanted, and what I should do, probably differed, but until now I was afraid to be honest with myself.

When that handsome man leaned down to kiss me, I cowardly closed my eyes. His lips touching mine felt wonderful. Was it the first time someone kissed me? Of course not. Was it the first time I gave a damn? Yeah.

After he kissed me, I opened my eyes and noticed his face was neutral. I sensed the poor thing was ready to either apologize—or run.

"That was nice, Danny," I placed my hand on his cheek. "Thank you."

Then I stood up and walked toward the back of the deck. *Thank you, Danny for a kiss?* Why in the hell did I say that? My stomach was full of butterflies, and it was either walk away or jump into his arms. I held my breath, turned around, expecting him to be standing there, but he was sitting back on the glider watching me. Damn, his patience was just what I needed.

In that quiet moment alone on his deck, I remembered something my raunchy sisters warned me about. I thought them silly—until now. They joked about something that I could feel awakening in me, and I was glad for this momentary hiatus. That day, I ignored their usual smut-talk about sex with their husbands or wanting to bang some hot actor, but now I was beginning to believe they knew what they were talking about.

At the time, I flippantly wrote it off as they either had too much wine, which we all did, or sunshine. Too much of either could make you say and do crazy things.

"Now that you are beautiful and available, Gabby, look out for the Sumpter curse."

I had just turned over on my stomach and was about to nod off under a hot, soothing sun, when I heard something about a…curse? I tried ignoring that, but I couldn't, so I turned toward Lea, the middle sister who always spoke her mind, and I loved her for that. We were sitting alongside my parent's swimming pool in rolled down bikini bottoms and loose tops, working on as much tan as we dared. The pool platform was raised offering us some privacy. Where I had some white skin showing, I noticed, without comment, neither of my nearly naked sisters displayed any. Thankfully, the rest of our family had decided it was too hot out and had smartly retired to the cooler house before they burned.

"She's right you know," confirmed Shay the oldest and, everyone acknowledged, the more level-headed Sumpter daughter.

"What are you too loonies talking about now?" I said to the women now lying on their sides facing me. "What curse?"

"The Sumpter curse. Remember when I dated Donald Vechio?" Lea asked.

I did. He was this very handsome guy from a wealthy and prominent family in the area who was completely smitten with Lea, and who could blame him? A lot of guys were, but this one she liked a lot. The two of them were so into each other that after they took a two-week vacation together in the Bahamas, everyone thought they might get married. They dated for a while afterward, and then he kind of stopped coming around. Lea met her husband Walt a short time later.

"Well, he gave up on me because of the curse."

My two sisters were holding their loose tops as they

looked at me with the same shit-eating grins on their lovely faces. I knew I shouldn't ask what the hell they were talking about, but if I was anything, I was always curious about things. But Lea beat me to it.

"See? Sumpter women are all oversexed. We only married the men who could keep up. Donald had everything I wanted in a man but fell short. Well, fell short in two ways, I discovered. One was the he tried, but couldn't keep up," Lea explained.

"Or rather…ah…stay," Shay added and then the drunken duo started laughing at something. I didn't get the joke.

I held my top, sat up, and looked at both of them. "Guys, I guess I'm the exception to the curse. I've had sex th—" I stopped when I heard a door close and thought someone was coming. We all had to adjust our tops. "—three times," I added after seeing no one was walking up the path toward the pool. "And that was with fat Harold Mires in high school. The only curse I have is, after that, I didn't want sex anymore."

"I remember that Mires kid. His brother wanted to take me out but would never ask. He would just stare at me across the room in History class. He was kind of cute. Well, anyway, it just takes a real man to light our fire. But once lit, mmmm, look out, girl."

"Shay, is right, Gabby. Once you really get fucked right—look out."

Lea's language stunned me. I'd never heard either of them curse before.

"Maybe it's better you've never gotten banged really good. Or is that really well? Anyway," Lea added, "you don't know what you're missing, girl. Because when it's good, it's very good."

"Amen," my other sister added.

"So, you and Wally were banging your brains out."

"That's the only reason I said yes when he asked me to marry him. Well, not the only reason, but a big one."

When they started pointing at each other and laughing, this time, I finally got the message. I couldn't believe the openly chaste and virtuous Sumpter women loved getting screwed. I'd never seen them even kissing their boyfriends. But it didn't take long to discern how smitten their husbands were with both of them. Now, I knew why.

"All we're saying," Lea added, after I lay back on my towel, "is that when you feel that fire growing between your legs, it could be the Sumpter curse awakening. Either resist it like you've been doing, or be prepared to indulge in it until he either takes care of business or—"

"Or runs away scared to death that he can't keep it up," Shay said, laughing. And when her top fell off and she didn't bother to pick it up, they both started laughing.

"Okay, no more wine for either of you flirts."

"All we are saying, Gabby," Shay said, after picking up her top and finally covering herself, "is that it's in our genes. Sumpter women love great sex. Why do you think Daddy is so smitten with Mom?"

"Yuck!"

"Yuck, nothing, Gabby, do it right and you never have to worry about your man cheating."

"Lea, is right, you know?"

"If the sex is so great, why do you call it a curse? Never mind," I added, unsure just how graphic these two bad girls would get.

"Because once unleashed," Shay explained anyway, "you will need somebody who knows how to make you happy, and there aren't a lot of men who can deliver. We both went through a lot of guys, trying to find Mr. Right. It can be very frustrating when he looks great, is rich, even hung, and can't last five minutes."

"And one final word on the subject." Lea held onto her bra as she turned over onto her back. "If you find him, marry him."

"Amen, sister."

I watched while both my sisters lay on their backs and closed their eyes, as if ending a discussion on…ah…world peace.

CHAPTER 11

Danny

T he attractive woman that Danny watched, as she stood up and strolled to the end of his deck after he risked her wrath by kissing her, was a complete contradiction. Yes, outwardly she had evolved from odd duckling to very attractive swan, but that was just embryonic. There was another birth, another awakening, that was virginal, but just as impressive, he thought.

People often changed for the better by losing weight or altering their outward appearance. The soldier that he was willing to risk his life for bore no resemblance to the attractive redhead in the alluring white dress. Like any man, he was grateful to be the recipient this evening of the shapely change. But it was the evolution of her personality that had surprised him the most.

Gabby, the soldier, became his little sister in Afghanistan. And, like a big brother, he was both very protective and, he was sure, a big pain in her ass at times. To even think about become intimate with her then he considered…incestuous. But he didn't feel that way now, not with the beauty he sensed was warring with her decision to allow their relationship to blossom. That was one reason he remained seated, as he watched her walk away, giving her space.

When he was filling their glasses with wine he came up with an idea, other than a second glass of wine, to help Gabby relax. Who could say no to dancing to a Marvin Gaye song? She was tense in his arms but, as they danced, he was able to pull her in closer, and she started to relax. Knowing the next few songs on his tape were fast gave him the perfect opportunity to get her to have fun. Her laughter was contagious, and her crazy dance steps broke the ice. She seemed to lose herself in the fast pace of the music. Gabby had clearly explained to him the dangers of any man touching her. It was that bright smile and her dancing eyes that gave him the courage to kiss her. The look of surprise on her face, and not indignation, was momentarily rewarding, her thanking him for the kiss…ah…momentarily confusing.

When she stood up and walked away afterward, he questioned his actions. But she did say "Thank you," he reminded himself. "Give her time, Danny," he whispered as the shapely lass slowly walked away.

Just the way she carried herself now—he found he transformation remarkable. In the army, she eschewed femininity and even walked like a guy. The graceful woman strolling to the end of his deck was the complete opposite. He never would have thought a person could change that much, but there was the evidence. Very attractive…evidence.

c∙∙∙∙∙∙

Gabriel

Once out from under the strong aura of that man, I

decided, when I noticed Danny was still sitting on the glider, that it was time for me to leave. Why? Because if I what my sisters claimed was the truth, I was in real trouble. Looking at that sweet man, I inadvertently covered my mouth with my hand, as if that could restrain the need I was feeling in my lower parts. *Now is the time to leave*, my conscience warned me, *while I still can*. He was having that strong an effect on me.

Too late! I knew it was too late as my heart started pounding in my chest when I saw that virile man stand up and start walking confidently toward me. I tried to figure a way out! *No, I can't run this time*, I berated my fears. But his every step was causing my blood pressure to rise. Those eyes of his were locked on mine, and I couldn't look away, I wanted to—no, no, I didn't.

This was the man who had foolishly charged out of cover, risking his life to draw the deadly gunfire of some Taliban thugs that had us cornered and surely would have killed me. He was the one who realized I was so badly injured, it was better to carry me to the field clinic than wait for help, and that saved my life. I trusted this man with my everything—or, so I thought. But as he got closer, I became afraid. Not afraid that he would hurt me, but that he would release that...part...of me—I was now convinced that what my sisters warned me about was true—a part of me I had never experienced. As he was now only a few feet away, that trembling part was in danger of exploding out of control. For a woman who always strived to be in control, that was frightening.

In the shadows, I couldn't read his face until he was close but, by then, I knew it was too late. The passion in his eyes even this amateur could read. He grabbed me up in his strong arms and, this time, he really kissed me. My mouth opened, as if obeying an unspoken command, and my tongue joined his in a dance that made my knees weak. Never one to French kiss a guy, I quickly became a convert. He was holding me so tightly I could feel his heart beating next to mine. I was loving the feel of his tongue in my mouth as it sought out mine. Then he released me but held my face in his rough hands as our tongues continued to dance and we tasted each other.

As passionate as that was, my mind was busy reviewing everything I did in preparation for this dinner date. A woman needed to have all her Ts crossed when there a chance of intimacy. I was green, but not that green. By the time we came up for air, I knew that if I permitted it to go any further or was unable to prevent that, my body was prepared.

"Danny—"

"I know."

No. you don't, I thought, *you have no idea what I'm thinking.*

And when he repeated that amazing kiss, as Lea's warning echoed in my mind, I felt the Sumpter demon slowly crawling up between my legs. I knew where it was headed, and I was both excited and anxious about what would happen when it got there.

That was when I decided to hell with my fears and threw my arms around his neck. He surprised me when he picked me up in his arms, as if I was a child, without breaking our kiss. Again, I was excited by that—and frightened. He stood there, holding me in his arms as we kissed and, when he carried me toward his bedroom, I didn't protest. Leaving the deck doors open, he placed me on his bed. When he lay down beside me, I wrapped my leg over him, and he pulled me closer, grabbing my ass in one hand and putting his leg up between mine. Feeling the pressure of his hard thigh between my legs made me close my eyes and groan. While in that state of ecstasy, he put his hand in my hair and pulled my mouth to his. I knew then, unless something else stopped us, he would be the second person I allowed inside me, and he didn't have to beg.

As we kissed, fondled, and started grinding on each other, I was lost in the how wonderful it felt. But I could sense he was holding back, as if granting me the right of every woman to decide how…ah…hot to heat the oven. If a woman left it up to a man, the dial would immediately be turn up to broil. Actually, at this moment with this man, that's where I wanted it set. Damn the curse, I thought as his powerful hand massaged my ass, his hard leg ground against me, and his wet kisses eroded my fears.

With the last of my willpower, I broke the kiss and looked into his brown eyes. Their wanton message was unmistakable, as his hot breath coated my face. But when I did, he relaxed his grip on me. I took that opportunity to roll out of his clutches and stood up beside the bed. I was breathing heavy, my clothes and hair were askew, and I couldn't have cared less. He was lying there, looking up at me, in the same disheveled condition. When he reached his hand out for me I teased him by shaking my head. When he moved toward me, I grinned and took a step back. This powerfully built man could have leaped from that bed and took what he obviously wanted. Instead, he allowed a woman who also wanted him to surrender to the moment.

I hesitated for a moment, questioning what I planned on doing next. My answer was in those eyes looking up at mine. I sensed he was as turned on as I was but in control. That was such a turn on. Reaching behind me, I pulled down the zipper on my dress. I paused, and not for effect like one might have thought, but asking myself if this was what I wanted. One look in his dark and brooding eyes, and I had to bite my lip. After a deep breath, I removed my arms from my dress and allowed it to slip over my body and down to my feet. I stepped out of it in the white lace thong and matching bra my sisters insisted I purchase. From the way he stared at my body, I realized sassy Delores had been right. I did thoroughly enjoy the intense expression on his face.

I had thought this was far enough, as bold as this trembling woman could get, and the next move was up to him., But then for some strange and crazy reason, at that intensely passionate moment, I remembered his silly skinny dipping escapade years ago. Reaching behind me, I unhooked my bra and tossed it...somewhere. I was craving this man so much I couldn't remember where, nor did I care. But being free of it felt *sooo* good.

I watched as his dancing eyes made love to my breasts, as they rose and fell with my breathing. Despite the rough army training and the beating I took, they had maintained their firm posture and were one of the few things about me my gorgeous sisters claimed they envied.

The final straw happened much easier than I would have thought. The man gazing at my body would be the first man I had ever taken my clothes off for. That thought wasn't on my mind then, but only occurred to me weeks later, when I was alone and looking back at that meaningful night. At that passionate moment, another thought entirely crossed my mind. I started wondering if what I remembered seeing when limp on that powerful man would fit when—*That's what a control freak does*. I cast away those negative thoughts before I could change my mind, pulled down my panties, and stepped out of them. Unexpectedly, he didn't stare at the throbbing space between my legs as I assumed a man would. He was looking into my eyes, as if still waiting on my permission. That warmed my soul and soaked my...space.

Then slowly his eyes drifted down my body. When

he stopped and stared at my lips, my mouth opened, as if touched, and I inhaled. Again, his eyes traveled down my body, halting at my breasts, moving slowly from one to the other, giving adulation to the twins. *Is it possible,* I wondered as I struggled to breathe under their intense onslaught, *for his eyes to physically caress my breasts?* Because my nipples hardened and started to ache, as if needing to be sucked. I bit my bottom lip.

Enjoying the hot passion of our kisses, I had climbed out of bed and removed my clothes as innocently as a seven-year-old playing doctor. But the way this mature man was ogling me, I quickly realized I was in way over my head. My previous sexual experiences were quickies in a car with my dress up, and my panties never got farther than my ankle. I had spent my life subduing the fire erupting between my legs and now, I feared that, in my immaturity, I may have given him the wrong impression. I wasn't the bold and passionate woman standing naked in front of him and obviously inviting him to take whatever he wanted.

Gawd! I groaned and my legs trembled, when his attention was drawn farther down my body. I was so jittery and unnerved, I quickly covered myself with my hands. He looked up at me and just smiled. Then he started to get up.

I inadvertently groaned and stepped back, putting my hand to my mouth when he moved. But he was only climbing out of bed. It was a reflex action. He stood on the other side of the bed, looking at me before smiling, and then started undressing.

Again, I sensed the slow and deliberate way he was removing his clothes was to give me a moment to reconsider, allowing me some control over what was about to happen while I still could, because once I surrendered my body to him, I was all his.

That vivid picture caused something to leak down my leg.

When he peeled off his black shirt, it was evident this cop didn't waste the last three years eating donuts. He was more buffed than I remembered. His abs were chiseled and his large arms evidence of a man serious about working out. But I also noticed this powerfully built man was also taking deep breaths. Call it naivety, but when he started unbuckling his pants I was a captive audience. As they dropped to the floor, the man was wearing all black and, from the large bulge in the remaining black item, was very aroused.

He took a moment to remove his socks before letting that thing out and, even though I was thankful for the reprieve, I was getting impatient. Finally, he looked at me as he placed two thumbs in the waist band on his briefs and teasingly grinned before pulling them down. What sprang out looked angry. I gasped at the size it was now. My body betrayed me as my legs went limp. I may have seemed impatient, when I climbed up on the bed, but I had to—before I fell on it.

When this large man joined me in bed, I wanted to explain my inexperience and fear, but something about the gentle way he took me in his arms said, "Don't worry." He gently pulled me closer and, as our bodies touched, kissed me. The kiss was gentle and carried none of the hunger and power of the others we'd shared. It was a calming kiss that also carried a message that I read, and it allowed me to relax. I was now able to concentrate on how wonderful it felt being in his arms and feeling his hard…ah…body against mine.

That changed the next moment when he started kissing down my face and neck. I closed my eyes and lost myself in the pleasure. I had expected another man climbing on board and whaling away at me with that powerful…ah…muscle for the required few minutes. The wet tongue and lips exploring my cheek and neck, as his free hand skillfully massaging my breast, whispered this would be nothing like that.

When his mouth reached my breasts and took one of my nipple between his lips, I thrust my chest up and gasped, while grinding my ass into the bed. That was so pleasurable. I closed my eyes and lost myself in the ecstasy as he sucked my nipple into his mouth. I had never realized how wonderful that could feel. No inexperienced fingers mauling me or tongue leaving a wet trail of spit down my neck. He then moved to my other breast but, this time, he just flicked his tongue around the nipple. I was so aroused, I grabbed his head and held it down against my breast.

But when he stopped and started kissing down my chest, I became frustrated. I wanted more. *Go back for a little longer*, I wanted to instruct him. I could feel my breasts aching for his lips. When he reached my belly button, that felt nice but nothing like—

Where is he going now? The answer to that question caused me to suddenly start panting as if I was having a panic attack. And then his tongue hitting my belly button was like pushing an automatic garage opener, my legs spread wide open. They didn't stop to ask me for permission. Damn, those traitorous whore legs.

All was forgiven when, moments later, he reached his destination. There was no way I could have ever imagined the pleasure derived from a man who knows how to make love. His dancing tongue, full lips, and large fingers had me flailing about in bed as if I was having a seizure—four of five seizures, maybe more. I lost count. And he wasn't in any hurry to move on to the next chapter in the book *Driving Miss Daisy…Crazy.*

Then he mercifully kissed back the way he had

come, and made me come, before I had to plead with him to stop. Raising his head, he peered into my eyes as if reading me. I took a few deep breaths and stared back at him. I was about to say how wonderful that felt when this powerful man's body moved up and overshadowed me. I knew what was next and was no longer concerned. I was so floating in the moment, he could have stopped there, and I wouldn't have protested at that point. But of course, he had other plans, and I was cool with that. I wasn't finished with making love to this man either. When I wrapped my legs around his waist, I could feel his hardness brushing against me. That woke me up out of my dreamy trance, because this wasn't some horny, amateurish, high school boyfriend fumbling around between my legs. Horny, I was sure he was, but thankfully he understood who the inexperienced woman under him was.

Physically, I was as ready as a woman could be for intercourse. When he gently pushed against me, I felt the pressure and told myself, *Don't clinch, just relax.* Lubrication wasn't a problem—I was soaked. He stopped a few times when I gasped, as my body adjusted to the large intrusion, and my nails dug into his back. His patience paid off as he was able to enter me. And as I relaxed, he then slowly pushed in as far as I could take and then pulled almost out. I was panting as much from fear as pleasure. As he slowly started moving into me again, the pleasure took over. As I hugged him, he repeated the act and, each time, I rose up to meet him. It felt both natural to do so and incredible. As the pace quickened, I realized there were other amazing pleasures I had missed these last few years.

But, like my sisters warned, something exploded out of me. I grabbed his ass and groaned as I tried to become one with the muscular body giving me such bliss. Where his flickering tongue made me dance, as if I was a marionette, his hardness turned me into a wild animal. I found myself growling at times as we picked up the pace. Soon his raspy voice joined mine as we reached out for culmination.

Nothing I'd ever wanted, nothing I'd ever tasted or desired, drove me like the fire I felt burning in my loins. A life of complicity and detachment had smothered my embers. Now, as he began to thrust even faster, his body was like bellows fanning those embers with each stroke until they started glowing red hot. I wanted to scream and announce my freedom now from conformity. Announce that I had joined those women willing to risk giving themselves to a man and trusting that gift was valued.

It was under like circumstances, that terrible day years ago that nearly killed me, that brought about the eventual change in my outward appearance. I sensed, after this wonderful awakening, there would be an even more drastic change inwardly. It had already started, as I tried to screw the brains out of the man who was wondrously screwing my brains out.

While his tongue had been like a butterfly on crack between my legs, teasing me until I exploded many times and repeatedly used the Lord's name in vain, his hardness started producing a deeper eruption that threatened to rip my soul from my body. It felt so powerful that I became anxious, but I knew it was too late to stop it, or him, from coming. When it happened, I was stunned by its power as it washed over me, and my body locked up. I audibly gasped and grunted out his name as tingling waves of pleasure washed over me. Then I went slowly limp and finally inhaled. Thankfully, the man who started me on this amazing trip was experienced enough to stop and allow me to bathe in its sunshine.

He held me as I collapsed in his arms. I felt so out of control I—I cried. They weren't tears of sadness or remorse. I was out of control but had never felt so alive. I was alive, and it was because of a man inside me that I cared deeply for. The tears that leaked down my face were tears of happiness. I was free!

When Danny started kissing away those tears and talking softly to me, I had already given him my body and now my heart was his. Why had I hesitated loving this man? I questioned as he whispered caring words in my ear. The answer was simple. I wasn't ready. Like the pain of child birth ushered in a wonderful little miracle, I had to evolve to be able to let go and release all the emotional trash I was holding on to. Three years ago in Afghanistan, I would have given him my body for sex. Tonight, I let go and gave myself out of love.

As I caught my breath, I grabbed the sweating man and tried to pull him even closer, deeper into me, as if welding my heart with his. When he slowly started moving into me again, I was surprised. I hadn't considered his needs in my awakening, but now I understood what he needed from me. I kissed his mouth, his face, his eyes, as our rhythm increased. I no longer had the fire in me. He had quenched that, but I realized he did, and he needed release.

I held on to him, as he slammed into my body, and whispered in his ear how wonderful he felt inside me. As the pace increased, his hands moved down my body and roughly gripped my butt cheeks. I could feel him tense up as he searched my body until he found release. Hearing and feeling this athletic man succumb to me almost stirred my embers anew. He groaned and his powerful body trembled, as he held me so tight I couldn't, for those few moments, breathe. As he relaxed, I rubbed his muscular back and shoulders.

"That was so wonderful, baby," I whispered.

His answer was to nuzzle against my neck as he

caught his breath. I wanted to say I loved him but decided this wasn't the best time in this exposed position.

Danny raised his head and softly kissed the tip of my nose and, finally, my lips. When he slowly slipped out and lay on his back, I climbed up under his arm and placed my head on his chest. He hugged me close to him, and I felt safe and cared for. Lying there, it wasn't like he had taken me, but rather I'd given myself to him and he did the same. That was a necessary concession to my pride. I took a deep breath. There were things we needed to discuss, but before I realized it, I had fallen asleep.

CHAPTER 12

Jose

Jose Paul Trujillo parked his car across the street from the building of those meddling bitches. He wasn't sure this was the one that his girlfriend Danita had called, but he was going to find out. He had all weekend, and if he didn't find her by then, first thing Monday morning, he was going to walk into that place and put a gun to someone's head until they told him where she was.

He had already decided to kick her ass and turn the bitch out on the street. She might as well make him some money after causing him all this grief. He couldn't believe she did this to him. "No, it my fault, Danita." He turned and looked around the street for her. "I should have kicked your ass the first time you did something stupid, and this would have never happened."

He had warned her about her smart mouth. Had she listened, he wouldn't have had to slap her around. The punches that blackened her eye and almost broke her jaw were forgotten. A woman needed to know her place. His drunken father had taught him that if nothing else…well, before the man was stabbed, fighting in some bar.

"I'm gonna find you, Danita, and when I do—" He backhanded the seat beside him hard enough to hurt his hand.

It wasn't until the fourth or fifth uniformed cop walked out of a building near the one housing the woman's shelter and drove patrol cars out of the lot on the far side, that he realized there was a police station a few doors down.

"They're not going to save you, bitch," he whispered under his breath, as if one of the cops across the street might hear him. What their presence did was veto his plan to storm into the shelter and kick someone's ass. Having had numerous run-ins with cops, he knew those gun-happy punks would love the chance to shoot him down.

Jose started up his car and drove past the police station, spitting out curses. He had another plan, a better plan. He would pick out someone working there, follow them home, and make them tell him where his bitch was hiding.

CHAPTER 13

Gabriel

I ended up in bed on the opposite side from my clothes when I woke up and slipped out of Danny's arms while he was sleeping. I wasn't sure what time it was, but the morning light was starting to break outside. There I was, the usually stolid Ms. Gabriel Sumpter, standing naked next to a man in bed. A smile creased my face as memories of why drifted across my thoughts. Looking down at the source of those naughty deeds stirred up desire for the sleeping man. "Gabby Sumpter, get a grip, girl. You're standing here naked in another man's house and thinking about waking him up and—this isn't you," I whispered as I studied his sleeping frame. The sheet was pulled up to his chest hiding his most interesting parts…or was that part? I giggled. "Okay, nudist, put something on."

Spotting his black shirt on the floor near me, I decided that would have to do for now. I had to pee and didn't want to be caught walking around naked. With his broad shoulders, the shirt fit like a night gown. I rolled up the sleeves and buttoned a few buttons. Looking in the closet mirror as I walked past, I had to laugh when I noticed it actually covered more of me than my dress did.

I flushed, wiped, and washed down there. There was only one tooth brush in his bathroom cabinet so I took some tooth paste on my finger and did the best I could to clean my teeth. He did have some Scope mouthwash that I used afterward. I liked the other popular brand because of the way it burned my mouth. It gave the false impression it was actually killing germs. I had left my purse downstairs so all I could do is run my fingers through my bedhead hair.

When I walked out of the bathroom and saw myself in the mirror, I looked better than I'd thought, so I felt good about that. After I noticed Danny was still asleep, I started posing in the mirror. I didn't feel sexy enough in his large shirt. The solution was to unbutton all but two buttons. Now my girls and thighs were partially exposed just enough to get attention.

Now what to do about Sleeping Beauty over there? If I kissed him, he would surely wake up and probably continue where he left off—I hoped. *Stop giggling!* Truth was, I was a little sore from last night, and I realized while in the bathroom, I was very hungry. Solution? I'd make us breakfast and later he could repay me two or three times. *Stop the giggling, Gabby!*

The boy must have been expecting company or had just gone shopping, because his frig was packed. I decided on eggs with cheese, red peppers, and onions. I opened a pack of bacon and was frying it in another pan. I found a can of fruit cocktail chilling in the frig. He had sour cream that still smelled fresh when I opened it, so I whipped some of that in with the fruit cocktail. I loved that combination. I hoped he did because, if not, I might turn into a bitch and say no. I started giggling again at that thought. He didn't have a coffee pot so I figured he used instant coffee, and that was fine with me. I was always complaining those drip coffee pots didn't get my coffee hot enough for me. I was a sipper and, by the time I took a few sips of coffee from those coffee pots, it had cooled from hot to lukewarm.

After I buttered the last of the wheat toast, I was ready to go and wake up the man of the house. But, when I turned around, he was standing there looking at me. He was shirtless and his pants hung so low I bit my bottom lip, like I did sometimes when uncomfortable. Damn, I could easily forget about those sounds coming from my empty stomach, jump into his muscular arms, and make others noises.

"Good morning, Gabby. The smell of—"

"Smell?" I asked with hands on hips and eyebrows raised.

The grin on his face signaled he was in the mood to play. That, or my outfit had done its job.

"The delicious scent of the food you are cooking," he apologized, "woke me up and I had to come find you."

"Come find me, or my smelly food?"

"Either or." He laughed. "Because I know they both taste amazing."

Yes, after that, and the look he gave me, I seriously considered reheating the food later. "Well," I decided, only after my stomach growled, vetoing another part of my body, "come sit down and enjoy."

"Let me slip into something more comfortable, wash up real quick, and I'll be right back."

I was going to protest the delay, but I liked a man who considered that a necessity. He was back quickly, and what he was wearing—a yellow wife-beater and black shorts—made the short wait worth it. So it wasn't a problem.

"Mmmm, this is delicious, Gabby. Thank you."

I just smiled at him as I ate. I expected some reference to what we did last night or just some small talk, but the guy sitting across from me had bigger things on his mind.

"Will you spend the weekend here with me?" he asked between bites.

When I looked up, something fell out of my mouth.

"We're both off," he explained, ignoring my lack of decorum. "And there are plenty of places we can go and things to do. There are a few movies I'm dying to see, and I think the musical *Superstar* is playing downtown at the Byham Theater. Or, gorgeous, we can just hang out here if you like. I'm open to anything you want."

It seemed like it took forever to chew and swallow the food in my mouth. That was what I got for stuffing my face. "I wasn't in a hurry to leave, Danny, but I hadn't thought that far."

"Please, consider it, Gabby. As I'm sure you could tell, I went shopping yesterday and there are plenty of great things we can cook to eat. We can snack and, tonight, I'll grill some steaks."

I knew what I wanted to do, and it was probably— no, it was the same thing he wanted, I was sure. But what worried me was the future. What did he want after tomorrow? Hell, what did I want? "I don't know about the weekend, Danny. Is it okay if we take it a day at a time?"

"Whatever you want, I'm just happy you're here."

His eyes were dancing and it made me feel good to be the cause. If I did stay, I had nothing to wear but the same dress.

He surprised me again by reading my mind. "Gabby, you can wear some of my clothes. You look amazing in my shirt, I noticed while you were cooking. I have some shorts and sweats you can wear if you'd like."

"Hell, your shorts would keep falling off my—that's your point, isn't it?"

He just smiled that endearing smile of his and, when he did, I forgot about being sore.

I cleaned up in the kitchen, after kicking him out, and took a long shower. And I did finally find a pair of his shorts that would fit...almost. Wearing one of his T-shirts, I felt clean and sexy. And yes, the shorts were constantly slipping low on my hips. He didn't mind and, after a while, neither did I.

We spent the rest of the day chatting about some of the good times we had in the service, avoiding what happened to me, and about growing up in Pittsburgh only a few miles apart. Our high schools were always in stiff competition with each other and sometimes fought after games. He showed me some pictures of his family growing up, some of the things they did, and the places they went on vacation, Myrtle Beach being a common denominator for both our families' vacations. We avoided talking about last night, but I caught him repeatedly sneaking looks at me. Wearing nothing under my clothes was my idea, and the way certain things were moving under my garments garnered his attention, and the response I wanted.

I knew he wanted me again, duh, but was trying to figure out what I wanted. We were very playful with each other and kept it light. Sometimes, I sat on the couch across his lap with his arm around me and, other times, his head was on mine while I massaged his tight shoulder muscles. I was happy just being with him until—

"Gabby." He sat up and looked at me. "There's nothing on TV. It's warm outside. Would you like to get a drink and chill out on the deck?"

It sounded like a good idea on the surface. But the last time we were out there, we ended up making love.

We had spent the last couple of hours watching a date movie. Each time they kissed in the film, we looked at each other and just smiled. One would have thought, after meticulously exploring our bodies last night, giving another kiss would be copacetic. But there was still a gap between us, and we had not yet figured out how to breach it without harming the high we were on.

When we walked out on the deck, there was a very soothing breeze that carried a hint of pine from the trees behind his property. I was a little nervous with what little I was wearing, until I remembered how private his deck was. "Mmmm, this feels great out here. I can see why you like it so much."

We walked over, placed our wine on the table, and sat close together on the glider. When I looked at him, it was obvious he wasn't thinking about the beauty of nature. I had caught the poor man staring at the T-shirt of his I'd been wearing most of the day, and I enjoyed taunting him by moving my shoulders side-to-side more than necessary. The Sumpter curse. That gave me all the incentive I needed. I climbed up, sat across his lap, and put my arms around him.

"Gabby."

I kissed him quiet. I didn't want to talk. I kissed him again when he started to speak, and this time, he understood and just held me.

I wasn't sure who I was after last night, or where we were headed. I just wanted to enjoy the now. This was all so new to me, dealing with intimacy with a man like Danny. In some ways, he frightened me and that felt great. Knowing he could take me places I'd never even dreamed about at the wink of my eye, or the loosening of a button, was awesome to me. But like Lea claimed, I'd gotten just a taste of the—until then, dormant—Sumpter curse. Would I regret allowing this man to help me reach as far into my soul as I could? I questioned while he rubbed my shoulders. And what would be the outcome? If he tired of me, then what? Like Lea said, "If you find him, you better marry him."

Surely, there had to be more to marrying a guy than his ability to rock your world in bed.

I was sitting across his lap with my head resting on his shoulder, sipping my wine. There were birds singing off in the distance and, other than that, it was very peaceful and quiet. Danny had one arm around me and the other resting on the bare skin of my thigh. In that quiet, I made a decision. Thankfully, it wasn't because of anything he did, like kissing me or after I looked into his seductive brown eyes. It was a decision where I thought through both the pros and cons first. My decision? I did want to search the depths of my being with this wonderful man.

There was probably a moment in everyone's life where you got the chance to swing for the fences. I kind of felt that way, sitting there. He wasn't pressuring me or hinting at some expectation. And I wasn't thinking of some obligation on my part. I'd talked with women who felt it was their duty or obligation to give a man…whatever. Just the thought of doing that made my skin crawl. Yes, I had surrendered my body completely to the man holding me. But at no point did I feel used. I felt worse after a few minutes with my boyfriend from high school, in the back seat of his car, with my dress around my waist and—yuck—his…stuff…leaking down my thighs.

Taking the last sip of my wine, I climbed off his lap, placed my glass on the coffee table, and stood there, smiling down at him.

The cute look on his face, as he tried to figure out the what and the why of this unpredictable woman, was endearing. I reached out my hand and took his when he stood up.

"Danny, I've been trying to figure us out. I don't have any answers." I gazed into eyes that appeared to be leaving any decision up to me. "All I know is, I want to spend this weekend making love to you. On Monday, however, I go back to my world and maybe, if you ask enough, I might go out on another date with you, maybe," I teased and he smiled. "But for this weekend, I'm all yours, babe, anyway you want me."

Boy, this guy loves to pick me up, I thought when I went to kiss him and, instead, was swept off my feet again. He carried me to his bed and spent the next two hours making love to me a couple of times with maybe a twenty-minute intermission in between. I quickly learned that last night wasn't a fluke. He skillfully helped me have an orgasm, maybe a dozen times in those two hours, and it wasn't very demure or lady like. *Are they supposed to be?* I wondered. I was flailing about again and some-times screaming into my pillow. I could only imagine what I must have looked like.

He has masterfully located my...everything, I thought as I lay there, catching my breath. It wasn't as if I directed him as some women had to do. He seemed to know where and when and for how long. And that was just with his tongue. When he entered me, it was an alto-gether different experience. That hard body just...possessed me. All I could do, at that point, was hold on the best I could as he moved me into different positions. I tried to give as well as I got, but I had to ad-mit I probably failed. He seemed to have an endless sup-ply of energy.

When he finally came, it was a relief and not because it was over. I was exhausted, but as anyone could tell you who'd been there, it was a wonderful exhaustion. But because, to me, it meant that he was also enjoying the experience.

Sex, to me, must have been like taking a sleeping pill, because I felt the tiredness sweep over me when he pulled those warm and soft covers up over us, and I instantly fell asleep again. When I woke up hours later—sore, of course—it took a moment before I located Danny. He was out on the deck with the grill lid up and smoke rising. On rubbery legs, I walked unseen into the bathroom, took a quick shower, and cleaned things. Wearing a towel, I located my—his—clothes and got dressed.

"There she is. Hi, beautiful. I was just about to wake you up and see if you were as hungry as I am."

I walked up to him and kissed him. "Yes, I am."

"Great. How do you like your steaks?"

"Medium will be fine. What can I do to help?"

He looked at me and I expected some smartass come back.

"Nothing. You make breakfast and I'll make the dinners."

"Deal. I guess I better be leaving tonight so I won't have to slave over that stove again."

"I hid your dress. You'll have to wear those little shorts home," he teased.

"No problem, the guys on my street will be very happy."

Danny laughed. "With your curves, I bet they will. I know *I* can't stop looking."

I batted my eyelashes, walked back into the bedroom, and started striping the bed. Not that I wouldn't have minded sleeping on those sheets again, but I didn't think there was a spot that our sweating bodies hadn't baptized. After last night, I'd learned where he kept his clean bed linen.

By the time he finished cooking, the bed had fresh, clean linen ready for…whatever.

"I figured we would eat downstairs," Danny volunteered. "It's getting a little cool out on the deck. And—" He was holding dinner between two plates to keep it hot, but something he was thinking caused him to grin at me. "—wearing that little T-shirt, I know what cold can do to those."

Those? Oh, you smart ass, I thought. "True, and I hear that cold sometimes shrinks…" I said, looking down at something. That wiped the grin off his smart-ass face. *Men, they're always worried about size.*

Dinner was so delicious, I could have let him screw me—wait, I already did. Okay, I was being silly, but I loved good food, and my steak was cooked just the way I liked them. Earlier, while I was recuperating in dreamland, he had made a tossed salad to go along with the steaks, and we shared an inexpensive, but sweet and tasty, red wine.

I knew I was still in the throes of passion, but if marriage was like this, hell I could do this. But I also knew this honeymoon was a mirage. It was when you returned home that a relationship reality started. This weekend was our honeymoon. Proof, while rinsing off the dishes, the man of the house stood behind me taking advantage by occasionally fondling my body parts. That was a first, but I did tell him I was his for the weekend so I couldn't protest—too much.

In truth, I was enjoying constantly being the center of his attention. How weird it was, going from cursing out any male getting within ten feet of me to allowing a man to stand behind me playfully grinding on my butt while gently cupping a breast in each hand and nibbling on my neck—and my loving every minute.

While we sat on the couch, I checked my cell phone

and there were no new messages, so I was hoping the world, better yet *my* world, was still turning.

Danny rented a first-run movie we'd both missed when it was in the theaters. I was enjoying the movie until it got boring and my thoughts started drifting. Each time I looked at the man sitting close to me, I had this thought. When we made love, it was him giving me pleasure most of the time until he entered me and then I tried to reciprocate. By then, I was so drained from my body's repeated flailing about, wonderful flailing about, I wasn't sure my effort was fair.

In high school, the girls whispered about what they did with their boyfriends in the back seat or in the dark somewhere in school or afterward. In the army, the women there made it plain what their men wanted and what they gave them. Both times, I found their explanations surprising and questioned if they were full of crap.

So, Ms. Curiosity had to do some research. There wasn't anyone I felt comfortable enough to talk to about it but my dad, and that wasn't going to happen. So I secretly watched some porn on my computer in the barracks and, eventually, came to realize how common some of the things they claimed they were doing actually were. I had to admit what I saw some of the women doing, and allowing to be done to them, wasn't for me, but at least I wasn't totally in the dark and stupid when the other female soldiers discussed the subject.

I was in my late twenties now, and no way in hell was still my attitude on some of the things they did with their men…well, before this weekend. Sitting here and reflecting on all he had awakened in me, I decided that, at some point in our relationship, I wanted to be the aggressor and make him flail around as if he was having a seizure.

I was sure I'd look weird doing it, but my body felt

so amazing, I didn't give a damn anymore what it looked like—or who saw me.

"Can I get you anything?"

"No, babe! I'm good." Caught off-guard, I answered him louder than I meant to.

He looked oddly at me for a moment, nodded, and returned to his movie while rubbing my leg. I watched his handsome profile for a few minutes and, again, my thoughts were centered on trying to give to him the same pleasure he'd given me. That meant trying to remember some of the things I'd seen on my computer because I had no real experience. Other than allowing him to pose me in different positions while making love, that was the accumulation of my involvement.

I had to look away as a huge grin formed on my face at the thought of my two sisters. I knew if they were here, those bad girls would give me pointers because I was sure there wasn't anything those two hadn't tried, and maybe a few things they invented.

When I leaned in closer, he put his arm around me. "You are in for another great night, my love," I whispered under my breath. There, I'd said it.

CHAPTER 14

The Pillowcase Rapist

He heard her drive up and waited anxiously behind her bedroom door to surprise her. It took excruciating minutes for her to finally transit her apartment and make it into her bedroom. She was humming a popular song that he also liked, and he casually joined in under his breath, as she approached. As her footfalls became louder, he became aroused with anticipation. It was this ephemeral moment that made everything worth the danger. These ephemerals, these brief seconds just before, would be the seasonings that flavored his lurid dreams for months. When she entered her bedroom, the scent of her perfume first tickled his nose as he stepped forward and grabbed her before she could turn on the light.

He quickly covered her face with the pillowcase from off her bed and delivered a vicious punch to the side of her head, knocking her to the floor, stunned. While she lay there moaning, he quickly tied her hands behind her with a cord from a bedroom lamp, turned her over, and tied the bottom of the pillowcase around her neck. He then shook her until she regained consciousness.

"Okay, bitch," he explained to the groaning woman, "here how this is going to work. I can either use my knife to kill your stupid ass—" He poked her in the throat with the tip of the knife and relished her gasping, frightened response. "Or you can do as you're told. Either way, I'm going to get what I want. Dead or alive doesn't much matter to me. Do you understand?"

It took a couple of slaps and backhands before she responded.

"Okay, okay, just don't hurt me anymore."

"Smart whore." He roughly grabbed her pants and pulled them down along with her panties, knocking her shoes off in the process.

Hearing him groan and knowing why, she tried to blindly kick at him.

He deflected her effort and sat on her. Grabbing her by the blouse, he punched her a few times, bloodying the pillowcase. She stopped fighting. When he released her, she moaned as her head moved from side to side in obvious pain. Taking his knife, he purposely cut her chest as he sliced her blouse and bra apart, exposing her breasts.

"Please don't do this," she pleaded as the pain from the cut cleared her head.

"You're not my first. I'm no virgin at this. Nor will you be my last. Stop squirming, bitch, you know you want this. You all want this but are too stupid to admit it."

"What makes you think I—"

She was silenced by repeated slaps to her face and head. When she went limp in defeat, he raped her. Near the end, she regained consciousness and started to resist his assault.

"Oh, still want to fight, huh? I have something special for you. You're going to like this, bitch." He turned her over on her stomach, slammed her head hard against the floor a couple of times and then sodomized her. "I know you like this, don't you, whore? What, cat got your tongue, or did you bite it off? I hope not because I'm going to ask you a few questions, and if I don't get the right answers, I'll start fucking you all over again. Do you hear me, whore? Maybe next time with a broom handle—all of it."

She didn't know when he departed. He had attacked her again, anyway, after she tried to answer all his questions, and she'd blacked out from his last punch. She awoke to pain and silence. It took her much longer than she thought to free herself, and then she locked her bedroom door and called the police.

CHAPTER 15

Gabriel

I was already at work when Beverly Davis, the head of the Pittsburgh office of Women Against Rape and Violence, walked in the door.

"Hi, boss."

"Hi, Gabriel, how are you this morning?"

"Actually, I'm great. I had a nice weekend."

"Nice weekend, huh? From that look on your face, it must have involved a man."

Like a swooning teenager, I fell right into her trap. I just looked up from my desk and grinned at her.

"Oh—oh my. You finally got laid, didn't you? I know that look. Stop it, girl, you look like it was your first time."

I shook my head and tried to appear peeved at her, but couldn't stop grinning. She walked into her office, laughing and talking about me. We were the only ones there, so I knew she knew I could hear her. I got up from my desk and walked down the hall to her office.

"Can we talk business now?" I asked while trying to ignore the smirk on her face.

"Only after you give me the juicy details of your weekend. Was it the cop? It was, wasn't it?"

"Boss, there are two women being transferred here today," I said, ignoring her inquiry and the smug look on her face. "My records show one is, Ellen S. from Dallas, Texas, and Linda W. and her little five-year-old girl from near Detroit."

"Yes, Gabriel, I have them scheduled to stay at the Shadyside house on Highland Avenue. I have a job reserved at a local grocery store as a clerk for one of them. I know the owner, she is a good person and there's a daycare close by for Linda W's daughter. We need to try and find work for the other young woman."

"I have a few places in mind that look promising. They aren't in Shadyside, however, but they *are* near public transportation."

"They aren't due here until around two p.m. Do you have anything planned this morning?"

"Only those job appointments I was hoping to secure for our clients, and there was another property I wanted to inspect. The price is a bargain, but I don't know if the property is."

"Okay, we will play it by ear. If you're here when they come for processing and counseling, you can take them, if not, I'll do it or Elaine, if she comes in today."

I quickly turned around and returned to my desk when Beverly gave me that inquiring look again. She wanted some gossip, and I wasn't about to tell her anything. Hell, I couldn't believe all the things I did to him, and let him do to me, much less tell someone about that. With the exception maybe of those two bad girls with whom I was related.

My job here was to review the monthly status of the

women we oversaw and help them with any problems that came up. Sometimes, they gave in and called the very people they were running away from and put themselves in danger again or worse, they were talked into returning to their abusive relationship. We'd had three women we had to quickly move elsewhere because their spouses located them from their phone calls.

I also recruited other volunteers, like Elaine, to assist these ladies. Then, finally, I visited potential job sites and tried to convince them to leave an opening for these displaced women. Often times, we needed them hired on our reputation alone, or the business person's personal concern about the brutality these women had endured.

That was important because, in most cases, they couldn't use their personal identification or they could be easily traced.

Some men even hired PIs to find their women, so they could continue the abuse. Any use of a driver's license, credit card, or social security number could lead them directly to our clients. Our only safety mechanism was that, when they left here, we connected them to others we knew and they passed them on to others we didn't know. So everyone working to help these women only knew who delivered them and who they, in turn, were delivering them to. There might be three or four additional stops to disguise their location, making them almost impossible to track—as long as they obeyed the rules and remained incognito.

Beverly had the tougher job. She had to constantly secure funding for the WARV house. Thankfully, she was very good at it. She had friends in high places and had financially supported many of the politicians that got elected in the tristate. But I'd swear the woman could stand on a corner downtown and talk people into giving away their rent money.

Beverly could tell gut-wrenching stories of the abuse some of these women had suffered and bring tears to a strong man's eyes. She could also make up some tall tales—so you never knew if she was being truthful.

⍟

Danny

"Men, today we are on stand-down," Captain Handover shouted above the din of conversations going on in the SWAT Action Room. "It means we'll only be called as a last resort, so I want all weapons inventoried, cleaned, and lubed. All vehicles checked, gassed up, and cleaned. I posted your job assignments on the board. Let's go. By noon I expect us to be ready to roll again."

"How was your weekend," Billy Thornton asked the man also assigned to cleaning weapons. Washington was one of the few men here that he found easy to talk with since his transfer to this unit. Being the youngest cop didn't help either.

"I had a great time, Billy. What about you?"

"I took my girl to visit my parents in Erie."

"Oh, yeah, how did that go?"

"They loved her, man."

"Hey! Did you say they loved her, man, or they thought that ugly broad looked like a man?"

"Screw you, Sellers."

"Help him out, Washington. Tell him you don't marry the first piece of pussy you get."

Billy looked at Washington as if expecting a confirmation or rebuke. He got neither.

"Come to think of it, Sellers, I just met a woman you might remember from Afghanistan."

"There's no one I want to remember from that hell hole, including you, Washington."

Ignoring Sellers's usual stupid answers, Danny asked, "Do you remember Gabriel Sumpter?" When Sellers didn't respond, Danny stopped what he was doing and looked over at him working at another table. The dumb expression on his face was answer enough. "Surely, you remember her. She was the reason I kicked your ass over there."

"You wish. I was drunk and you sucker punched me. I would like to see you try that now."

"No, you wouldn't." Danny placed the weapon he was cleaning down on the table and turned toward Sellers. "The results would be the same—your punk-ass flying through the air."

They glared across the room at each other.

"What about this girl, Washington," asked Ian, the other officer in the room assigned to the same tedious job, trying to defuse a possible dangerous confrontation.

Danny didn't answer him as he traded stares with Sellers, then he went back to cleaning the weapon he had dismantled.

"She was this ugly fat dyke that Washington had the hots for," Sellers said, ignoring Danny. "Like most of the women over there, she turned him down."

"We were just friends," Danny said to the other two men in the room who had stopped working and were staring at him. "Like me, she was an amazing shot with an M-16. Anyway, pencil dick here's wrong." That got Danny the response he wanted as Sellers scowled at him. "She wasn't gay—" He studied the response to that news. "—but everyone thought she was because she dressed and acted like—"

"Thought, my ass." Sellers laughed. "She had bigger balls than you, Washington. And didn't some Taliban boys do a number on her? I heard she was going after one of their women, and they caught up with her and taught the dyke a lesson, really buggered the bitch."

"Where in the hell did you get that stupid shit, Sellers? One, she wasn't a dyke, and two, it wasn't the Taliban who raped her. It was some good old cowardly American soldiers, taking what no woman would give those fags. They weren't even sure if it was rape."

"I thought you said—"

"I did," Danny continued. "The problem is, Billy, usually there is some sign of bruising with a rape attack, but with those limp dicks, there was none. It was more like tickling."

"That's bull," Sellers said after the laughing died down. "Those women over there were always shouting foul after they gave it up to real men."

"Bull? You stupid shit," Danny shouted at Sellers. "She was nearly beaten to death. That's not bull. She was in a coma when they shipped her off to Germany, you idiot!"

"How do you know it was our soldiers?" Billy asked the big man who was growing more demonstrative.

Danny just looked at him. The kid was green so Danny swallowed the crude remark he was about to spew on him.

"You are the one full of shit, Washington. The brass investigated her supposed rape and said it was the Taliban."

"Investigated. my ass. It was another cover up."

"With our government, I can believe that," Billy injected.

"They never even asked her if she remembered who it was. They just quickly shipped her home. She was found with an army-issued pillowcase over her head." Danny informed the young cop. "It was a cover up. When did the Taliban get army-issued pillowcases? But I saw her here in town the other day, and if you knew her you would not believe she's the same person," he revealed, starting to calm down. "She's knock-down gorgeous-looking now. And take my word for it, she's no dyke."

"Whoooooo," Ian said and was joined by a grinning Billy.

☙❧

Sellers

Sellers slammed down the rifle he had just finished servicing and stormed out of the weapon's room. One day, he swore as he stepped outside for some air, he was going to get even with that black bastard.

Lighting up a cigarette, he blew a long string of smoke in the air above him. "That bitch just got what she deserved," he rambled as he flicked the ashes off his cigarette and continued muttering to himself, "with her smart ass mouth. If you're going to act like a man, you better be able to back that shit up. I guess she learned her lesson that night. We don't need those kind in this man's army, then or now."

He took another long drag of his cigarette and continued mumbling as he paced in front of the SWAT building. "So she's no longer into pussy. Well, after getting ripped up, she likes dick now. That's probably what happened. She likes being dominated." He took a long drag of his cigarette and slowly blew out the smoke, "Wouldn't be the first time a woman was dominated and learned she liked it. Hell, my last two wives loved getting their flat asses kicked by me."

Well, the first marriage only lasted six months, until she got religion, and the second only a little longer, until some do-gooder convinced her to leave and get a restraining order on him.

That left a black mark on his career, and one on her jaw. He planned to get even with her—if he could find her useless ass.

"So Sumpter is screwing Washington."

Sellers had always suspected that was why they were so buddy-buddy over there. She was a white dyke that liked black meat and thought herself too good for white soldiers. Well, apparently, she didn't learn her lesson over there. "Maybe she just needs a bout with the champ," he gloated as he tossed his cigarette down and crushed it out under his shoe. "It takes a real man, not some ghetto trash, to make a woman out of a dyke." He grabbed himself and, as he walked into the station, devised a plan to make that happen if he ever found her.

⁊ↄ⁊ↄ

Danny

The day ended as quietly as it started for the SWAT crew in Zone Number Two. They didn't receive any calls and had finished servicing the equipment a half hour before the captain wanted. Driving home along Carson Street, Danny's thoughts, as they had all day, centered on a redhead who had spent the most awesome weekend with him.

As he stopped at a red light, the memories of that weekend returned. He shook his head, unable to believe the complete transformation in Gabby. After joyously exploring every delicious inch of that woman's body, he could confirm, other than her tattoos, she was a different woman. In fact, he realized, it was only those tattoos that could tie Gabby to Gabriel.

Working out, the girl went from bulky to built. Her hair was now its natural red, much longer, and beautifully styled. Even when heavy, she was attractive but just hid it. Now she was smaller and very toned. In the throes of their passion, he'd been impressed with her strength when she locked her body around his. Dressed and undressed, she was beautiful. The terrible image of the battered woman in that hospital bed was erased by the female who stripped naked beside his bed. She appeared unmarked, her skin smooth and flawless. Having spent time with her breasts in his mouth and hands, he could attest they were large but perfect. No sagging or—

A slight horn blast sent whoever was distracted in the car ahead of him moving forward at the green light. A moment later, Danny rejoined his daydream.

The woman had a flat tummy but those hips…Wow. He was a leg man and hers were amazing, but those hips. The round curve of her butt was eye catching. He remembered sitting up in bed, while she was lying there sleeping on her stomach, and admiring her heart-shaped rear end. The girl had distracting curves. One night, between love-making, she was lying on her elbows talking about…something…and he was using two fingers to walk up and down those two mounds. She allowed him to play butt-soldier until realizing he wasn't listening.

At first, when making love, she seemed content to allow him to be the aggressor. He understood this was new to a woman who had shunned intimacy for most of her life. Her allowing him to make love to her with little reciprocation was a compromise, and he understood it would require patience. That patience was rewarded. Danny knew he had a stupid grin on his face as he remembered the past weekend, starting with Saturday night in bed. The aggressor became the hunted that night. And for the next twenty four hours, until she went home late

Sunday evening, Gabby became the one dictating how and where in his bed. He just let her lead and occasionally nudged her in the right direction when she—

"Oh!"

He had to brake hard, not realizing traffic ahead of him had stopped at a red light. When the traffic started moving again, he allowed some distance between him and the car he'd almost rear-ended before he continued driving home. "Danny, get it together man."

After taking a deep breath and admonishing himself for not paying attention, and after his pulse slowed to normal, he relived the distracting memory of her pushing him down on the bed and bathing him in wet kisses. Lying there, he questioning just how far the inexperienced young woman planned on going with those kisses.

Inexperience aside, she traveled down his chest, stopping between his legs. She didn't surprise him with her lack of technique, that was to be expected, and—from all the pleasure he was deriving—that was forgiven. But there was no lack of effort. The road getting there might have been a little bumpy, but the girl helped him reach his destination—repeatedly, without stopping—and that was a first. With no hesitation, she took, revived, and took him again without coming up for air. Then afterward, she lay in his arms, smiling at her achievement. From that point on, they were equal partners when sharing each other's bodies. Orally, they reciprocated, and she allowed him to show her a few of the many different positions possible when making love.

As Danny turned onto his street, he realized he'd had more sex this past weekend than he had the last three months. And none of those other trysts were as satisfying as with the inexperienced, masquerading, former dyke.

The big question was, what now? Like she said, that wonderful weekend was something that ended when she drove home. They had experienced almost everything a man and woman could together, from A to Z. But now they were starting over at A. And A, she had teasingly informed him, would require him starting from the beginning and asking her out for a date. Would that first date end in great sex again? He doubted that. She was now a woman wanting her man to pay his dues to get in her pants. There was nothing wrong with that. Just with them, he humorously thought as he climbed out his car and locked it, they had started at Z and worked their way backward to A.

That was how he wished every relationship had worked. Especially with Lenora, he thought as he stopped and remembered a woman he had come close to really falling for. That beautiful brown rose never wanted to get past ABC unless he married her first, and there was no way he was going to gamble if the woman he married liked sex. Having sex before marriage wasn't a prerequisite, but it would surely destroy any union for him if he discovered later they weren't on the same page sexually. No once every Saturday night in only the missionary position for him, like some married couples. He craved spontaneity and a woman who obeyed the laws of physics in bed. "For every action there is an equal and opposite reaction." Newton's Law of Motion.

Danny stepped in the door and turned off the house alarm. Walking into the living room, it was as if he could still sense her presence and could inhale her essence. He stood there for a moment picturing the shapely lass bouncing around his house wearing just enough to give him a constant—

"I miss you, Gabby." Taking a deep breath failed to center his thoughts in another direction. "What an amazing weekend with lots of laughs, fun, food, and great sex." He realized that all the hidden passion that was in

Gabby, as she tried hiding her real self, exploded out, and he was the lucky recipient of her coming-out party.

He planned to shower, make dinner, relax with a drink, and then call her. That would give her time to do the same and, maybe, just maybe, give her time to think about him.

഑ഛഝ

Gabriel

I arrived home from work and checked my answering machine for messages. I had to install a house phone and answering machine for business calls. There was a message from my sister and a few nuisance calls. I was a little hungry but decided to shower first just in case I had a surprise visitor. I hoped.

Showered, I found some leftovers that looked okay after being in my refrigerator over the weekend. Sitting on the couch, watching the news while eating dinner, was more often the norm for me after work. The only part that wasn't was constantly looking at my cell phone for a message.

My reasons for doing so I ignored. To admit I hoped he would call, was an insult to the female code. Maybe before this weekend, but afterward? Why wouldn't he? I questioned. *Because I gave him everything a man wanted from a woman on our first date,* those voices of guilt whispered. *He doesn't have any reason to call now.*

Finally shedding my naivety on Saturday night, I'd done things to him I had never considered doing with anyone. It wasn't easy for me at first, but I persevered, and the results more than compensated. And the funny part was I began to enjoy doing them almost as much he did receiving them. And from the way he repeatedly whispered my name while adding "Oh" in front of it, he was definitely enjoying it.

I had to smile when I thought about my searching the internet and the shocking things I saw that made my mouth drop and the words, "No! Never! Not me," escape my lips. But the only other way to actually gain experience hadn't been an option for me in my past. I wasn't gay, but I might as well have been with the celibate life I was leading.

Just as whispers of guilt tried to make me regret the last few days, my cell phone sang my "Danny's Song" ringtone.

"Hello," I answered while trying to hide my enthusiasm.

"Hi, gorgeous, missing me yet?"

"I'm sorry, who is this?"

Hearing Danny laughing on the other end buoyed my spirits. I was sitting on my couch in PJs and suddenly felt overdressed, even though he wasn't here to tease.

"Okay, well, I'm just a guy who missed the lady in white with the awesome legs."

"Excuse me, I do have awesome legs, but how did you get my number and what do you want?" I was having fun, pretending I didn't know him. Truth was, if he had insisted on coming over, I would be running up the stairs to shower—again. And my hair was still damp from the first one.

"Ah, yes, how I got your number? Well, I saw this beautiful woman walking across the street by my station house, and I just had to meet her."

"Oh, you did huh? What was so special about her?"

"Well, she was lovely and had an amazing figure."

"So, you noticed that?"

"Not to sound crude, but I'm sure every guy on the street did."

"I doubt that, but I'll take it that was meant as a complement."

"More of a thank you."

"A thank you?"

"It's a guy thing."

When things got quiet, I thought maybe he had changed his mind.

"Ah, yes, the reason I called was to ask if you would permit me take you out for…ah…dinner or something?"

"Well, maybe dinner sometime," I teased. "But I don't know what something is."

"Ms. Sumpter, will you go out with me to dinner and maybe a movie or dancing. With your legs, I'm sure you are an amazing dancer."

This time, I started laughing. He remembered I said I was a lousy dancer. I did like the comment about my legs, however. "That sounds nice, but I know nothing about you. I don't even know your name." I heard him curse. *What, Danny, are you thinking with your other head?* I was thinking it was a nice other head, then I re-membered—how in the hell would I know with the few I'd seen?

"Sorry. My name is Daniel Robert Washington. I'm twenty-five years old with a birthday next month. I'm six foot three and weigh about two hundred and twenty pounds. I am a city cop in the SWAT unit. I served four years in the army and met some wonderful people there, like this certain one young female soldier I was friends with. You won't believe this. She was a great soldier but actually thought she was a better shot than me."

"The crazy woman. So, you proved she was wrong by winning all those competitions."

"Well, no." He laughed. "But I had an ulterior mo-tive in letting her win so I could get in her pants."

I shook my head at him. He always seemed to have

an answer for everything. "Oh, you did, huh?" I chuckled. "Well, how did that work out for you?"

"How did what work out?"

"You know what, you smart ass. I should hang up on you. Did you finally get in her pants?"

"Unfortunately no, and those where some very big hips in those pants. They were then, anyway. But you know what?"

"I know I'm going to be sorry for asking again, what?"

"I saw her recently and she is now a fox."

"What, no more big hips?"

"Nope, they're very shapely now."

"How do you know that, did you get that close?"

"What…ah…no, I saw them from a distance."

Liar. "If you are so interested, why didn't you ask her out then?"

"I was going to—and then I found out she prefers women."

I quickly covered my mouth to stifle a laugh. I didn't expect that come back. "So, I'm your second choice?"

"No, I never thought a woman as pretty and classy as you would even consider giving me a date so she was the next best thing."

I should have known a guy who dated half the women at our base would never be lost for words, except a few choice ones.

"So, beautiful, would you let me take you…out?"

I shook my head at his intentional play on words. But it was fun having a handsome man trying to get into my pants. I thought about stretching this out but I was starting to ache for him again. It was as if I could feel his large hands searching out my body under my PJs. From memory, I knew he had the strong hands of a lumberjack and the gentle touch of a surgeon who knew just how to operate on my body. Damn! My resurrection was complete, I was thinking more and more like the other horny Sumpter women.

"Ms. Sumpter?"

"Ah…yes, I would love to, Mr. Washington."

"How about tomorrow?"

"That would be nice, Mr. Washington, but I'm still sore from…my…ah…" *Think, girl,* I admonished myself, distracted by those memories. Honesty was not always the best policy when starting an intimate relationship. "Ah…weekend workout. I'll need a few days to recover."

"Over did it with the exercise, huh?"

Okay smart ass, I know where you are headed with this. "Yeah, it felt so good, I couldn't get enough. My trainer was amazing, gifted, and knew how to work over a body." *There,* I thought, *eat that up.* I could just image him grinning from ear to ear.

"I know what you mean. You do have to be careful about how many reps you do."

I could hear the laughter in his words. "You're right, as always." *Okay, smart ass.* "Ah…the next time, I'll remember that and stop before I get too sore."

"Ah…okay. But remember, each time it gets easier so you were right to keep pushing…ah…your limits."

Yeah, I knew you would think that, you turkey. "How about Wednesday evening?" I asked.

"That would be great, Ms. Sumpter. I'll see you Wednesday night. Is seven okay?"

"Seven's fine. I'll call you if I have to cancel."

"That would be a real bummer. Remember, I carry a gun, and I'm not afraid to use it."

I shook my head and laughed. "Bye, Mr. Washington."

I should have been ecstatic, when I hung up, but I wasn't. It was my idea to take it slow, but I missed him.

After a weekend in his arms, and him inside me, I longed for that again. He was so sweet and gentle with me that, even in the heated throes of passion—as that powerful man sometimes…manhandled…me—I loved it. I knew the last thing Danny wanted was to hurt me. Hell, he treated me kindly long before I slept with him, but wasn't that the point? People changed when they got what they wanted. But was it fair to prejudge him? Hell, I'd changed, was that a bad thing? Screwing or not screwing someone never guaranteed the relationship would work out. Life was a gamble, regardless of being a virgin or a whore. The odds of relationships lasting were very poor these days for various reasons, but great friendships could last forever.

"A day at a time, Gabby, take it a day at a time," I whispered.

CHAPTER 16

I had just turned onto Penn Avenue after visiting a hardware store that was advertising for help wanted, when I berated myself for getting frustrated. I couldn't get a firm answer from the owner on giving that job to one of our women, but he didn't say no, so that was something. But he was willing to give it to me on the spot, that grinning letch of a proprietor said, while ogling my breasts. Maybe this wasn't the right opportunity for our ladies. Knowing their lack of options, that letch might take advantage of the circumstances, and them. It wouldn't be the first time we found out later that we had put a vulnerable woman in a compromising situation.

Two blocks down the street and I got a call from Beverly.

"Hi, Bev, what's up? Are the women there yet?"

"Yes, they arrived a few minutes ago, but that's not why I called. Something terrible has happened."

My first thought was the usual problem we had—some angry guy had found one of our women and hurt her or her child. I wasn't too far from the truth.

"It's Elaine. She was beaten up and raped."

My stomach turned. Elaine was one of the most kind-hearted people I'd ever met. She was an unpaid volunteer who lived alone after her husband divorced her for his secretary five years ago. They never had kids, and she blamed that for their break up. She never let that slow her down and had, on occasion, risked taking some of the younger women home with her until we could move them to a safer home or shelter.

"She's near you, in West Penn Hospital, Gabby," she said to my shock and silence.

"I'm heading there now, Bev. I'll let you know what I find out."

"Okay, Gabby, I can handle everything here."

Elaine attacked? I couldn't believe it. I thought about calling Danny for help. I would have, but the anger I had for all men when one of them hurt a women vetoed that. I struggled with not placing all men in that sick category. Right now, my sweet Danny was also a lowlife, cowardly, gutless, woman-raping bastard of a man. I would reason that away in time, but it was one of the things I worried about in any relationship I might have with him or any other man since my attack.

When I arrived at the hospital, Elaine was already in her room, but it took about an hour before I could see her. When I entered her room, her face was badly bruised, her lip cut, and one eye almost swollen shut. I thought she was asleep, but she opened her eyes as I approach her bed.

"Oh, Elaine, I'm so sorry." I tried hiding my shock at seeing her condition, but I never was good at that—like most people who allowed anger to surge through them.

"I know, Gabby, so am I."

"What happened?" When I saw the tears in her eyes, I changed my mind. "No, you don't have to tell me. I'm sure the police have enough information." When she nodded her head, I just walked over and held her. We cried together for a while.

"I walked into my apartment and he was there," she said, after we dried our eyes. "I had left my bedroom window open like I always do. I never thought anyone could climb up there on the second floor. Apparently, it was very easy to climb up, the cops said. Stupid, stupid me. When I walked into my bedroom. he placed a pillowcase over my head and started punching me in the face. When he stopped, he said if I just submitted, he wouldn't kill me. So, I did, Gabby. I did whatever he wanted."

"You did the right thing, Elaine. Better to be bruised and alive, than dead."

"I know, Gabby, but some of the things he did to me I never—not even with my husband Frank when he was around."

"I know, honey. I was attacked in the service." She looked up at me as if I was making it up for her benefit. "Three years ago in Afghanistan."

"Then we're both scarred."

"If we let them, yes. It took me a long time to get over it, but I had a wonderful woman help me. I'll do the same for you if you need me."

"Thank you, Gabby."

We talked for a while and, when I noticed she was falling asleep, I kissed her and left, promising to drop by tomorrow. I called Beverly and told her what I knew. She must have noticed how angry I was and demanded I take the rest of the day off and go home. She was right about the angry part. It took hours of pacing my house before I could calm down. Not to mention my urge to shoot some loser who took that moment, while I was driving home, to blow me a kiss from his car. When I reached for my purse, he had accelerated away. Lucky sucker, he didn't know how angry I was after what happened to Elaine.

"Hello? Hello? Hello—"

"Danny," I said, after finally calming down enough to talk.

"Gabby, is that you?"

"Could you stop by for a few minutes, I need your help with something."

"I'll be over in an hour, okay?"

I hung up without answering. Again, I was angry with my best friend. I had an hour to stop blaming him for what another asshole did. Thankfully, it didn't take that long. I was showered and had put on some sweats when he rang my doorbell.

"Hi, Gabby."

I pulled him into my house, wrapped my arms around him, and started crying.

"Gabby, what's wrong? Did someone hurt you? Son-of-a-bitch, I kill the bastard!" I shook my head as I cried on the angry man's chest. "Then what's wrong? Are you having my baby?"

Okay, that came out of nowhere, but I shouldn't have been surprised. Not from the man holding me. I stopped crying and looked up at him, wondering where that came from. He smiled at me. I knew, from that moment on, nothing could ever make me hate him—nothing. I pulled his head down and kissed him.

The man was a mind reader and, apparently, loved to pick me up. I had no objection to where he was carrying me. My kiss was his invitation. I would tell him every-thing about what happened to Elaine, just not now. Noth-ing that happened outside this house could change that—not now.

We patiently undressed each other, taking time to stop with each garment removed and kissing the revealed flesh. That was the most exciting undressing I could have ever imagined. I was so turned on, I wanted him inside me before he finished removing my clothes. His carrying me to my bed didn't bring about the immediate entwining as I had hoped. But I had no objections to where he spent the next half hour. I hoped he didn't mind, but I would have to reciprocate later because now I had to have him. He didn't resist when I pushed him over and climbed on top of him.

My only real experience in bed was with the man I was now wildly riding, but I gave him what I knew. Aside from the obvious pleasure I was seeking in his arms, it was the physicality of being with this powerful man that I needed. In a gym, I would work out my anger and frustrations on a heavy or speed bag until I was soaked with sweat and my arms ached. But it was the man moaning under me, shaking his head side to side as he thrust up into me, that was the beneficiary of my anger. My pleasure won out first and I collapsed on him.

My man allowed me a few minutes to recover and then took over. He flipped me over on my back and climbed between my legs. Did he sense what I craved? I didn't know. But there was nothing gentle about the way he attacked my body. Locked in the grip of his powerful hands holding me by my hips, I became his speed bag, as his body pounded my flesh, and I loved every stroke. Yes, I would be sore later, but it was what I needed to eject the angry in me. We had made love much longer, as our goals then were to give pleasure to each other. But this time our motivations were different, and we quickly exploded.

I would never admit it to my bad sisters Shay and Lea but, damn, now I understood the curse. The man panting on top of me had freed my body and soul. I didn't know if he could go again, but I was sure hoping he could because—wow, that felt amazing. I just closed my eyes, wrapped my legs and arms tightly around him, and reveled in the moment. Thankfully, that was enough for him. I knew he was everything I needed. Later, he took his time and proved that, three additional times, before he released in me.

When I felt him lifting up off me, I pulled him back down and squeezed, before releasing him a few minutes later. When he rolled over on his back, I moved with him, not wanting to be free of his touch. Remaining in his arms, I placed my head on his chest.

"Danny, I need your help," I said after I sensed we both had caught our breaths and relaxed.

"Give me a few minutes more, and we can go again."

I pinched his nipple.

"Ouch!"

He knew that wasn't what I was asking.

"Okay, help with what?"

I sat up and looked at him. Mistake. From the way his eyes were staring at my breasts, there was no way he was listening to whatever I had to say. I resumed my position, lying on his chest.

"One of the women who volunteers at the women's center where I work was raped in her home."

This time, he was the one who sat up. When I joined him, my breasts weren't their usual eye magnets. Inwardly, I smiled at that axiom.

"What happened?" he asked.

I explained to him what Elaine had told me.

"Gabby, that sounds similar to some other reported rapes. I'll need to check, but I think at least two of them happened to women who worked with organizations like yours."

Now, I was the one surprised.

"Why don't you come and stay with me for a while, until we can figure out if you're in any danger?"

"Do you think this is some husband or boyfriend,

angry because he can't find his woman to beat up on?"

"I don't know, babe. I just would feel better knowing you were safe."

"In your bed, I'm never…safe."

I was going to tell him why when he pushed me down on the bed, his gaze traveling from one end of my body to the other and back again, stopping at my eyes. What he was thinking about doing warmed me. But he never got the chance. It was my turn to give. I knew I surprised him, but for sure he wasn't going to stop me. Well, not for the first few minutes, anyway, and then he had other ideas and, when he lifted me off him, I was all for whatever he wanted next.

☙◌❧

I woke up dwarfed by the large body of the man spooning me. I never felt safer than I did hidden in his arms. I didn't want to move, but I needed a shower. When I gently lifted his heavy arms off me, he rolled over on his back. I waited until I was sure he was asleep before climbing out of bed, walking into the bathroom, and letting my shower pound my sore body. The man, who took me on my knees this time, was asleep. Believe me, he earned it. We went from that position to my being on top of him to changing positions again, before he finally ran out of gas…or something.

While I was drying off, I debated his suggestion to move in with him. Just to be in his arms every night would be worth it, I figured. But I did love my independence and freedom. When I walked out of the bathroom, Danny was sleeping soundly. I pulled the covers over him and went downstairs. I sat on the couch in my robe with a glass of wine, debating if Elaine's attacker was someone we were familiar with. Was I in danger or was Beverly?

She also lived alone. Maybe she should also stay with Danny. An option, I humorously thought, she would love. Probably insist that it would be safer if we all slept on one bed with Danny in the middle.

I decided to make dinner and then wake up "Sleeping Booty" with a kiss. The only question was should I risk going upstairs to change into something more comfortable and maybe wake up my visitor. I would be too hot in the kitchen in my robe so I decided to risk it. Tiptoeing softly, and trying to be quiet, I walked into the room. Like a magnet, I was drawn toward the man in my bed. He had kicked off the covers and was lying on his stomach with his head facing the other way. Feeling brave, I crept up closer to the bed. Being able to be this close to him without wrapping my arms, legs, and lips around him gave me time to study his body. It was beautiful. His skin was a smooth light tan, his shoulders and arms very muscular and toned, and mmmm what a shapely ass. I wouldn't have ever imagined that I would be standing in my bedroom staring at a naked man's ass, especially a naked brown man's ass. *From playing a dyke to a voyeur, you've come a long way, baby.*

I walked away, shaking my head, before he woke up from my lips kissing those muscular cheeks. He wouldn't have minded, that was for sure. I slipped on a Steeler black and gold knit night shirt and some white cotton socks. The loose knit shirt was airy and cool, just what I needed as I cooked over a hot stove.

Now, what could I quickly cook was the question. I had a taste for spaghetti, but making the sauce right took time. My promise to try the readymade sauce I'd purchased crossed my mind. Looking in my refrigerator, I tried to get some ideas. Frustrated, I decided on the spaghetti. Thankfully I had red and green peppers, onions, and ground chuck to add to the ready-made sauce. Quickly, I got the ingredients together and started my sauce. Its taste would depend on how long it could cook. I figured Danny might sleep another hour and then take a shower, so that should give dinner time to simmer. My timing was damn close. I heard those heavy footsteps coming down my stairs right on time.

"There she is."

When I turned around, there he was standing there shirtless—again. And of course my eyes immediately stared at his hard stomach and those muscles that curved down in a V toward his…

I had to clear my throat. "Hi, Danny, hungry?"

"For both."

"For both what? Oh, never mind, I should have known better. Come take a seat, and I'll serve you. We're having spaghetti for dinner."

"Great, I love spaghetti."

Of course, he would say that. What guy wouldn't after what I just gave him. But I smiled and kissed his cheek. It wasn't my best spaghetti, but he liked it and that made it good. We laughed and joked around while we ate, avoiding the ugly things happening in the world. I tried to remain somewhat aloof, figuring it was a female's duty, but this boy, who rocked my world in bed, also made me laugh and feel alive just chatting about everyday things.

He helped me clean up the kitchen and put the leftovers away. I poured us the last of the wine in my house and we retired to the couch.

"What do you think of my offer?"

"That's sweet of you, Danny, but I think I'm safe here. But if, for any reason, I begin to suspect something, I will take you up on that."

"Come here."

I climbed onto his lap.

"You have my cell phone number. If, for any reason, you feel uneasy here at home alone, or about someone hassling you at work, call me. If I don't answer, leave a message. Sometimes I have to turn my phone off when at work, but I check it often."

I kissed his face, laid my head on his shoulder, but I didn't comment.

"Thank you for dinner, Gabby."

I didn't like the tone of that, so I sat up in his lap. "Are you going?"

He smiled at me, but that wasn't going to work. I had more plans where to place that smile.

"Don't look at me like that, girl. I have to work tonight."

"Really, or have I worn you out?"

"I still have an hour to go, lady. Do you want me to prove it?"

From the look in his eyes, and that teasing smirk on his face, I sensed he meant that, and the truth was I was the one worn out.

"Well?"

"I believe you. Thank you for coming over. I really needed someone—"

"Someone? So, you aren't going to admit you needed me."

"I needed you very much today, Daniel Washington."

"That's better."

We kissed as his hands gently traveled over my body. It seemed to me he wasn't trying to blow on my embers, just soothing them, and I appreciated that.

"Go get dressed, knucklehead, before I change my mind." I removed his wandering hand, climbed off his lap, and pointed upstairs.

I watched him stand up and, when he went to kiss

me, I shook my head and stepped back with my hands on my hips, tapping my foot. Watching him smile and then walk up the stairs, I felt something new to me that I didn't like. It got worse when he returned, kissed me on the forehead, and then walked out my door. I had to remember this was a part of a relationship. The coming and going, and there was a lot of the first, the ups and the downs, the ins and—

"Okay, bad Sumpter woman, you have got to stop." Those words had only one meaning and not the one I intended. The Sumpter curse!

In a life of extremes, sitting in his arms on the couch was my favorite. I'd had the era of lost identity, when I played the part of being gay. Then I joined the army and became a killing machine. And taking a life then became as easy as drinking a beer. Protecting myself and the soldiers depending on me removed any guilt. Surviving a near-death attack, I spent the next three years trying to mend myself and other broken women. Of all those abrupt changes in my life, none affected me as deeply as the man who'd just walked out my door.

The high wall I placed around my heart survived all of these dramatic events until—he walked back into my life. I never knew that just sitting in his arms, and his nurturing me, could feel so cherishing. His face in my hair and his breath in my ear, as he whispered loving and teasing things, moved me more than those violent changes. His hand softly rubbing the skin of my thigh became as rewarding as when he roughly clasped those same thighs in the throes of passion. In those gentle moments, more thoughts passed between us than all the words we'd shared.

Now, I was feeling worse, letting him leave with an hour to—

CHAPTER 17

Danny

Danny walked into the Zone Number Two police station. "Detective Cable?"

The detective looked up at the uniformed officer standing at his desk. "Yes, Officer, can I help you?"

"I'm Danny Washington. One of the ladies who work at the woman's center, a few doors down, was attacked and raped in her home. From what her co-workers said, it was similar to some of the ones you alerted the zone about."

The detective frowned. "I didn't get any notice that he had struck again."

"Struck again?"

"Yes, that MO sounds like a new rapist who just started a few months ago—that we know about in our area, anyway. He has attacked four women who we've learned are connected with help centers. Apparently, he has some grudge with women working in that field. What do you know about the latest attack?"

Danny gave him all the information he had.

"That sounds like our boy, Officer Washington. I'll add that building to our list and stop in and alert the women there to be very careful walking to their cars and while at home. Apparently, most of the attacks occurred in or near their homes, and I expect this guy will strike again. He's a vicious SOB. He's ruthlessly beating up his victims, and I'm afraid he's going to kill one if we don't catch him. He's smart, so far anyway, and hasn't left any clues or DNA. He's obviously wearing condoms, gloves, and maybe even a mask. None of his victims can identify anything about him. Some thought he was white, others black, and some—" He threw his hands up. "—had no idea."

"I don't know how many women might be targeted," Danny suggested, "but maybe we can put them or their homes under surveillance."

"Yes, if I had the manpower, but the murder rate is up this year, and most Zones are spread too thin. What I'll do is look up all the women's aid centers and alert them to this possible threat."

"Thank you, Detective, at least that's something."

They shook hands and Danny headed home, planning to get some much needed sleep.

のめの

The Pillowcase Rapist

The Lexus was easy to follow as it pulled out of the police station parking garage. Fortunately, the trailing vehicle had that common tan color and universal GM shape that made it all but indiscernible from other makes and models in traffic. Keeping back four of five car lengths, he was confident the pig in the Lexus never knew he was being followed. His plan was to follow him home and then double back and follow his whore to her house when she got off from *her* job. Then he could get to them, after finding out where they lived, regardless if they were alone or together.

Yesterday, he had followed the older woman working there and discovered where she lived, so now he would have two to choose from, or he could do both broads the same night.

Parking a few houses from the house where the Lexus stopped, he studied the cop as he exited his vehicle and walked into his house. The man took his time studying the cop's house and thought he'd found a fairly easy entrance in from a basement window. From the way the cop stood motionless, once the front door was open, indicated he was shutting off the alarm system. If the house had security alarms, he would have to time his entrance for when they were shut off.

The older broad's house a blind man could enter without being caught. He decided, when it became her turn, he could play with her all night. While picturing what he had in mind for her, he drove away from the cop's house.

There was an apartment and another house belonging to some other bitches that he wanted to check out. This was becoming fun, he decided as he headed for the first of those potential destinations.

ﾂﾂﾂ

Gabriel

I didn't learn any additional information from Elaine on my visit earlier today. She did state that two detectives had departed just before I arrived, but with little news about her attacker. She also informed them that she had tried, but couldn't add anything to what she told the police yesterday.

Thankfully, our schedule at the center was clear today so we left work early. Tomorrow would be different. There were three or four possible cases arriving that we would have to take on from different cities, but they were only transfers. Meaning we received them and moved them on to another place.

Beverly was stopping by the hospital to see Elaine, so I just headed home. There were some sheets that needed washing from the last few nights.

Yes, that normal function turned my thoughts around 180 degrees. If I wasn't driving, I would be crossing my legs, hoping that calmed the growing itch between them at the thought of that man.

It was a curse. I was beginning to believe that now. Did all women have this reaction when they thought of the man in their lives? I went years and never felt this…this aching…for a man. It was very pleasurable, but for a woman who needed to be in control, it could be a curse.

The way I felt now, if he was standing there when I got home, I would jump him right there with the door open, and that wasn't me. Well, it hadn't been me, and I wasn't sure I liked the new me sometimes. This wasn't something I needed counseling about, searching my soul to see who I wanted to be. Both sides of me had their better points. I loved running my life my way, and I loved the way he made the woman under him float in ecstasy. Could I have both? Could any woman? But weren't they conflicting? Could you lose yourself in his arms and allow your man to do whatever to your body and yet climb out of bed and be in command of your life? To be true to either, didn't that require taking some from one to complete the other?

I did know, when I was floating in the pleasure he gave me, I didn't give a damn about anything going on outside his warm body. Yet when I was in control, my thoughts were about making life better for others. One was obviously nobler and made the world a better place, maybe one person at a time. The other—damn was all I could say. If you had never been that high, you wouldn't understand anyway.

I took a quick shower when I got home, threw on some loose sweat pants and a T-shirt, put my hair up in a haphazard ponytail, and then started my wash. Two hours later, I had the house clean and my laundry finished, folded, and put away. But my stomach felt like I should have eaten something first. My weakness for fast food whispered a quick solution, which also meant I would be spending more time running around the track at Mt. Lebanon High School, or with the very skinny women at my fitness gym.

I was debating which fast food establishment would be getting my money when my phone ringing moments later trumped either delicious decision.

I heard that familiar song on my cell phone but, being a woman, I had to play the part. "Hello," I said on the third ring.

"Hi, Gabby."

"Who is this?"

"The man who takes your breath away."

"Is it you, Santa Claus? But I'm mad at you."

He played along, like I knew he would. "Why, little girl?"

"I asked for the Rock in my bed, and you gave me Pee Wee Herman."

"Smart ass." He laughed. "I was calling because we have a dinner appointment tonight. You said Wednesday, it's early, but I thought you might be hungry."

It *was* Wednesday, I had completely forgotten. Maybe it was because of what happen to—

"I am, Danny. Can you give me an hour to get ready? I didn't expect you this early." I couldn't tell him the truth.

"Nope."

"Nope?"

"Nope. Look out your window, I'll wait. As you can see, I'm sitting outside your place right now. Throw on a sweater or a jacket. The wonderful place I'm taking you to doesn't have a dress code and couldn't care less, as long as you're civil."

Throw on a jacket? Wearing just this T-shirt, I'd have to carry my gun—in my hand—cocked and loaded. Wait—poor choice of words.

"Come on, Gabby, trust me. It'll be fun. I'm just wearing sweats myself. See, I had this craving all day for some delicious ribs and the best potato salad in the city and thought you might like to go slumming with me. Please."

That nudged me into grabbing my purse, checking that my weapons were in there, taking out my spray bottle of perfume and hitting a few places, grabbing my keys, and then stopping at my door. *This is crazy*, I admitted then gave my breath the hand check and started laughing. I shook my head, locked my door behind me, and hurried out to his car. I stopped half way, returned to the house, unlocked my door, grabbed my jacket to cover my perky girls, and hurried back to his car.

"Okay, where are we going that couldn't wait until I got…respectable?"

"Gabby, you have to relax and trust me. I would never take you some place you wouldn't enjoy."

"But I look—"

"Girl, you look amazing in—in whatever."

"I think you have the wrong Sumpter woman."

"Maybe years ago, but not now."

He turned on his radio and, by the third song, was singing. His confidence was both appealing and irritating. Anyway, despite my aversion to this trip, I was humming along with him after the next song.

"This is Wilkinsburg," Danny explained as we drove through the town. "It used to be a very nice area but has fallen on hard times. Most of the small towns in the Pittsburgh area mainly functioned on the taxes generated by the steel mills and those who worked there. When the mills started closing in the seventies and eighties and moved to the mid-west, these towns suffered from lower tax revenue. As responsible people moved out, following other opportunities, less responsible people, in most cases with much lower incomes, allowed towns like Wilkinsburg, Braddock, and some sections of Pittsburgh, to decay from a lack of financial investment."

My next question would have been, "Then why are we here?" but I'd promised to trust him—and I was armed.

"There's this mom-and-pop restaurant that serves the best home cook food I've ever tasted. I've been going there for years. Just another block."

The neighborhood looked like the hood, but I was with him so I wasn't too worried. But I was armed and, with him being a cop, I knew he was required to always be armed. And I had seen him in action and knew he could handle himself.

"Okay, we're here," he said and parked in front of this store-front-looking building. The bricks were painted white and the windows were decorated, preventing anyone from getting a good look inside. *Home Style Restaurant* was printed in black and gold letters on the windows. I looked at the place and then at him.

"Don't judge a book—"

I was sure he said that because of the stunned look on my face. I smiled at him and waited until he walked around and opened my door. He had once frowned and chastised me when I was about to let him forgo that courtesy. He opened the restaurant door and about a dozen people of color, seated at four or five of the tables, turned and stared at the white woman standing there. I only took another step when the man behind men pushed.

"Danny!"

I heard someone calling him and, like clockwork, most of the faces that were staring at me smiled. Then an older, heavyset woman started walking toward us from behind the counter with her arms outstretched.

"Mama Jones, you look beautiful. Are you sure you won't marry me?"

"Oh, stop it. You know I'm married. Who is this little flower?"

"This is my best friend, Gabriel. I told her I know a place that makes the best soul food and she was dying to come here and try some of your cooking, Mama Jones."

"Come on, honey, I can tell, from that leery look on your face, he probably railroaded you here. But don't worry, I'll take good care of you," she said, taking my arm and ushering us toward a table. "Come, sit near me."

Her upbeat manner did calm me as did the other patrons who were now ignoring us and enjoying what they were eating, from the music of forks hitting china. We sat at a table and, when I looked around, I saw that everyone was dressed casually and more into each other than this stranger.

"Okay, what can I get for the two of you?"

"The works."

I looked nervously at Danny, having no idea what the "works" were. I would hate to have something offered to me that I didn't like and offend someone. I loved sea food, but not fish on my plate with the heads on them and their eyes looking at me.

Yuck! I'd catch them, gut, scale, and cook them, but it would be, for me, like leaving the head on a turkey at Thanksgiving. One of my idiosyncrasies, I guessed.

"Danny, maybe this little lady doesn't like soul food."

"And we won't know that unless she tries some, now will we?"

"Sweetheart." Momma Jones smiled. "I'm going to give you a little taste of some of the food we offer. I won't be upset if it's not to your liking, okay?"

"Don't believe that, Gabby. Do you want me to tell you what happened to the last person to say they didn't like her cooking? They didn't eat the lunch special the next day."

He then turned and looked around the restaurant. I got caught up in his actions and nervously looked around too.

When I turned to ask him why, he leaned toward me. "They *were* the lunch special the next day," he whispered.

I didn't know why—he had tricked me—but I found that very funny. But I didn't laugh out loud until Mama did.

"Whatever you do, honey," she said, frowning at him, "don't eat anything from his 'special' plate tonight."

"Just joking, Mama, you know I love your food," Danny pleaded to the back of the woman walking behind the counter.

From the way she rolled her eyes at him, I knew he was in trouble. That meant no one would be eating me for the lunch special tomorrow…well, with the possible exception of the repentant big-mouth sitting across from me, if he was lucky.

I devoured everything Momma Jones placed in front of me. From tender and delicious ribs that fell off the bone, thick and very cheesy mac and cheese that I could have cut with a knife, some type of very tender leaf greens, the best potato salad I'd ever tasted, candied sweet potatoes, and some things I still didn't know what they were but I tried everything, and it was all delicious.

"I'm so glad you liked my cooking, Gabriel." Mama Jones expounded, sitting down at the table after we finished eating.

I was sipping on a hot cup of coffee. Danny had asked if he could excuse himself for a minute to say goodbye to a friend of his who was leaving.

"Everything was delicious, thank you. I'm stuffed. And please call me, Gabby."

"Gabby, you are the first woman my Danny has brought here for me to meet. You must be special to him."

"I don't feel special, dressed like this. I had just finished washing clothes when he stopped by. Rather have dressed up a little."

"Not for my place, darling." I watched as the proprietor looked lovingly around this small building. "I've had plenty of opportunities to move to a much larger place, with a more elite clientele, in an upscale neighborhood, but that's not what I wanted," she continued. "You're dressed perfect for my place…well, as long as your jacket is closed." She looked real seriously at me and then playfully smiled.

Yes, that made me look down, and she laughed and apologized when I closed my jacket over my erect nipples.

"See, Gabby? I wanted to retire to a place where I

could serve people my recipes and sit and chat like we're doing. I'm not in it to just make money. Sure, enough to stay open, but that's not the reason I'm here. I wanted a place where my customers could finish washing clothes," she said with a big smile, "wash their face and hands if necessary, splash on a little smell good, and come sit down and eat until you can't move."

"Well, I'm close to that now."

"Good."

There were a few minutes of silence as we both looked to see what Danny was doing. The way he was laughing with two guys, we both realized we had a few minutes to kill.

"How long have you known, Danny?"

"We were close friends in the army and just bumped into each other again after a few years."

The look on her face said she wasn't buying that. "He's a great guy. He helped my two sons who were always getting in trouble. Now one's in the service and the other's off to college." She placed her hand on mine. "I always hoped he and my only daughter would hook up, but that never happened. Now, I think maybe he has found the love of his life."

I was so surprised by that I was speechless.

"Look at you, how sweet. I think the feeling is mutual. Well, I'm going to stop meddling before he catches me. You're welcome here anytime, Gabby, okay?

I nodded my head and, as she walked past, she squeezed my shoulder. Then she went over and started chatting with her other customers.

"I'm sorry, Gabby," Danny said, arriving just as Mama Jones departed. "She doesn't mean any harm, but I know Mama, she was asking personal questions, right? She loves to set me up or inquire about my love life."

"Don't worry, she was cool. I like her a lot, and I can tell from the gleam in her eyes she loves you."

"We have gotten close over the years. She's a good friend of my mom's, and I helped her with her sons when they were growing up. And showing up here on occasion with some other police officers helps keep the riff-raff away and is good for business. You'd be surprised how many cops now eat here with their families."

"Yeah, she told me you were close."

"Well, are you ready to go?"

I nodded and stood. I had a great time and the food was amazing, as was the company. A book by its cover, that was very true here. We hugged Mama Jones and said our goodbyes to some of his friends. Danny opened my door and, as I got into his car, I realized there was so much about his life that I didn't know. I felt bad, because I was so quick to judge what I saw. The people in that old building treated me better than I would have received in a five-star restaurant.

"Thank you, Danny," I said was we drove down Penn Avenue toward the Parkway.

"See? I knew you would like the food."

"No, not because of the food, but for introducing me to some nice people."

"You're also nice people, or I wouldn't have brought you around them."

As we drove off, his kind words had the opposite effect on me. I was falling deeper for him and, all the while, fighting it. *Why?* I asked myself. The answer was the same—control. The guy driving smelled so good, I couldn't stop imagining him taking me. That's who I'd become, but how did someone whose life was emotionless and stolid, become driven by feelings of intimacy. He was slowly stealing my control. It wasn't a devious deed on his part, I was sure of that. From what I knew about Danny, he was just being himself. The problem was with me.

"You're very quiet, are you okay?"

"I'm sorry, Danny. I was just thinking about some things."

He didn't bother me about that the rest of the trip so I avoided the subject. I appreciated that so much, but by remaining quiet, I relinquished even more control. How? Because he was so understanding, there was nothing I could deny him if asked. To me, that was relinquishing control. *Tell this wonderful man no? Why would I? Yes, it's a woman prerogative, and that also of a man, but not when you've possibly found your soulmate.*

"Are you working again tonight?"

"Yes, I am, beautiful. Then I have a three-day weekend off. Hint, hint."

"Can you—no, you need to rest before work."

"What did you want, Gabby?"

"You," I brazenly told those questioning eyes.

He could only take quick looks at me while driving. But those brown eyes didn't need but a moment to reveal they desired the same thing.

"Not what you're thinking," I had to lie to save face, for some stupid reason. "Well, that also, but just sitting in your arms is what I was talking about."

"Hey, lady, like I said, I'm always here for you."

Yes, you are, I was thinking as we pulled up in my driveway. "Look, Danny, I'm okay," I confessed before he could get out the car. "You go home and get some rest before work. I'm having trouble getting what happened to Elaine out of my mind. I don't have Friday off, but I would love to spend the time I do have with you."

"Okay, Gabby." He seemed disappointed but agreed. "I'll call you later."

I kissed him, climbed out the car before he could,

and walked to my house. It surprised me that he had agreed to leave so quickly. Only after he was gone did I realize my mention of poor Elaine had polarized his decision.

Danny did call later and I apologized if I made him feel uneasy. He said I hadn't, but hearing that from him did little to convince me. It wasn't intentional, but I was having troubling thoughts about Elaine and also what happened to me. Maybe it was women's intuition, I didn't know, but I sensed something bad was in the air. After checking that everything was locked, I took my gun to bed with me.

CHAPTER 18

The van carrying Lynn Anderson, Sharon Jones and her two kids, and Elsie Wynn arrived at the woman's center Thursday at a little past noon. They arrived from Kansas City, Dallas, and Detroit. I had two houses set up for them on Neville Island, but only one was ready for occupancy.

After processing, I took Lynn Anderson, Sharon Jones, and her two kids and set them up in one of the homes. Beverly, or one of the other volunteers, would take the other lady and set her up temporarily in a motel, or I would when I returned. That went as well as could be expected.

"I hope the four of you are comfortable here," I said. "Mrs. Sample, who lives downstairs, can help you with whatever you might need. We placed food in the frig. I'm not sure what you like to eat, but it's something to keep you for a while."

"I'm sure everything will be fine, Mrs. Sumpter," Lynn Anderson said as she walked around the living room on the second floor, looking at the old furniture in the furnished apartment they would be sharing.

"Well, there are two bedrooms on this floor," I explained.

The Anderson woman seemed relaxed and open. Mrs. Jones, maybe because she was more worried about her children, was uptight and very nervous. Not knowing what these women had endured, I never let that bother me. Sometimes it takes a while for them to realize they are finally safe.

"Mrs. Jones, we have set up the larger of the bedrooms with a bed for you and bunk beds for your kids so that each will have their own bed. The rest of this apartment you will have to share for now. We are working on finishing the other house so you'll each have your own place."

The way Mrs. Jones looked at me, for a moment, I thought she was ready to bolt out of here. When her two kids started running around the room and having fun, it seemed as if that was the final straw.

"Thank you, Mrs. Sumpter," Lynn Anderson said, "and thank that other nice lady at the woman's center. This will be fine, and I'm sure we will get along just fine until…well, until we find our own way."

"She's right, Mrs. Sumpter."

"Okay enough of this Mrs. stuff. I'm single, my name's Gabriel, and everyone calls me Gabby. Now if you have any questions about anything, Mrs. Sample is downstairs and understands the situation. What we have to insist on is that you don't make any calls home to either friend or family, or use any credit cards or cell phones. That'll enable people to trace you here and could put you and the others in danger. As of now, no one knows where you are. We want to keep it that way, and I'm sure each of you do too."

They nodded at me and each other.

During the drive back to the center, my spirits were

lifted. It was always a great feeling when we were able to turn around the lives of women living under the tyranny of some crazy man. I parked and had to admit that, while walking toward our building, I was blissfully looking toward the police station for a certain handsome police officer. That would have put the cherry on top.

That sweet thought turned to shit when I walked in the woman's center door.

"Is this the bitch?"

"What's going on here?"

There was a man with a knife in his hand threatening Beverly. He had her backed into a corner when I walked in the door.

"I'm going to cut up this bitch if someone doesn't tell me where my woman is."

"No, you're not!"

"What did you say to me?"

"I said, 'No, you're not!'" I repeated and started walking toward him. "You're going to leave her alone and get your useless ass out of here before I call the police."

"Gabby, get out of here."

"Don't worry, Beverly. In the army, I used to eat punks like this for breakfast."

He responded as expected. I had already sized him up and knew I could disarm him. He was all mouth behind that knife and only about twenty-five pound heavier than me. I was trained to fight in the service and spent weeks practicing self-defense when I took this job—just for moments like this.

"Are you dissing me, you bitch?"

"You're a lowlife punk, pulling a knife on a woman half your size. Come here—" I motioned with my hand. "—and I'll take that knife away from you and castrate your little pecker." Yes, my anger had returned and I wanted to kill this bastard. Yes, I was stupid for taunting him, but I had my reasons. He shoved Beverly against the wall and growled at me.

I decided to take another path when he started walking toward me with this enraged look on his face. My plan had been to kick him in his balls and then counter with a swinging sidekick to his head. Thankfully, I was wearing jeans today. Instead, I pulled a weapon out of my purse and Tasered the punk. He flopped around on the floor like a fish for a few seconds before lying there unconscious. I walked over, never taking my eyes off the…fish…and comforted a frightened Beverly before calling the Zone Number Two police station.

"Did he hurt either of you?" Detective Maroney asked.

I looked at a still-shaken Beverly and waited until she shook her head.

"No, Detective, we're okay."

"Well, ladies, he won't be bothering anyone any longer. He's wanted for the murder of the brother and sister of the woman he was after. Apparently, they wouldn't give up her location. Excuse me, ladies, I'll be right back."

Admittedly, I was shaken by that stunning news. We were safe, but another family was brokenhearted at the actions of that lunatic. Now I felt remorse because I should have shot him in the head and sent him straight to hell. This wasn't just a deranged boyfriend or husband we faced, that nut had already killed members of the family of the woman he was looking for and probably intended to do the same to Beverly and me. And oddly enough, we still had no idea what woman he was looking for.

"The car out front—" Detective Maroney walked over to Beverly and me. "—that he was driving was stolen from Atlanta and will be picked up and impounded until its owner can make arrangements for its return. Mrs. David, it was a good thing Ms. Sumpter came along when she did. I have no doubts he would have killed you."

Beverly looked at me as if she believed that was a real possibility.

"Well, ladies, that should wrap everything up here. The prisoner will be shipped back to Atlanta to face charges there. We'll probably waive the right to prosecute him here, so you won't have to testify. With all that he faces in Atlanta, a few more years on his sentence for attempted assault won't matter much." Then, with a nod and a smile, he walked out the door.

Beverly sighed and rubbed her neck. "How did it go with the two ladies?"

Her voice sounded normal, but the twitch in her eyes gave it away. "Bev, why don't we call it a day? The ladies and the kids are set up and seem happy there."

"You might be right. I took care of the other lady. There's nothing scheduled until Monday. Isn't tomorrow the day you meet with your sisters for lunch?"

"Yeah, every second Friday we meet for lunch somewhere."

"In that case, don't bother coming in tomorrow, Gabby. I'm on call for this weekend, so you're free until Monday. That's an order from your boss. Let me get a few things out my office first, and I'm also out of here. Hey, why don't you give that new guy a call?"

I just stared at her. She smiled, genuine this time, then turned and walked to her office. After what just happened, spending time with Danny was a great idea. Just my luck, he was probably reassigned to work nights this weekend.

"Call him."

"Mind your own business, nosey," I jokingly said to the voice shouting into the lobby from her office. I would call, but only after following Beverly home and making sure she arrived safe.

"Don't get out of your car," Beverly shouted at me when we arrived at her house.

I waited to leave until she walked into the house and then waved me away. I sat there an additional few minutes, just in case. "Okay, girl, are you getting paranoid? Hey, after today who wouldn't. Okay, now you are talking and answering yourself. The straightjacket is next."

Looking back a few times after I U-turned, I headed home. But I had to make a few stops first for some much-needed groceries and alcohol for the weekend for me and maybe a visitor.

When I pulled into the parking lot and called Danny, the call went into his voice mail so I hung up. He might be on a dangerous stake out, and I didn't want to distract him. *I'll call him tomorrow*, I decided. *Now, off to the store*.

CHAPTER 19

The weather was perfect today for lunch with my sisters. There was plenty of sunshine and it was very warm with a nice cool breeze blowing. I decided to wear my white shorts and show off my toned legs. I had made running a few miles around the high school track near my home an every-other-evening routine for the last six months and it showed. My calves were chiseled and Danny was smitten with the muscularity of my thighs when I wore anything short. A pink tank top under an open yellow short-sleeved shirt and sandals completed my outfit. It felt comfortable and captured the breeze.

We were meeting at the Double Wide Grill on Carson Street, which was Lea's favorite outdoor restaurant on the Southside, so I thought I was perfectly dressed for that typical Burgh neighborhood. Living closer, I arrived first and was able to reserve a great table in the sunshine that also offered a good view of everyone walking and driving past.

A better reason for this table was I would be able to judge my sisters' attire as they walked from the parking lot toward the restaurant. After turning down two nice guys who playfully offered to buy me lunch, I spotted my sisters a block away and had to chuckle because they still had that runway model gait of theirs. Lea, the braver of the two, was wearing a tiny white mini skirt that of course either of them could have pulled off with their tall frames and very long legs. She'd added a dark blue blouse and white sandals. Lea's blonde hair was cut shorter than she liked, she claimed, but it made getting ready for work in the morning easier. Shay looked great in white Capri slacks with a sleeveless tan blouse. Her blonde hair was pulled back off her face in a long pony-tail. Both ladies, even after five kids total, still carried themselves with class. They seemed more uptown and out of place to me in this urban section of Pittsburgh.

"Hi, Gabby," they both said as we hugged and then they sat down.

"Hi, ladies. You both look great. Lea, I love your hair that short. And, Shay, after three kids and you can still fit those skinny Capri pants. You guys look good."

"And I feel good today," Shay added, placing her purse under the table.

"Same here, but I'm really looking forward to this weekend," Lea revealed. "I've been working too much this week. But I did close four deals, so it was a great week."

We chatted about family, their kids, the husbands, and Mom and Dad over roasted chicken salads. That was the norm for us and I enjoyed their stories. Their kids were a handful, lots of fun to be around, and loved their Aunt Gabby. Admittedly, I spent too much time away from my parents. I called often and enjoyed chatting with them, but I didn't spend nearly enough time at their house. But they weren't stay-at-home parents either. Those two wild oldies were gone more than home, so we all understood and accepted our sometimes-distant relationship.

We'd finished the salads and had ordered coffee when I knew it was time to say what was on my mind.

As if on cue, Lea opened that door for me. "So, what's new with you, Gabby? You seem to still be losing a few pounds."

I finished stirring the sugar in my coffee before answering. "You may be sorry you asked."

"Are you gaining weight?"

"No! No. If anything, I'm losing. It has nothing to do with my weight or health."

"I'm never sorry to hear hot gossip," Lea admitted with that naughty grin she sometimes got.

Another trio of guys stopped at our table to chat. Again, we gracefully declined their attention as my sisters displayed their wedding rings. The three determined guys then turned their attention to the only single Sumpter at the table.

It took a more-blunt objection from Lea before they moved on. One even wrote down his phone number on my napkin before excusing himself. The boy was good looking, I had to admit.

"I've met someone," I volunteered when things went back to normal.

"Is he…ah…worth marrying?" Shay asked, grinning.

My "*Yes*" produced high fives between my sisters and head shakes from me.

"But? I know that look on your face, Gabby."

"Yes, there's a but, Lea. There are some things I'm not sure of, and no, he's not married," I said to the look on her own face. "Actually, it has nothing to do with him. He's amazing. Well, there might be a problem with my family about him, but not with me. He's a person of color."

"Whoa! I thought you were going to say he wasn't Catholic."

All three of us laughed at my crazy middle sister. But that did help alleviate some of the consternation I had in confessing my secret.

"Look, Gabby, I dated a black guy in college. Oh, Shay knew." Lea looked at Shay and then me. "We talk about everything. I had no problem with our differences, but he did. Reluctantly, when it started to become an issue with him, I had to end it, and I spent many a night regretting not waiting until I found a worthy replacement first."

"What she's not telling you is she didn't sit in her dorm pining over him. She went out and found plenty of replacements, but not worthy ones."

Lea stuck her tongue out at Shay.

"His name is Danny Washington," I said, getting back to my problem. "He is a city SWAT police officer in the Zone Number Two station near where I work. We met in Afghanistan while both of us were in the service and became best friends. He saved my life over there a few times."

"And how did you thank him?" bad girl Lea asked, while hinting at something else.

"I was still in my rebellious stage, Lea, so nothing intimate happened between us over there."

"*Nothing?*"

"Nothing. Then three years after being home, the woman's center moved into a building down from his station. Crazy, huh? If he hadn't risked his life to save mine over there, I would be dead. So—so when he asked me out I couldn't say no to him."

"That's great, baby, you needed someone to get your love life jump started again."

"Lea's right, honey. If this Danny person is ringing your bells, I'm—we're—all for it."

"What aren't you telling us?" my perceptive middle sister asked.

"He's a great guy, and I'm really stupid for questioning our relationship but…"

"But what, honey?" Shay asked.

"I grew up intimidated by my wonderful sisters' great looks, poise, and inner confidence. Lacking all of that, I lost my true identity, rather than try and complete. No, guys," I said to the apologetic looks on their faces. "It had nothing to do with you guys, honestly. The two of you were always sweet to me. But I did lose my identity. Weirdly, after I was attacked, I became very determined to be myself. Losing weight and, with your help, dressing better allowed the real Gabby to come out."

"And you—"

"Wait, Lea, I know what you are going to say. My point is, with Danny, I feel myself surrendering parts of the new me to him—gladly, mind you. But I'm not sure if that's what I want now. If that's who I want to be."

"Then keep him at a distance until you are sure."

"That's my problem, Shay. He doesn't deserve that. Even back in my rebellious days in the army, he treated me with the same kindness and friendship as he does now. My wearing something sexy is a turn on for him, but what makes him special is that the look in his eyes never changed. Three years later, and a completely different me, and it never changed. Finally, a guy that sees me as more than just a great piece of ass, and I am that."

"Duh! Of course you are. You're a Sumpter female."

"Right, Lea. But do you see where I'm coming from? You don't find guys like Danny every day. Sometimes, the way he looks at me, I would do anything he wants. I trust this man. What I don't trust is—"

"You, right? That's why, when you find someone like him, you—"

"I know, Lea, you—"

"Marry them, yes."

I wasn't sure my sisters grasped my dilemma. And I wasn't sure I wanted to elaborate further. "I just wish I knew what to do. I don't want to over analyze this and alienate him."

"No one does, Gabby, but you have to be true to yourself first, right, Shay?"

"She's right, honey."

"I know she is, but—"

"It's the curse, isn't it?"

All I could do was smile at them, provoking a duet of head shaking and I-told-you-so looks on their perfectly made-up faces.

"Yes, I could—" I stopped when they started laughing. "I could do him ten times a day, every day, and still daydream about him. But it's more than just great sex, you bad twins."

"Hey, we warned you. Now, it's going to be very hard to put out that fire."

"Tell me about it, Lea. That man rocks my world every time and barely breaks a sweat doing it. He came over for dinner one night and we spent the weekend in bed. Or was that when I was over at his…regardless, I have a problem, sisters. I don't want to lose my identity again in his strong arms."

"How do you know you're not still evolving into the real you? Sis, you have come a long way. My beautiful youngest sister is only a few years old. Give her time to mature before judging her choices. I think she'll get it right."

That was something I hadn't considered. I nodded because that was a possibility.

"Have you thought about dating other guys?"

Looking at Lea, who'd asked, I sensed both of my sister were playing psychiatrist to see if my revulsion for men surfaced. A twinge did but I ignored it and smiled. "I'm in love with Danny, guys."

That shocking news caused a couple of wide eyed looks.

"Okay! Ten othar guuys ar—verboten!" Lea said in a terrible German accent.

Shay and I laughed at our silly sister.

The conversation lightened up after that.

"Oh!" I was elated to tell them before they left. "Danny really loved the white dress you picked out. He couldn't stop commenting on how nice I looked."

"Yeah! Do we know how to shake up our men, or what?" Shay boasted.

As I was telling them how much Danny loved the dress, bad Lea grinned. "Just how quickly did he take off your new underwear?"

I had to laugh at that, remembering I was the one who'd brazenly stepped out of them.

"See? If you had worn the black number I first picked out, you could have skipped that last part and gone straight to getting—"

"Raped, right?"

"Exactly," Lea admitted, licked her lips, and then gave us the "What?" face.

I just shook my head at her. It was a wonder the single-minded woman didn't have ten kids.

"Gabby, be honest with yourself," my usually sane other sister said as we stood to leave. "Give it some time before you make a decision you might regret. He sounds like someone who doesn't deserve to be hurt if you are wrong either way."

"I will, Shay," I said and hugged her.

"If you love him, marry the curse."

"I'll think about it, Lea."

She kissed my cheek, and I watched as my sisters walked away. I noticed just about everyone in the restaurant, and those driving past, also watched them leave. We Sumpter women were eye catchers.

It was my turn to pay for lunch, so I left a nice tip and walked to my car. I still had an hour to kill before my hair appointment and to get my nails done at The Mall at Robinson.

CHAPTER 20

Danny

Danny had overslept after a late evening shift that ran well past midnight as they stood by at the station as backups for Zone Number Three SWAT team, who were trying to get a man with a gun to release his family. They spent seven hours talking that intoxicated man into releasing his wife and coming out with his hands raised. Thankfully, their patience paid off, and they didn't have to kill anyone or get shot at. Every cop in this city remembered the senseless violence in 2009 when two cops were callously gunned down as they were innocently walking up to a door to investigate a nine-one-one call in the Stanton Heights neighborhood. When the call came from a mother having an argument with her son, it was believed they didn't expect a confrontation and never drew their weapons. But the unexpected murder of those two officers was always on the thoughts and minds of cops in this city.

Danny hadn't planned on it, but he slept downstairs on his recliner when returning home early in the morning.

His bedroom was allocated to his houseguest. When he woke up and stretched, he realized it was still dark out. From the wall clock over the fire place, he saw it was almost five in the morning. "Wow, I've only been asleep for less than two hours." In the quiet of the room, he heard something other than the ticking clock. He heard his guest moving about upstairs in his bedroom and no longer had to be quiet. Walking upstairs to answer the call to pee that woke him up, he noticed the door to his bedroom was cracked open. Peeking in to check on his guest, he was rewarded with seeing the naked police officer lying on her side with her back to him. That position gave him opportunity—and pause. Apparently, she was still recuperating from last night and the liquid fire she drank, making the covers too hot to sleep under.

The SWAT team had stopped at Jake's Pub two blocks down the street from the police station, as they often did after a long shift, for a few drinks and ended up closing the place as they sometimes did after hours. Danny had only a few beers, but Janet Mann, one of three police women there, had too much to drink and was so blasted that he offered to drive her home, not knowing she had abruptly turned down two other offers earlier.

"Officer Mann, would you permit me to give you a lift home?" he asked the woman leaning on the bar.

"Hi, handsome Dan. Ah…no thanks. Ah…I drove."

"Of course you did. But in your condition, you can't drive home, or I'd have to arrest you."

"Arrest me, handsome." She stood up and flirted. "And don't forget the body search. Boot I will decode if I cam drive."

"*What*?" he asked the officer, who was slurring her words. She then waved him off and returned to her drink and stool.

Danny was about to accept her put down and leave

when, walking to the door, he turned around and spotted Officer Gloria Steward interceding. Watching them arguing, he debated getting involved. Only when Gloria looked past the inebriated woman and anxiously waved him over did he question ignoring her and leaving or trying one more time.

"Here he is," he heard Gloria announce and watched the object of their concern turn around and face him with an angry stare. "Danny, would you give Janet a lift home?"

"I offered, but she turned me down," he explained, hoping that would free him of that responsibility.

"She has turned everyone down. I asked, but she won't let me drive her home either."

"You—but you live in the other—you know," Janet mumbled.

"In the other direction, yeah I know, but I told you I didn't mind. Anyway." Gloria raised her hand over Janet's head displaying a treasure. "I took your keys out of your purse, girlfriend, so you're not driving home tonight."

"No." Janet tried to snatch the keys from Gloria's hand, stumbled, and almost tripped. "I'm not going anywhere with some pervert—a pervert like DiNardo, no way."

Danny looked remorsefully at Gloria. Both knew of DiNardo's bad reputation for sexual harassment, Gloria personally, and neither could they blame Janet for turning him down when he volunteered. She wasn't that drunk yet, apparently.

"Well, Danny isn't a pervert, he's a good guy."

"Yes, he is Glor—" the now-smiling cop agreed and walked up to him. "Okay, Danny," she said too loud to blame it on the alcohol. "You can take me." She grinned.

The howling sexual accusations by a few other

buzzed cops, overhearing what they wanted to hear, gave her the audience she desired.

"Take her, Dan, or I will," was repeated differently, but often.

Somehow, once in his car, Janet coerced him into driving to his place instead, explaining it was much closer and she could sleep it off on his couch. With his drinking near the legal limit, and his house being much closer, it made sense at the time.

"You have a lovely home here, Danny," she announced as she walked around the living room. Then she kicked off her shoes and sat on the couch.

"Thank you. Look," he added, reading her intentions. "I can't have you sleeping down here on my couch. Come with me."

"No, Danny," she halfheartedly protested as he helped her to stand and she followed him up the stairs. "I can't put you out of your own bed."

He insisted she take the master bedroom, after turning down the very tempting invitation to share his large bed. He walked out, closed the door behind him, and made the recliner downstairs his sleeping quarters.

The spare bedroom was available, but he had washed all the linen and, after a very long night, wasn't in the mind set to walk down to the basement and get them out of the dryer. They were probably too wrinkled to use now anyway, he convinced himself. Sleeping on the recliner was the best idea for two reasons. One was putting distance between him and the shapely lass, whose shapely ass he was now unabashedly staring at, lying on his bed. And the other, because the recliner was very comfortable and often became his resting place when he was tired after a long night at work or play.

After imagining the obvious, he quit staring at the alluring curve of her brown hips, as guilt finally nudged him, and he quietly closed his bedroom door. And while in the bathroom, urinating, he remembered why it was probably left open. Just as he was finally about to drop off to sleep in the recliner, he'd sensed something moving, something—close. Too tired to care what, he allowed his mind to drift off. Just before the darkness claimed him, a delightful scent floated down and relit his consciousness. Questioning the origin, he opened his eyes to a set of bare brown thighs inches from his face. Realizing who it must be, he followed those shapely legs up to pink-lace bikini panties, a tiny waist, and, to his surprise, two large and perfectly shaped bare breasts. He stared up at the beautiful illusion, not surprised the fellow officer invading his dreams looked so good. He'd always thought…

"Danny?"

"Oh!" Danny kicked in the bottom of the recliner and abruptly stood up when her voice pierced his hallucination.

"Danny, I can't sleep," the woman in the impressive sleepwear announced to the now-wide-awake man with the now-wide-open mouth. "Do you have something I can take?"

She must really be drunk, he thought of this usually chaste fellow police officer, to stand there, asking him if he had something to help her get to sleep, wearing only her panties.

He wasn't angry at the obvious skin show because the girl, drunk or not, was a damn brick house.

"Ah…yes, I have something that…ah might help," he muttered as his eyes traveled repeatedly from breasts to eyes. "Come with me." Trying to slip between her and the chair, his arm accidently brushed against her breasts. He turned to apologize and realized from the look on her face that it was unnecessary. In the kitchen he took out a bottle of wine from the refrigerator and poured her a cold glass of red wine. "This should help."

"More alcohol?"

"Yes. Any sleeping aid, like Benadryl, taken with alcohol, can be very harmful or even fatal. The cold wine will cause your body to relax" he said, while struggling not to stare.

"Okay, Danny, I trust you aren't just trying to take advantage of me."

"*What*? No! I—"

"I'm just joking." She smiled. "Thank you for the wine. I do feel more relaxed." She handed him her glass, smiled, kissed him on the cheek, and walked alluringly away.

Danny watched as she ambled out the kitchen. She didn't have Gabby's curves, but what woman didn't look great in just panties? He hurried to catch up and get another look at her as she climbed the stairs.

Struggling now to get to sleep himself, with that enticing picture of her standing over him seared into his thoughts, his next move would have been to take the same remedy he gave her. He finally drifted off while staring at the stairs that led up toward his bedroom.

Let the records show that, had I not already fallen for a certain former army private first class, I would have gladly climbed in bed with Janet and, afterward, we both would have slept the deep sleep of the exhausted. But Ms. Mann was a very nice-looking woman with a sexy body that…ah…gave rise to his…ah…interest, regardless of his deep affection for another.

Maybe if the inebriated nude nymph was sober and teased her way into his arms, he might have yielded to that temptation. But taking advantage of a very drunk fellow police officer, staggering around his home was, thankfully, a turn-off. What people did drunk never surprised him. He had seen people do some crazy things they never would do sober, never.

Working together those few times with Janet, they joked about dating sometime, but it never went any further, mainly because they seldom saw each other. She was a very competent police officer and was respected by most of the officers who worked with her.

Standing at his bedroom door, Danny, admittedly, took a longer look than proper etiquette dictated. Thankfully, he reasoned as he closed the door, she would never know of his lapse of proper discretion.

Wrong.

ⴰⴰⴰ

Janet

Janet had flirted with Danny all night at the bar. But nothing too blatant that might come back to haunt her or give her fellow officers drinking there anything to tease her about later. Enough, however, she thought, to have made it clear she might be interested in him. The way he played it off caused her to question why? *Maybe that's it,* she debated. Wouldn't be the first time a guy as good looking as Danny was...in the closet. That thought prompted knocking down two or three additional shots when offered.

Not being much of a drinker, she was inebriated long before she realized it.

Danny's offer to drive her home was at first met with resistance, like with the other offers. Only after Gloria, another female cop she had often worked with, took her keys from her and gave them to Danny, did Janet finally relent.

"Thank you for this ride home, Danny."

"Any time, Jan," he said as he helped her to his car and opened his door.

"Hey, Danny?" she asked as he started driving, "I live on the other side of town. Would…ah…would it be an incon…ah…would it be presumptuous of me to ask if I could sleep it off at your place? Don't you live nearby?"

"Yes, I do, and that would be fine if it's okay with you."

"Well, it will, be if you hurry." Then she added when he looked curiously at her. "I have to use the little girl's room. Or—or—" she added, giggling, "—the little boy's room in your place." And then she mumbled something while looking out her window. "Hopefully, you're not a little boy."

෴

"You have a very nice place here, Danny," Jan said while walking into his living room.

"Thank you."

"Do you live alone? I'm only asking—" She staggered over to his couch and sat down. "—because I don't want to cause you any problems."

"Yes, I do, and no, you won't be causing me any problems."

That's what you think, Janet mused as she looked around at his home.

Everything looked very neat and clean. That was always a prerequisite before she slept with any guy. One time even pushing a guy off her, when she got a whiff of his strong body odor, and then got out of his bed, got dressed, and left. Walking those ten blocks late at night, before catching a bus home, she considered the gamble of being alone in that bad neighborhood worth it, because she was armed anyway.

Danny, from what she could tell, was always neat, and whatever cologne he used was a wonderful distraction in the close confinement of their police vehicle when they did work together. Tonight, she decided to find out if all that muscle in that tight shirt he's wearing was good for things other than police work.

"Janet, you can have my bedroom for the night. It has its own bathroom and shower, so feel free to use whatever you need."

"No, Danny, this couch feels comfortable enough." Janet felt the material of the couch. "I can just—"

"No way is my lovely guest going to crash on my couch."

It was then she remembered her lie about having to pee. "Thank you, Danny, that's sweet. All right, lead the way."

"I hope everything is okay for you. Don't worry," he added when they walked into his bedroom and she started looking around. "The sheets are clean. I washed everything earlier today and ran out of time making up the spare bedroom, so I'll just crash downstairs."

Janet removed her gun belt and laid it across a chair then turned and gingerly walked over to him. "No, Danny, I wouldn't think of putting you out of your own bed. We can share that huge bed of yours. Remember," she said, grinning and grabbing his shirt, "if you're bad I have a gun. And if you're not," she added with a snicker and walked over to the bed, "I have a gun."

Danny laughed. "If you need anything," he said, as he walked out the room, "just holler."

The words formed in her mouth but, when he turned his back, her pride wouldn't let her say what she wanted to—above a whisper. "I want you to screw my lights out."

Hearing those words would have made her intentions

clear, and he would either have to take her or take her home.

Climbing into his bed after he departed, she found it very comfortable, but maybe too comfortable, because she couldn't sleep. Lying on cold and smooth sheets in his bed in just her panties, she imagined what his response would be if he was lying there beside her. That picture produced the sensation she started feeling between her—

Janet sat up. "One more chance, Mr. Washington," she vowed.

Her first steps out of bed were on rubbery legs. She giggled. "Whoa there, girl."

But after stopping for a moment to get her balance, she continued walking out of the bedroom and stopped at the top of his stairs. The what-are-you-doing question crossed her mind and was just as quickly ignored, unanswered. Grinning, she quietly started walking down the stairs until she could peek around the wall and look into his living room. A lamp, in a far corner, apparently set on dim, illuminated the object of her pursuit. As promised, he was completely reclined in the recliner wearing…as little as she was. Well, wearing the same thing, just not as little. Janet smiled at that truth.

It was now or never. She took a deep breath and stopped to ponder what she was doing. Looking down at herself, another very important and obvious question surfaced. Her pride and need battled with the answer. In the middle was common sense, suggesting getting dressed in her bra first. Yielding to the winner, her first step almost ended her plans when the alcohol in her system caused her to misstep and almost tumble down the rest of the stairs. She just caught herself on the banister, sparing herself possible injuries and, even worse, a very embarrassing tumble.

Quickly looking down at the still-sleeping man, she guessed he didn't hear her faux pas.

Walking over to him, wearing next to nothing, with each step, she became more nervous. Janet knew this was the point—actually, standing at the top of the steps in what she wasn't wearing was the point—when she should have debated what would happen next if he woke up.

Nearing the point of no return, she made her decision. Standing next to him, his face inches from her thighs, she could feel his hot breath on her skin as he slept. Envisioning taking an even bolder step momentarily crossed her mind as his deep breathing gave her an injection of courage. He was lying there on his back with his arms up over his head. Other than the black briefs he was wearing, he was naked. She took that respite to imagine what it would be like to have this virile man's muscular frame wrapped around hers. He looked great in his uniform, unlike some cops who let themselves go too quickly after joining the force. The sleeping man was not only handsome but impressively built. Her eyes traveled down his large chest stopping at his taunt stomach. The desire growing between her legs egged her on until she was staring at the budge in his shorts. The alcohol in her system was the fuel that fed her imagination as she stared, but what she wanted to do next couldn't be blamed completely on that sexual lubricant.

She was just about to shake him awake when his eyes slowly opened. He stared at her for a moment before his eyes slowly trailed up her body and gazed at her breasts, seemingly mesmerized, before suddenly sitting up so quickly she froze as his panic turned her passion to mortification. For a moment, when he stood up and his hard body brushed against hers, she gasped, thinking he was going to take her in his arms and force himself on her.

At least that was what she both feared and hoped, as her heart pounded in her chest.

"Ah, Danny, I can't sleep," she quickly admitted, a version of the truth, when he failed to react to their closeness. "Do you have anything I can take?" she asked, placing her arms across her bare breasts, vacating the objects of his attention, "that can help me get to sleep?"

In the moment it took him to peel his eyes away, she knew if she pushed a little harder he was hers. That intense moment passed as embarrassment replaced her desire. He had quickly stood up, bumping into her when she didn't move, mumbled a suggestion he had, and then hurried into the kitchen.

Janet had hinted about a relationship before with the handsome man now looking for something in his refrigerator. After two failed relationships, she had decided to wait for Mister Right. It only took chatting with him on a few of their patrols to recognize that Danny was almost everything she wanted in a man. She had always fallen for the great-looking guys, some ending up as one-nighters, and he was that. But chatting with him first, she was able to see a future with him beyond lying on her back with her legs wide open. But working different shifts and jobs at the station had prevented their friendship from growing.

"If this wine will help." Janet stood there unashamedly and slowly drank his sleep solution while he fumbled around the kitchen, using every opportunity to sneak looks at her. Even more so when captivated by the few drops of red wine that dripped from her glass and ran slowly down her bare chest.

"Thank you, Danny," she said and then handed him the empty glass, kissed him on his cheek, and strolled out of the kitchen and slowly up the stairs as he followed, giving him another chance to see opportunity. Softly tiptoeing down the hallway, she listened for footfalls behind her and heard only silence.

Frustrated, when he didn't follow, Janet lay in his bed, pounding her fist against her pillow. Her pride considered her actions appropriate, but the growing ache in her body vetoed that. After she calmed down, the thought occurred to her to resort to an established, and very often lately, method of relief. Pulling off her panties and tossing them haphazardly across the room, she kicked off the covers and let her fingers give her what that virile man downstairs spurned. But it was the image of him lying in that chair that quickened her release. When he suddenly stood up, she felt engulfed by his large muscular frame and the stunned look in his eyes. As her fingers touched her moistness, she imagined him tossing her down on that chair and forcing himself into her, and that produced the toe-curling response she craved. After a third time, which, for her, was a record, relief, or the wine, finally started working.

Waking up with the bright morning light shining in her eyes, Janet grabbed a pillow and covered her face. It only took her a moment to remember where she was and why—her parched mouth and headache answering the why.

Taking a deep breath, she realized waking up alone in bed was for the better. She had wanted him badly last night and remembered what she did multiple times as a poor but necessary alternative.

Maybe it was a good thing they didn't. Getting drunk and seducing him might have ruined any possibility of a real future together. Yes, she liked him, but not enough to use that bait to snare him. Not him or any man, she had often resolved—when sober.

"Well," she admitted, tossing the pillow off the bed, "it wasn't the first time I've done something stupid when drinking." That embarrassing sorority party initiation always came to mind.

That became a moot point when she thought she heard someone walking up the stairs and down the hallway. As the sound became louder she was sure of it. The sight chill in the room had already informed her that she was lying naked with the covers tossed at her feet. She sat up, went to reach for them, and spotted the bedroom door, that she had purposely left partially open last night. Having had more time, she might have dismissed the naughty thought that crossed her mind. Maybe.

Door three, like the game show on TV, Janet hastily decided would be the final door she would allow him to open. Lying down on her back with her head looking away, she pretended to be asleep. If this picture didn't entice him, maybe he was gay, she jokingly mused, believing, as most women would, that no man could resist a naked woman lying in their bed. But as the footfalls became louder, she yielded to her pride somewhat, turned her bare backside to the door, closed her eyes, and pretended to be asleep.

Silence. The footfalls stopped. She could sense his eyes scrutinizing every inch of her backside through the partially opened door. The fire of desire, that took three times to relinquish last night, was reignited. Janet struggled to control her panting and appear to be asleep. As the seconds stretched on, she had to squeeze her legs together to quench a growing need and prayed he didn't notice, or maybe it would be better if he—

When she heard the bedroom door close, her eyes popped opened, and she slumped with disappointment. Then she had an epiphany. What if he had entered the room before closing the door? Her panting returned, as did moistness in certain places, when she pictured him standing there staring at her nude form. What would he do next? Was he stepping out of his black underwear? She tried talking herself into turning her head and pretending she just woke up, but couldn't muster the courage. What if, she questioned, he was now walking toward her naked and aroused? The question became should she turn over and offer herself or continue to play asleep? There was a growing need for somebody to quench the fire between her legs. In a failed effort to turn over and act seductive, she squeeze her eyes closed and just listened. She heard nothing but her own panting. Where was he? What if he was standing over her like she had him last night about to reach out and—

Hearing footsteps in the hallway and then another door closing, abruptly answered those questions. Funny thing was she began to feel cheap when she heard that other door close. He would never know it, but that also was when she desired him the most and would have given him whatever he wanted. Whatever!

❧❧❧

Danny

Danny quickly showered and, before he started to cook breakfast, decided to check on his guest again. Hearing his master bedroom shower running, he didn't have to knock before walking into his bedroom.

"Janet," he said when opening the bedroom door.

As expected, she was in the bathroom when he peeked in. He quickly walked to his closet, got a clean robe out and placed it on the bed for her. It also gave him a chance to gather a change of clothes for himself and hurry out of the bedroom.

Ten minutes later, the young woman walked into his kitchen, wearing a short white cotton robe and a towel around her head. And even without makeup, she was still very attractive.

"Hi, Danny."

"Hi, Janet, how are you feeling this morning?" he asked and then quickly turned away from the desirable-looking woman.

"My head is throbbing and my stomach's turning, but that food sure smells great."

"Hungry?"

"Starving. I had plenty to drink last night but haven't eaten anything since lunch. I think that's why I got plastered."

"Well, grab a chair and I'll make you a plate."

"Whose robe is this?" she asked after sitting down as he placed a plate of food in front of her. "It is very soft and feels great, but it's definitely too small for you."

"Yes, I know," Danny admitted as he put the rest of the scrambled eggs on his plate and sat down across from her.

"Is this the normal attire for women who sleep over?"

She was snickering when he stopped eating, for a moment, and looked at her. "That so rarely happens I wouldn't call it normal, but yes. I did purchase it for moments like this."

They traded stares.

"Truthfully," he jokingly added, "when I realized my robes would be too long for any female guests and might cover great looking legs like yours, I had to purchase something smaller. The first one I bought was actually a wash cloth…ah…with sleeves."

As he'd hoped, she laughed

"I bet it was, you—you pervert."

He laughed.

"But if I embarrassingly recall," Janet admitted,

without looking up from her plate, "last night I walked around, revealing even more."

Danny was surprised by her frankness. "You were— we were—very drunk," he explained to the young woman occupied in playing with the food on her plate. "I'm sure it takes more than just getting you drunk for a man to enjoy that amazing privilege."

"Usually." She smiled, looking up after that consoling remark. "But last night I let my guard down."

He was trying to think of the right words to say when he noticed her head drop again. "Well…thank you."

A grin appeared on her pretty face. "No, thank you, Officer Washington, for not taking advantage of me last night." She looked in his eyes and repentantly added, "I would probably feel much worse now had I added indefensible sex to my sins last night."

"Darn it!" he teased. "You're welcome Janet." When gazing at the mournful look on her pretty face, he added. "But I hope we can still be good friends"

"As close as you would like."

Two hours later, after a hug and kiss on the cheek, Officer Mann was climbing in a cab to pick up her car in Jake's Pub's parking lot after flatly refusing a ride from her willing host.

After she departed, Danny sat down on the couch with a fresh cup of coffee. Last night, he realized, and what happened this morning with Janet, was a reflection of where he was, or better yet, who he was. Drunk or not, the old Danny would have gladly banged the shapely Ms. Mann when she came on to him after he offered her his bed, and she was tugging on his arm to join her. Not to mention the enticing vision he saw after opening his eyes in the recliner. That was crazy. And then, even after she thanked him for not taking advantage of her, when she stood up after breakfast and allowed her robe to "accidently" come partially open, wasn't the inviting curve of her beasts another invitation?

Yet it wasn't the very attractive brown woman in the cab that cornered his thoughts, but the redhead that had transformed herself from dyke to dynamite. Being with Gabby was, at first, just fun, as they teased each other about anything and everything. But after they made love, he knew she was special. Inexperienced, yes, but she lacked nothing in effort and that touched him. If she could love him, he wanted to make her his world, but only if she could love him.

"But be patient with her, Danny," he said to the silence in the room. "She's still fragile, and you could scare her away. You never know what her family would think, and what their opinions, pro or con, would mean to her."

Another sip of coffee signaled his determination to pursue her until one of them vetoed the relationship.

CHAPTER 21

Beverly

Beverly Davis, the head of the Pittsburgh branch of WARV, looked at the clock again. The weekend was calling. She had nothing planned for that time off, but just being off was what motivated her. It was some unfinished paperwork that prompted her to come in today. She had given Gabby the day off and had planned to take it off also. Some of her friends had invited her to a bingo tournament, and she politely refused. But that did give her an idea. She was thinking about leaving early and going gambling at the casino.

There were two reports she had to finish and send to the home office in LA before leaving work today. The music on the radio, turned down so as not to be a distraction, failed. Beverly stopped writing and started singing along with an old Whitney Houston song.

"Okay, work before pleasure." Frustrated with that outlook, she sighed and walked out of her office and into the lobby to lock the front door. With a half hour of work to finish the reports, she didn't want any interruptions now. Gabby had continuously berated her for leaving the front doors unlocked. The rule was, when alone, or suspecting any trouble, lock the doors. It was her failure to do so that enabled that nut from Atlanta to catch her alone. "Thank God for Gabby," she whispered at that scary memory as she walked into the lobby and peeked in the corner where that nut had leaped out and surprised her. He was gone but his ghost remained, sending a chill down her spine.

Door locked, Beverly was returning to her office with her head down, humming the same tune, when something was placed over her head and she felt a sharp pain on the back of her neck before things went very black.

420423

Gabriel

Traffic was backed up even worse than usual on the Parkway. Then I remembered something about another lane closing on this always-busy, and seemingly-always-under-construction, highway. Going out to the mall at Robinson had seemed like a good idea at the time. I was able to try on a couple of nice dresses and purchase some more sexy underwear with a certain man in mind.

I knew it was probably a bad move because everyone would have the same idea for a short cut, but I took the next exit anyway. Doubling back, I made a right turn onto Highway 60 East. To my surprise, the traffic was actually lighter. I cut through Crafton and down to the West End. I was on the same side of town, so I decided to check on the center before heading home for the weekend.

I should call Danny and see what his plans were for those off days, I was thinking as the traffic on my short-cut through Crafton became heavy, but at least we were still moving. Finally, I was able to turn onto Steuben Street and drive down into the West End. When in the area, I often detoured past the women's center just to check that some irate dickhead hadn't lost his mind and tossed a brick, or worse, through a window.

As I drove past the building, I had to quickly look in my rear view mirror before hitting my brakes. Thankfully, there wasn't anyone tailgating me. I had almost missed Beverly's car in the shadows of the parking lot beside the building. What was it and she doing here today? Backing up, I pulled into the lot and parked next to her car. Other than our two vehicles, the lot was empty. Looking into her car provided no answers. It was empty.

I checked my purse then hurried toward the office. The lights were on in the back, but I couldn't see anyone inside. Common sense said Beverly changed her mind and came in today to finish some paperwork in her office.

"Workaholic." I turned to leave but I sensed something was wrong. The door was locked when I tried it, and that was a good thing. I put my key in the lock and it turned. I started to open the door, and it didn't move. I tried it again. The lock turned, but the door remained locked. For the safety of the women that we helped, we'd installed keyless locks that could only be locked or unlocked from inside the building. That meant Beverly had to have used those locks on the front door.

After looking around and seeing I was alone, I took out my phone and called the office. I could hear the phone ringing, but no one appeared to be in the lobby.

"Okay, Bev, I'll try your phone."

Again, I thought I could hear the ring tone of her phone but she didn't answer it. Now I understood why my stomach was turning. Something was very wrong. The street was basically empty when I nervously looked around for help. I was about to dial nine-one-one when I stupidly remembered the police station a few doors down. I ran to the station and in the front door. There was this large officer behind a desk, and I was about to walk over to him when I spotted, walking out of a room, the same detective who had arrived at the women's center after I Tasered that murderer. What was the detective's name? I tried remembering. "Excuse me…ah…Detective Maroney?"

Puzzled, he looked at me for a moment and then started walking toward me, smiling. I was about to explain the problem when another man walked out of the same room. It only took a moment and then I recognized him. I took a step back and covered my mouth. It was him, there was no doubt it was him. He seemed ignorant of who I was until—

"Hi, there. Ms. Sumpter, right?" Detective Maroney said, unfortunately loud enough to center the attention of everyone in the room on me. "It is nice to see you again. I hope you haven't had to Taser any more attackers."

I heard him but my eyes were on the man behind him, now frowning at me. Then the questions in my head started. What was he doing here? He was in plain clothes, but was he also a cop? If he was, did Danny know? If he did, why didn't he warn me?

"Ms. Sumpter, are you all right? What can I do for you?"

"Something…ah…is…wrong."

"Excuse me?"

"At the center," I was able to say, after looking away from that asshole Sellers. "I noticed the lights were on and the doors locked, but no one is answering the door or the phone."

It was when the smiling detective suddenly lost that fake smile, that I really got worried.

"John, and…ah…Bill," he said, "come with me please."

The two large uniformed officers seemed to appear out of nowhere. I stepped out of their way, but when I took one last look at Sellers, he was gone. Not seeing him anywhere, I quickly followed the officers out the door and down to our building.

"I have a key," I explained when we reached the building, "but the doors are locked from the inside. My boss's car is still in the parking lot, but she isn't answering the office phone or her cell phone."

"Before we have to break down the door or a window, John take a look in the back. Maybe that door is unlocked."

"Right."

I was going to say that door was always locked, but decided to let him check it anyway. We all looked in the windows, hoping for the best. For me, that went up in smoke when the officer called John appeared in the hallway. I'd never seen that rusty old door in the rear opened. Never. He walked toward us and then stopped suddenly and disappeared into a room that I knew was Beverly's office.

When I gasped, Detective Maroney placed his arm around me.

Officer John reappeared and, when he hurried toward us to unlock the door, I noticed he was on his phone with someone. "This is a crime scene, Detective," he said as he opened the door.

"No!" I screamed.

"There is a female deceased in one of the offices," he coldly added, looking from the detective to me.

"Ms. Sumpter, you will have to stay out here."

"She's—my—friend," I cried.

"I understand that, but we need to gather clues on

what happened. The fewer people in there the better. Do you understand?"

I did, but that didn't make it any easier to remain outside. Poor Beverly. *What is going on here?* I wondered. My thoughts were interrupted by the sound of a siren in the distance. Help was coming and that gave me hope, despite what the officer claimed, that Bev was going to be all right.

The ambulance pulled up to the building and two paramedics climbed out, opened the rear doors, and I screamed for them to hurry as they raced past me into the building with their equipment.

I was pacing in front of the building trying not to throw up when Detective Maroney walked out. I knew from the blank, emotionless, business-like expression on his face what he was going to say.

My tears started in earnest before he could utter a word.

"She has passed," he said. "Someone attacked her. The paramedics couldn't save her. She was already gone."

I thought I was prepared to hear that but his words stole the strength from my legs and he grabbed me just as they buckled.

"I've got you. Come on in and sit down."

He took me into the lobby, sat down with me on the couch, and asked some questions as I tried to get myself together.

Between sobs, I told him what I knew and about the last conversation we had. "As you know, we sometimes get angry men asking about where their women are," I explained, wiping errant tears from my eyes, "but nothing—nothing like this."

"I don't think this was some random punk looking for his woman like that last nut. Some of the—" He hesitated. "There's evidence that links this to other sexual attacks."

"Sexual attacks! Like Elaine Abbot?"

"Yes," he answered reluctantly. "Hers, and maybe three others that we know about. This nut is singling out female advocate workers to assault. We found a bloody pillowcase at each of the—what is it, Ms. Sumpter?"

I couldn't breathe. "What? Ah…nothing, Detective," I said, taking my hand down from my mouth and trying to hide my surprise. "I just remembered something about that happening to someone in the military. They—they couldn't have a—" Then I shook my head. *It couldn't be a coincidence twice*, I thought.

"Well, anything you can remember might help, you never know."

I heard him and wasn't about to go through that again. With a man? No way! Even knowing he was here to help couldn't completely suppress my revulsion at sitting this close to a—

"Detective?" a uniformed cop interrupted. "The coroner is here if you want to speak to him."

"Thank you. Will you excuse me, Ms. Sumpter? Do you need a ride home or to somewhere?"

"No." I shook my head, wiped my eyes, and explained. "My car is parked outside."

"That's right. Well, I'll be in touch and, if you can think of anything else that might help—" He handed me a card and added, "—anything, call me."

Sitting there, I could feel that old anger resurfacing. Some bastard had raped and killed one of the most caring people I'd ever met. He didn't have to kill her, as frightened as she got, she would have done whatever filthy thing he wanted. He only beat and raped the other women. Why kill Beverly? No, he had to have planned to kill her all along, the bastard, but why?

I got up to leave. I knew I had to get out of there before they carried Beverly's body past me. I didn't think I could have held it together seeing her all bloody. I hurried out the building without looking back. Who gives a damn now about that building when the heart of the place has stopped beating?

ↄ෨ↄ

Detective Maroney

Detective Maroney stood at the door to the crime scene and, after looking in and shaking his head at what he saw, turned and watched the shaken woman rush out the office front door. Who could blame her? But thankfully, she never saw the immoral condition of her friend.

"Detective Maroney?"

He took a deep breath, turned toward the voice, and winced at the strong stench of death that permeated the room.

"I'm Assistant Coroner Donald James."

"Yes, Coroner James?" Walking into the bloody crime scene, Maroney avoided looking at the grossly displayed victim again and was greeted by a small man in a white lab coat and glasses. Oddly, in this room of despicable horror, he questioned the age of the young-looking assistant coroner. "What can you tell me about all this?" Maroney asked, getting back to business.

"The victim probably died of strangulation," the doctor said, motioning for him to walk around the desk. "See the hemorrhaging in the eyes?"

"Was she sexually assaulted?"

"From a preliminary examination, yes."

"Before or after she was murdered?"

"Hard to tell, Detective, before a more thorough examination. Let me show you this." Walking around the desk he pointed to cuts on her body. "See these knife wounds in her back and thighs? They were probably administered while he was raping her. They weren't deep enough to kill her, but bloody and very painful. Yes," he said to the cop, shaking his head, "she was probably also sodomized."

It was shocking enough, the veteran detective thought, to look into the office and see the poor victim tied across her desk with her privates displayed for all to see. Her legs were tied to the legs of her desk, her nude body bent spread eagle and ass up across her desk, and her arms tied down the other legs of the desk. In that very exposed position, he had violated her long before he…violated…her.

"The way he tied her down," the coroner pointed out, "she was powerless to do anything but submit. These bruises on her rear were probably a result of his punching her with his fist. We couldn't find any other weapon." The coroner moved around to the other side of the desk. The detective hesitated but, at the coroner's beckoning, followed him. "He probably beat her face until she did him."

Detective Maroney frowned at that display of disrespect. "Did him?"

"Sorry. See the bruising here and here. Also look at the marks behind her ears. He was probably holding them while he was—"

"I get the picture, dammit!" the detective snapped, waving off further evaluation and looking away from the battered victim's face. "Any finger prints or body fluid we can use to identify her attacker?"

"He was smart. He wore gloves, and from the spermicidal fluid we found in her mouth, and in her—a condom. But I think our victim was smarter than he gave her credit for in her helpless condition. She bit him," he explained at the questioning gaze on the detective's face. "Maybe not enough to enrage him, I think, or maybe that explains the bruising on her face, but enough to puncture the condom." The coroner walked back around to her rear and pointed at her right leg. "When he…ah…finished—" The coroner knelt down and pointed at a drop of something wet on her ankle. "We found one single small spot of sperm that was dripped here." Avoiding looking at the red and bruised ass of the victim, Detective Maroney leaned down closer to the potential clue. "If he is in the database, we might just get lucky," the coroner crowed.

"Let me know as soon as you can."

"Sure thing, Detective."

Detective Maroney walked from the room, hoping to get the picture of the grossly displayed woman's battered body out of his mind. "I'm dealing with an animal."

He had another question for the young coroner, but decided it wasn't worth returning to that room and violating the victim's right to privacy again.

Walking into the lobby, he was greeted by four members of the Crime Scene Investigation Unit walking in the door.

"Hey, Maroney. We have to stop meeting like this. My wife is going to think you have a thing for me."

"Yeah, Jeff. She knows better. Now with her, maybe. She's not ugly like you. Hi, Harold." The other two he didn't know and just nodded. "Apparently, the killer exited out the rear door," he explained. "My officer came in through that door so—"

"Well, hopefully," Harold said, "there are other fingerprints."

"Yeah, hopefully. We sure could use a break." With that said, Maroney walked out of the building into the sunshine. Looking around, he noticed that, even with all the flashing lights of emergency vehicles parked in the street, none of the locals seemed interested. The street was empty. Closing his eyes for a moment and inhaling the fresh air, only then did he realize how strong the sickening smell of death permeated that crime scene.

The angry Pittsburgh Police Detective turned and started walking toward the police station. The murder of a woman he'd just met, who dedicated her life to helping others, weighed down his steps. Was there something they were missing about this felon? he questioned. Was her killing to send a message this time? Maybe it was the fresh air, but as he entered the police station, he decided to review all the information they had on these rapes. This guy was now a murderer.

CHAPTER 22

Danny

Having spent the day with his mom, taking her out to lunch at the Monroeville Mall and then shopping at the Giant Eagle grocery store, Danny got into his car for the drive home and finally had the chance to turn on his cell phone.

It was one of the few stipulations his mom insisted on when they were together. It was *her* time, she would berate him when it rang, interrupting anything they were doing, from planting her flowers to just shooting the breeze on the back porch swing while drinking coffee, during one of his visits.

Danny had once put it on vibrate, but she felt that, as they were sitting on the swing, so he had to promise to shut it off. And for her, he would keep it his word.

"So who are you seeing now," she'd asked as they were putting away the groceries.

Danny hid a grin as he continued to put away the can goods. Making her wait was part of the fun. When she didn't ask again like she normally would, he relented. "A young lady I met while in the service. I think you'll like her, Momma."

"Oh, so you are going to let me meet this one."

"Yeah, maybe, because she won't be afraid of you like the others would."

"No one's afraid of this old lady."

"Hell, I have a gun and I'm afraid."

"And you should be with your hard head."

They both smiled. There was little doubt about how they felt about the other. He hugged and kissed her at every chance, and they shared loving words at each greeting or departure, either in person or over the phone.

Sitting in his car, Danny turned on his phone and checked it before driving off. He was trying to break the habit of using it while driving, after seeing a couple of terrible accidents believed to be related to the distraction of cell phone use.

No messages from Gabby, and that was the main reason for checking.

"Oh, well," he said with disappointment coloring every word. "Home for a quick shower and, afterward, I'll drop by her place and see if she's free for tonight or maybe this weekend."

෴

Gabriel

I didn't know how I got home. Well, I was driving, of course, but the voyage was a fog. Thankfully, I didn't kill anyone along the way. I was about to get out of my car when reality hit me like a sucker punch. The tears flowed and there was nothing I could do to stop them. "Dead! Beverly dead. My God, why?"

I must have spent a half hour parked in my driveway,

crying. I started to call Danny and hung up at the last minute. I wasn't angry with Danny, but he was a man. Yes, that part of me was resurrected—somewhat. I needed his strong arms holding me, but that thought made me picture what poor Beverly had endured at the hands of a man, and it turned my stomach.

I dragged myself into my house, so depressed and confused that my guard was down. But when the pillowcase slipped over my head, just as I stepped in the door, I instinctively dropped down to one knee, avoiding what I imagined was going to happen next. That helped, but didn't save me. The glancing blow sent me flying across the room. I was stunned, but I was able to yank off the pillowcase, roll over on the floor, and face my attacker.

He stood there, gloating. "Hi there, bitch. I know you remember me."

I did, and all the pent-up rage, that I struggled for years to overcome, surged up in me, and I wanted to kill him.

"I was your first, remember Afghanistan? I followed you home, and while you were sobbing like a bitch in your car, I broke in the back and waited on you. And guess what? I still have a hard on for you." He did his Michael Jackson imitation with his hand. "Isn't that great? Just like old times, right?"

Hearing him gloat sent me up off the floor and charging at him in a fit of rage. "You asshole!"

"Whoa there, girly." He sidestepped my rush, grabbed me, and tossed me down on the floor. But I got off a punch to his face, sending him stumbling backward against the wall.

I was on my feet as he regained his balance.

"I'm going to kick your ass and then give you something I know you are going to like, you *bitch*!" he shouted, after wiping his nose and seeing blood.

"Do you want me to turn around, pencil dick? I know you like to sneak up on defenseless women from behind, you cowardly punk!" I screamed. I knew this was foolish, because he was a highly-trained soldier, and almost twice my size now. But this was the man who defamed and defiled my humanity. I wanted revenge.

"What did you call me?" His face became flushed with anger, and the veins on his neck protruded like worms.

I wanted his hate to blind him and mine to give me strength. "You're a cowardly punk, Rockhound," I sneered, attempting to get him off his game.

"I'm going to shove everything I can find up your ass, you bitch!"

It worked. This time he was the one charging recklessly at me. I studied the angle of his charge, looking for an opening. I stepped back from his wild swing, turned, and gave him a hip, using his momentum against him, like I was taught in self-defense judo class, and flipped him over on the floor. He groaned when he hit it hard but was quickly starting to stand. But this time I kicked him in the head, sending him flying backward over my coffee table. With my heart pounding in my chest, I ran over and kicked him in the head again as he struggled to stand. He grunted and fell face first on the floor. He mumbled something and tried to get up again. I couldn't believe him. So I stomped my foot down on the back of his head, trying to drive his damn face through the floor. This time, he wasn't moving.

I walked toward my open door to escape, but my unsteady legs buckled so I leaned against the wall trying to steady my trembling legs and pounding heart. *Bend over and breathe slowly*, I reminded myself from my training. I was trying to calm down and catch my breath, but I was breathing so heavy, I never heard him approaching. When

I stood up, he grabbed me from behind. I couldn't believe he recovered that quickly. This time, I was in real trouble, as he had me in a head lock with his arm tightly locked around my neck, choking me as he lifted me up on my toes.

He laughed and the stuck his filthy tongue in my ear. "Got ya, bitch. I'm going to do to you what I did to your boss. You got some rope, cowgirl?"

Hearing that, I was more angry than frightened. *Think Gabby, remember your training.* I struggled to get an advantage. I tried kicking back at him and then stomping down on his foot, but he seemed to know exactly what I was trying to do and countered my moves. I was still fighting, but things were starting to get dark. I wasn't afraid of dying as much as I was of what depraved things he would do to me when I was helpless. I gave it one last try and elbowed him in the ribs breaking his hold—or so I thought. Actually, my legs had buckled and he dropped me to the floor.

My head was spinning as I lay there, almost blacking out. I had a terrible headache and was gasping for breath. My throat burned when I tried to swallow. Everything was blurry. I looked around, trying to escape him. Before I could move, he placed a knee on my chest, preventing me from breathing,

"How do you like me now, huh?"

He was laughing at that pun, when he viciously backhanded the side of my face. I was dazed and gasping for air. As I fought to breathe, he climbed off me. When I tried crawling away, he grabbed my pants and his filthy nails scraped the skin on my thighs as he started to pull them down my legs. I was very weak and struggled to raise my head. I was looking for an opening, and I spotted it. One kick in the nose, as he was removing my pants, and the bastard was mine. There, there! Kick him in the face! But my leg—my leg wouldn't move.

I felt cold air on my legs when he yanked off my pants and panties. Then he grabbed me by the ankles and twisted them, easily turning me over on my stomach. *Why am I so weak?* I wondered.

"Ahhh, there's that tight ass I loved. Remember how great that felt back then, bitch? I hear it turned you from a fat ugly dyke, to a spook-loving whore, remember? Oh, you are going to like this."

Feeling my strength slowly returning, I started crawling away from him.

"Where are you going, bitch?"

Searching for something to defend myself, I spotted my purse where it had fallen on the floor near the up-turned coffee table and the handle of my gun was sticking out. I whispered a thanks to the Man above and, with what little strength I could gather, crawled toward my purse. My fingertips touched it, and then I was pulled back by one of my legs.

"No, you don't. Big Daddy's not done with you yet, whore."

It was then I realized that he'd had me in a sleeper hold, and I had nearly fainted. That was why I was so weak. It would take a few minutes before my body could recover from the loss of blood to my brain. A few minutes I didn't have. I would need to stall him.

"Okay, okay, you win. Don't hurt me anymore," I pleaded in my best defeated-female voice. "Don't hurt me and you can take me like you did in Afghanistan." I turned over and spread my legs. Surprisingly, the only embarrassment I felt doing that was realizing my front door was wide open.

My ruse worked. His eyes bore down on me…well, a private part of me. After staring for what seemed like forever with his mouth open, he started unbuckling the belt to his pants. From the lump in his…ah…throat, he was definitely distracted. I was just about to leap for my purse but, overanxious, I gave away my plans when I turned my head and looked first. He quickly stepped over me, beating me to it.

"What? Is this what you wanted?" he asked, holding my purse just out of my reach. "I was just playing you fool." He dangled my purse over me. "Did you really think I was that gullible and that stupid? You—someone like you—is not going to just give up, spread her legs, and let me screw her. No way, bitch. Now your boss, after I beat her ass, offered me all her holes, and I took them and even more. But an ex-military broad like you? No way. Oh—" he said, after looking in my open purse. "What do we have in here?"

When he pulled out my gun and aimed it at me, I wanted him to shoot. I almost begged him to shoot, and I knew he would, it would just be the last terrible thing he would do to me.

"This must be my day," he gloated, after reaching in my purse again, and pulling out another item. "What's this? A Taser? Mmmmm, are we going to have some fun?"

The heavy weight of my predicament caused my body to yield to the inevitable. I lay flat, staring up at the ceiling, wondering how I was going to get through this. *Is this fair?* I wanted to ask the Man above. *I guess lightning does strike in the same place twice*, I thought that was funny for some odd reason. And while lying there, staring at the ceiling, resigned to my fate, I was dumbfounded when former US Army Private First Class Richard "Rockhound" Sellers went flying over my prone body and crashed against my upturned coffee table breaking off one of the legs. I looked over at his crumpled body and then sat up stunned.

"What the—"

"You son of a bitch!" someone shouted.

Shocked, I turned and looked toward the sound of that voice.

"Are you okay, Gabby?"

Standing there was my brown knight and, from the scowl on his wonderful face, a very angry brown knight. All I could think of was covering myself. I was ashamed. But the way he looked at me, I knew I had no reason to feel that way. Like a light being turned on, his angry face turned to concern, and he took a step toward me. That's when I heard this thunderous loud noise coming from behind me, and I flinched. When I opened my eyes my brown knight had a growing red spot in his chest and was tumbling backward. He landed hard on the floor and didn't move.

"Danny!" I screamed.

When I turned over and saw that grinning bastard Sellers sitting up staring at me with blood running down his face, I didn't care if he killed me. I wanted revenge. I spotted my opportunity, out of the corner of my eye, a few feet away. And this time I stared at him, not giving him a hint about what I was planning to do.

The cocky bastard took his eyes off me for a moment, as he stood up and callously blew on the gun's barrel like in those old western movies. "Eat that, Washington."

When he looked down at me, he quickly lost that arrogant sneer, and his mouth dropped opened in surprise. Before his gun hand could lower and point at me, I Tasered that asshole.

The gun in his jerking hand fired off three times as he danced at the end of 50,000 volts. Unfortunately—and I really "hated" what happened to the dancer doing a poor imitation of the "Electric Slide"—two of the three shots ripped into his thigh. I knew, from the large amount of blood pouring down his leg as he collapsed onto the floor, he'd probably severed a vein or an artery and needed immediate assistance to save his life.

I slowly stood up and kicked the gun out of the unconscious bastard's hand. I was naked from the waist down and, as I looked down at that bleeding asshole, I had the strongest urge to piss on the man who killed my Danny. Resisting that wonderful impulse, I knew I had to do something I dreaded. I had hurried out of the women's center before seeing Beverly's bloodied body being carried out. Now I wondered how I could possibly look at my Danny.

There I stood in the middle of my living room, half naked, with one dead man and the other dying if I didn't call for help and place a tourniquet on his legs. I found my pants and put them on. Only when fastening them, did I realize I was so disoriented I forgot to put on something else first. I cried. I did so with my back purposefully to the open door and man I loved. There I stood, fighting the urge to fall to my knees and just cry my heart out. *Not for me*, I thought and wiped my eyes. Breaking down would dishonor the wonderful man who gave his—

Maybe if I hadn't stopped sobbing, I would have never heard a small groaning sound behind me.

"Danny?" I turned around and ran over to the prone body of the man who always seemed to be there for me when I needed him the most. The wound in his chest was bloody, and his breathing labored. I thought, for sure, the way he'd quickly dropped to the floor that he was dead. I saw something red lying near him, picked it up, and held my panties against his wound while looking around for my phone. I remembered he probably had one. I found it in his pocket and, thankfully, it didn't need a password.

I sat there and pulled him up into my arms as we

waited for the ambulance. Funny, I wanted to say my goodbyes to him, just in case, but I worried if I did, it might really be goodbye. I made a vow, the root of it from the pain I felt in my heart, that I would never love anyone like this again. Then the tears came. I wiped my eyes with the back of my bloody hand and took a deep breath. This wasn't the time to cry, that would come later.

Looking over at the man who shot Danny, I was careful not to put any additional fingerprints on the weapon on the floor beside me, but if that bastard moved a muscle I was going to shoot him in both eyes. When I heard the sound of emergency vehicles turning into my driveway, I looked down to tell Danny. He was staring up at me, and then his eyes slowly closed.

CHAPTER 23

O fficer Washington will survive—by just a fraction of an inch," Doctors Zorn told a hospital waiting room full of cops and a woman, shielded and weeping softly at the news, behind a wall of huge men in blue. "The bullet had partially severed a major vein near his heart. It was a miracle he survived and an even bigger one we were able to repair it. We lost him twice on the table, and on the third desperate try, we succeeded before we lost him for good."

The cheering died down after the doctor raised his hand to quiet the throng. "The problem is," he explained, "there is still the chance the stitches won't hold and he could bleed to death before we could save him again, so the next few days are very important."

Dick Sellers's DNA eventually confirmed that he was the pillowcase rapist. Amazingly, he'd lost a lot of blood but lived—long enough to reach the hospital. The bastard was more critically injured, but I insisted Danny be placed in the first ambulance leaving.

Danny had also lost a lot of blood and his condition was so critical that the doctors took the unusual step of placing him in a coma to allow his injured heart to heal. I was there all day for the first four days, in case he took a turn for the worse. It was on the fifth day that we got great news.

"Mrs. Washington, everything looks great. We X-rayed the incision and everything looked fine. His pressure is normal and there's no trace of blood in his urine or feces. Tomorrow, we will double check, but I'm sure he will be just fine. He'll have to take it easy until he gets his strength back," Doctor Zorn explained to his mother, "but I'm positive there'll be no problems."

"When can we take him home?"

"Well, tomorrow we will slowly bring him out of his coma. It could take up to a few weeks for a patient to feel strong enough to leave. So, let's say, we will know by Friday, if everything goes well."

"Thank you, doctor."

Danny's sweet mother walked over and took a seat. I was sure those encouraging word lifted a huge weigh from her small shoulders. We had just returned to the waiting room from getting something to eat when the doctor walked in behind us. I went over and sat beside her.

"Gabriel, I can't thank you enough for being here for my Danny and me."

I just smiled at her. I had picked her up each morning, spent most of the day here with her, and then dropped her home afterward. As Danny fought for his life, I was warring with my feelings for him. Well, not actually my feelings, but I was struggling with why I still got angry at *him* when someone else hurt other women close to me. Last night, the first one not filled with tears and prayers, I came to a decision that was more painful. "Mrs. Washington." I took her hand. "I won't be coming to the hospital any longer to see Danny."

"That's okay, honey, you've been wonderful. I can get my nephew Nate to bring him home when it's time."

"I just wanted you to know—"

"Honey, I could see it in your eyes. You don't have to tell me how you feel about my Danny. Did he ever tell you about his father?"

I shook my head.

"Well, he was a white man. A very handsome and well-to-do white man. I met him when my car broke down and he stopped to help. He was so good looking that when he drove me home and asked me for a date, I said yes."

I saw her eyes suddenly sparkle with life and her cheeks become flushed as she talked about him, reflecting how deeply she must have loved him even after all these years.

"And in my day," she explained, "that was really frowned upon—by my parents and society. But he loved me so much that, even after me telling him no for a year, he kept coming around to see me. He would be at my job, sitting in my church. The brave man even risked getting shot by my dad when he came to visit me at my parent's house. Today you might call him a stalker. But the caring look in his eyes spoke something different to my heart. He finally wore me down because I did love him. Then when the kids were young, he was in the wrong place at the wrong time, and someone shot him sitting in his car. The police thought it was a robbery. They never found his murderer. I think when they realized I was his wife, they weren't going to go out of their way to arrest anyone unless they walked in and confessed with his blood still fresh on them."

I felt her pain as she lowered her head for a moment and then raised it proudly. It was obvious he was dead, but not in her heart.

"That's what we had to deal with back then. But my Danny has his father's sweet spirit," she said, those smiling eyes returning at that memory. "It would have been a crime having another good man shot to death. I know you are troubled about having a relationship with my Danny. Been there, done that."

As she shifted her concern to me, my eyes watered up and my throat burned as I tried to talk. "Mrs. Washington, I'll be going away for a while. I just wanted you to know I wasn't running away and leaving him." I tried to be strong and resolute, but a tear leaked down my cheek. "Now that he's going to be okay, I need to figure out—"

"Honey, I've seen the trouble you're battling with on your face. You go and, if you realize he is the one for you, come home and give it a try. If not, find the one man who can make you happy out there somewhere like I did," the sweet old lady said, while pointing toward the world outside the windows. "After my Joel died, I missed him so much. And after all these years," she revealed, softly patting my cheek, "I was never with another man. I tried to move on with my life, but I couldn't see giving myself to another man. So, I lived for my kids. That's how much we loved each other. You are a wonderful lady and deserve to be happy, my dear."

The tender way she looked at me wasn't surprising. Neither was the concern for me in her words. This sweet woman had a way of winning you over.

She was a smaller version of Danny, with that quick smile. Her hair was peppered gray and usually pulled back in a tight bun. I could see why her husband couldn't take no for an answer, she was still a very attractive woman.

Later, I walked her to her door, kissed her goodbye like I always did, and walked out of her life.

Driving home, and constantly wiping tears from my eyes, I detoured from that destination and headed back to the hospital. Apropos, the elevator was empty and unusually cold when I rode up to his floor. I nodded at the nurses at their station as I walked past. We never shared names, but became very familiar with each other as I'd spent each day last week here until asked to leave.

Looking at my watch, as I walked down the hall toward Danny's room, I saw I had about twenty minutes of visiting time remaining. Even if they threw me out, I needed to say goodbye to him—personally. That sweet man deserved that. But I knew it was placating my guilt that had redirected my steps.

As I approached his room, nausea gripped my stomach and my legs became weak. I had to stop short and get ahold of my feelings. I leaned my head against the wall as my tears threatened to return en masse. But the worse part was the guilt that burned in my chest. I was leaving because I desperately needed to find myself again. What happened to Danny, although his doctor claimed he would completely recover, took a lot out of me.

I stood up, when I saw a nurse walking out of another room. Reaching Danny's, I had an epiphany. I suddenly pictured him sitting up in bed waiting to ask me why I was running away and leaving him to—

I actually held my breath, as I peeked in his room, as if that was a real possibility—the irrational actions of a sane woman stressed out. Danny was still comatose, of course. Dispirited, I took a deep breath, forced myself to walked over to his bed, and silently studied him for a long time as I searched for the words to try and defend my undefendable plans.

"Danny, I have to get away from all this. I'm sorry," I whispered as tears leaked down my face. "But I'm an emotional wreck. You tore down my walls of hate and

revulsion I used to keep most people away. Especially—"
A giggle escaped my pain. "—any man stupid enough to
try to get to know me, right? But you—you were able to
seduce me into opening up and letting life in. I've never
known such joy as when I did. Baby, after you first made
love to me, I was ready to die right then and there, because I believed nothing could ever top that moment. And
when I think of how close I came to rejecting you, my
heart pains me. It's me, Danny, no one can blame you for
my leaving. I'm in this depressing funk, and I can't seem
to break free. I've gone to church and prayed. No relief. I
spent time with my wonderful family, and no relief. I
don't do the get-drunk thing, so booze won't help. I grew
up hiding these negative feelings behind the fat, tattooed
girl that looked and acted tough. Continuing that charade,
I did the same thing in the army—until I met you. I can't
go back to being that confused girl again, and I don't
want to. After being in your arms, no way. I loved wrapping my arms and legs around you. Learned to use more
than just one part of my body to captivate and, at times,
subjugate you. In your arms I became a woman, a woman
who enjoyed giving of her herself as much as receiving.
It was never a duty for me giving you my body, as some
women think, but a privilege. But I need to find the
woman who giggled with you in her mouth. And not the
one that can only see you bleeding to death, and Beverly's funeral, whenever she closes her eyes.

"Baby, I can't shake the fact of how close you came
to dying just because you loved me. I've spent many
sleepless nights worrying that the brightness of the morning sun out my windows when I wake up, might be from
the angels who came to carry your soul to Heaven, leaving me alone. Your mortality was just that fragile."

I touched and gently rubbed his hand. "Tomorrow,
Danny, the doctors will bring you out of your coma. For a

few days you might be disoriented and then hurt when you realize I'm gone. Please forgive me. You are the most wonderful person I know. Seeing you shot and near death almost broke me." I felt his spirit in the room asking me why. "The thought of losing you tormented me," was my only response. "Each time an alert sounded in the hospital or a doctor ran past the waiting room, I died. Day after day after day, that just wore me down. I have to go somewhere and heal, like you're going to need to heal, over the next few weeks. But there isn't a hospital for what ails me. Wait—maybe the looney bin."

I leaned down and kissed his cheek. Oddly, I expected to get a whiff of his cologne, the norm when I was this close to him, to carry on my journey, but apropos for me—nothing.

I couldn't look over at the nurses, as I skulked past, sensing they knew I was abandoning that sweet man fighting to regain his life. This time, when the elevator doors opened, it was nearly full and every eye was staring at me, judging me. Fleeing, before any of them could announce to those in the lobby about my despicable deed, I rushed out of the hospital door and right into a heavy downpour. The cold rain was a welcome disguise for the tears that had started—again.

CHAPTER 24

Danny

Danny debated going home first and changing clothes, but it had taken him all day, hell all week, to get up the nerve to drive to here, and any diversion might cause him to default on his mission for the third time just this week. Every other mile, he had questioned where he was going, and every other mile, he changed his mind and decided to turn around. Thankfully, the highway didn't offer him an exit at each mile when his goal reversed.

Another good reason to remain in his police uniform happened when two local North Hill Police cars slowed when he drove past on one of their more exclusive streets. Out of uniform, he would have been stopped for sure. Even as he pulled up into the driveway of an impressive-looking residence, got out, and looked around, a patrol car pulled up and parked directly across the street.

Something else was happening that made his choice of today maybe bad timing. There was a large gathering of people, he noticed after he knocked on the door and was lead out to the back yard by this cute teenager with her cell phone glued to her ear, wearing an orange bikini that barely covered her youthful assets.

It was funny, as if an alarm had gone off, when he stepped out the back door into a very large property with a beautiful swimming pool off to the right, tennis court off to the left, and tables filled with people in the center. Everyone seemed to stop what they were doing and looked his way. He was taken aback by the thirty of so people seemingly having a great time until he—

Danny was sure the uniform, even more than the color of the officer walking out of their house, was the main reason everyone became distracted. A policeman walking out your house was rarely a good thing. And for this family, considering their missing link, a very bad omen.

Other than some kids ignoring him, as they played in the pool, the adults noticed him right away, and some of them started walking in his direction.

"Excuse me," he said as he walked toward the largest group of adults. "My name is Danny Washington and, as you can see, I'm a Pittsburgh Police Officer. I'm not here with any bad news, so please relax." He smiled at them and tried explaining. "I'm here looking for someone, and I'm hoping you can help me find her."

Silence. Well, other than some mumbling among them. And then a tall, striking-looking blonde placed her hand on the chest of an older gentleman, keeping him there, and started walking toward him. He had little doubt, from Gabby's description of her sister Lea, who this lovely creature was. But her sisterly depiction of her failed to convey just how impressive-looking this very attractive woman was.

She was a few inches taller than he expected and, even at a distance, she was captivating. She was wearing a white bikini under a shear coral tunic, and he couldn't stop staring. With her blonde hair and blue eyes, the thought *Playboy's Miss July* came to mind

"Hello."

"Hi, Lea." From her wide-eyed and opened-mouth gaze, he figured that took her by surprise. She smiled. *Good*, Danny thought, feeling a little less nervous as she walked up to him. The others apparently were allowing her to dispense with this interloper.

"I'm sorry. Do I know you?"

"No, but your sister described both of her beautiful sisters." Danny held in a chuckle when the woman in front of him grinned at that complement and struck a pose.

"Right, right." She smiled again. "You must be Danny. My sister did mention you are the brave cop that saved her life. Are you here looking for Gabby?"

Her words gave him hope he might have missed her among her family. He looked past the tall blonde at the others there, intently searching the faces behind her, searching for the reason for his visit. "Yes, I am."

"She's not here," she said, "but she told us about what happened." She touched his arm, getting him to look at her. "We're so glad you saved my sister's life, and that you're all right."

"Thank you."

"Walk with me," Lea said, after motioning to the others that everything was all right. She took his arm, leading him around the side of the house. "Gabby, isn't here. She decided she needed some time to herself, but didn't tell us where she was going. She wanted to be alone and figure out where her life was headed."

"I don't understand. I wish she had waited until I could talk to her before she left."

"Danny, she was there at your bedside every day, all

day, until she was certain you were out of danger before she left town."

"I know, Lea. My mom said she would pick her up each morning and drop her off at home each night. My mother said she was wonderful."

"After all my sister has gone through, with the terrible things that happened to her in the army, to her boss at work, and then to you, I think she wanted to clear the air and figure what she wants to do now with her life, free of problems."

Danny hid the pain those last words caused. He didn't think it was intentional.

"We love her, so we all agreed that she should do whatever she thinks is best. How is your health, Danny?"

He knew she was trying to be courteous, but he didn't find Gabby here and that superseded everything else. "I'm back to normal, Lea. In fact, today was my first day back at work. I was very lucky and have a clean bill of health to do…whatever."

Lea turned and looked at him. "That's great, Danny," she said as they reached his car.

"Does she call?"

"Yes, every few days. She's doing well, she says. And no, Danny, we don't have her number. She asked to be alone but calls from those throw-away phones that are impossible to trace. I know." She shook her head. "My sister is protecting her privacy but being a little over-dramatic about it, but we're giving her space. She asked us to only call her phone if it's an emergency."

Danny looked from the attractive woman to the large and expensive house. Nothing was going as planned. "Thank you for talking with me. I didn't mean to interrupt the get-together."

"No problem. We do this a couple of times a month with family and friends, weather permitting. Hey, your showing made a boring party interesting," she joked. "I can imagine you're on everyone's lips back there."

He was sure of that. It wouldn't have surprised him if two or three additions police cars sped around the corner, lights flashing, and raced up to this beautiful dwelling. "Well, thank you for talking with me about her, Lea. At least I know she's okay."

"It was my pleasure." She then surprised him by kissing him on the cheek. "Take care." She started walking away and then stopped. "Danny?" she asked, not surprised that he was staring at her…exit.

"Yes?"

Lea lowered her head as if debating something. "Don't give up on her—yet."

He smiled and nodded at the lovely creature who then playfully gave him her Queen of England wave and walked away. The lady was married and a mom, and it was obvious why Gabby felt intimidated by her sisters. They were strikingly beautiful women, he admitted. Wow.

Looking across the street, Danny noticed there was now a second police car parked a block away. *They do protect the rich and famous*, he jokingly acknowledged.

He was about to get into his car and leave when the idea of Gabby being alone somewhere stole his thoughts. Instead, he leaned back against his car, looking down at his feet, trying to figure out his next move.

✂✂✂

Lea

"Why is he still here?"

"What?" Lea asked her father as she walked around to the side of the house and saw him standing there. Turning around, she quickly realized what he was talking about.

"Who is he?" her father asked, the frown on his face superseding the question.

"He was the soldier…well, and cop…Gabby told us about who got shot saving her life. He just wanted to know if she's okay. I told him she wasn't here and that she just wanted to spend some time alone."

"Okay, but why is he still here? You go back with the family, honey, I'll take care of this."

"Daddy, he's only concerned about—"

"I'll take care of this, Lea. Obviously, he can't take a hint."

"Daddy, don't—"

She stopped when he raised his hand as he walked away. She knew it was no use convincing him he was wrong when it came to his Gabby.

CHAPTER 25

Gabriel

My last few weeks here had been revitalizing. I came here confused about my feelings. Did I really love Danny? There was no doubt I did.

What troubled me was that I had lost the delightful joy I found for the first time in his arms. Maybe for good reason, after what had happened to us, but at one point, I was so caught up in the glow of our relationship, I didn't think it possible anything or anyone could come change my feelings for Danny. When I was more relieved than overjoyed he would recover, I knew something was wrong. I became anxious that the old me, minus the buzz cut, smelly cigar, and fifty pounds, and now a size six, was starting to resurface.

The one thing that had survived my sabbatical here was my deep feelings for that wonderful man. He was the only guy to rock my boat, in other words, drive me insane with pleasure, but it wasn't the great sex that I missed. Well, I did miss that very, very much, but what I missed even more was the gentle nature of that former army bad ass. There were times he tossed me around in bed like a rag doll and I almost reached the limit of physical endurance, but I loved him for that. I had lost weight, but I gave as good as I got—almost. It was the gentle way he would hold and caress me that I yearned for. That man, almost twice my size, had large hands that could sooth as well incite my body.

My time on this beautiful island had restored my joy. Finally, I was at peace with myself.

I'd gotten so tanned, laying out on the beaches every day, I could almost—almost pass for a native. Not really, of course, but this redhead had gotten a major tan. Looking at the white tan lines around my ass and boobs, I was tempted to go to one of the nude beaches here and make that an all-over tan. My main reason, dreaming about the passionate look in Danny's eyes at my unveiling. True, I might regret it years later when things sagged and wrinkled, but what the hell? The heat had purged me of all the negativity I was feeling as I walked along the beaches and shopped in some of the very interesting local outdoor markets here in the Bahamas. The natives had been overly friendly, knowing tourism was the livelihood of the island.

But today was decision day. I woke up in my hotel room this morning, thinking it was time to sink or swim. The first few weeks here were spent wandering around the island, basically confused about what I wanted to do with my future. Now, I realized life wasn't about waiting for a better hand. It might never happen. If anyone's life should reflect that truth, it was mine. So, you just played the cards you were dealt or you folded. I'd lost a good friend, but I also had a great family to lean on and a guy who thought sunshine shone out of my ass. At least he did before I ran away.

I'd been able to ignore my confused feelings the first

few weeks here by staying busy, but the reason I came here hadn't changed. After learning Danny would survive, I took a break from my hospital room diligence and attended Beverly's funeral. It was while standing over her casket, and saying my last goodbyes, that a taste of male revulsion flavored my mouth. The talent of the funeral director had erased most of the damage to the face of my friend, but I learned from one of the cops at the hospital, there for Danny, some of the terrible things that were done to her. *What's wrong with some men?*

I knew I was troubled when, after later learning my Danny would recover—where was the joy? I had prayed each night before bed for his recovery and, after my prayers were answered, where was the joy? Getting away and searching my soul for the answer was the only response I came up with. As expected, my family was in my corner and, even though they hid their concerns, they allowed me to leave with their blessings.

If the cause of my melancholy attitude was because of something Danny had done wrong, or had lied to me about something, or failed to live up to my faith in him, then I might be able to reason away those questionable feelings. But the man had been a saint to me in every way I'd wanted and a devil in the other way, and that was wonderful. *Then, obviously,* I finally reasoned as I spent time alone here, *the problem lies with me.*

With Danny recuperating, it gave me this opportunity to get away from all the sadness at home and clear my head. I'd done that. This month here had been nothing but very relaxing. I didn't have any clocks to punch. I could, and did, stay in bed some days as long as I wanted and also some days stayed up late into the night. There were days I went scuba diving and that was wild. On a whim, I signed up and took a couple of breathtaking boat rides around the islands. Feeling brave, I finally got up the nerve to take the amazing cave tours on the Islands. But just staying at the beautiful Atlantis Paradise Island Resort Hotel was exciting in itself. There was so much to do here. I even spent days winning, and then losing, and winning again, at the slot machines in the casino. I worked up enough nerve to slide down the highest water slide and laughed when my bikini bottom started to untie as I stood up. The men were staring and the women were frowning. *Tough shit, ladies*, I thought as I held on to my bikini, smiled at the men, and strutted my stuff walking away.

A couple of nights, after befriending some of the other women on vacation alone here, we went dancing at some of the clubs, and I was constantly hit on. I wasn't here for that, but I could have gotten into a lot of fun—trouble—because the guys were great looking and came in all colors. I did turn down all drinks delivered or purchased for me while I was sitting at the bar or a table and was careful to only drink what never left my hand. But every night when I went to bed alone, it was the brave police officer who I prayed was still recovering, who made love to me as I cuddled up with his sweet memory. After a month of imagining that, it was time to go home and make those saucy dreams come true. I was finally ready to face Danny and decide what I really wanted.

Had he moved on? Maybe. I could understand a man like Danny finding someone else to enjoy his strong arms. I knew that was a possibility when I boarded that plane and flew away. But this was what I needed to do to be whole. To be the woman he fell in love with. To learn to forgive and, most of all, to forget. I would be happy for him whatever he decided…well, after kicking myself for leaving.

Normally, I was up at sunrise and had a delicious breakfast out on the hotel veranda with the other early risers, or back in my room. Last night, I couldn't get to sleep, thinking about my decision. It was early morning before I finally dozed off and ended up sleeping in. Getting a late start today, I had to forgo eating breakfast and decided to go for a walk on the beach before it became crowded. It was already hot out as I walked down to the water's edge. It was a beautifully clear sunny morning like many on this breathtaking island. The air was fresh and I had already fallen in love with the salty ocean fragrance blowing in from the blue water. Standing there, looking out at a calm ocean—something I'd done many times in the last month—this wonderful island paradise was telling me it was time to face my feelings for Danny. It was time to go home.

This was paradise, but I was always alert not to be caught in any dangerous situations here. If I was alone, I kept to the areas where there were plenty of other people. Today, might be an exception because I was completely alone as I walked along the beach away from my hotel. After repeatedly turning around and confirming the few people out were much farther down the beach, I started to relax—but maybe too much. Because when I started back toward my hotel, I saw a lone figure also walking along the water's edge, coming in my direction.

I shrugged off any apprehension because he was also alone and looking around, apparently also enjoying the beautiful scenery, at least that was how it appeared to me. That changed when he stopped and stared at me. He was between me and the Atlantis Paradise Island Hotel where I was staying. My stubbornness pushed me to ignore him and just walk further away from the water. That lasted until he changed direction and started walking directly toward me. I continued walking, until I noticed he was apparently trying to intercept me.

Rather than face a possible confrontation, regardless

of how innocent and well meaning, I turned around and was about to head for one of the other hotels when something about the man seemed familiar. Ignoring that observation, I was about to hurry in another direction when I stopped and looked at him again. When I did, he waved at me. It was one of the guys I danced with the other night, I was sure of it. But even if it was, that was then and this was now. In a crowded club? Maybe. Alone on this picturesque beach? No!

Resolved to keep my distance, I turned to walk away when I—

It can't be, I thought as he quickly closed the distance between us. My fluttering heart knew before I did that it was him! I stood there on shaky legs as the tears started leaking down my face. All sorts of questions ran through my mind. He started running toward me, as if he knew of my dilemma.

"Gabby," I heard him calling out to me.

"Danny," I whispered and started running to him. I jumped into his arms, knocking him down in the sand. "Danny, Danny, I love you—I love you." I held his face in my hands and planted kisses everywhere.

"I know," he answered between my kisses when he could breathe. "And I love you, Gabby."

Okay, what happened next was my doing, I'd take the blame if pictures of it ended up on the internet, but he didn't seem to mind. I didn't even look around first to make sure we wouldn't be arrested for indecent exposure. I pulled off my shorts and panties, and then I unbuckled his cargo shorts. They never got down past his hips as I climbed on him and made love to my man. It wasn't legendary visual passion, on a beautiful sun-bleached beach, as the waves rushed in over us, like in *From Here to Eternity* with Lancaster and Kerr.

But it *was* very passionate, and only lasted a few

minutes for both of us, as we were so fired up, there was no holding back.

"Danny, Danny," I whispered, struggling to catch my breath as I collapsed in his arms.

It took a nice breeze blowing over my ass before I realized I'd better get dressed. When I did, he pulled me into his arms and hugged me so tightly I couldn't breathe.

"Gabby, I knew I would find you."

"I'm so glad you did. But how?"

"I'll tell you later. Right now, I want to go to one of our rooms, wash the sand out of my ass, and make love to you."

"What did we just do?"

"That was an appetizer, my love, I want the main course."

"So do I, so do I."

He took my hand and, as we started running, I pointed at my hotel. He smiled. *Great, we can wreck two rooms in the same hotel.* We didn't wreck any rooms, but the beds took a beating as we spent the day renewing our relationship over and over. I asked him—only afterward, I was ashamed to admit—if he was healthy enough for sex.

"Well—" He laughed. "—we did the research and proved that a few times."

Other than meals, showers, and sleep, our bodies were continually clenched together, either in the dance of love or just sitting in each other's arms. Either way, I couldn't get enough of him. The wonderful feeling of him on, in, and under me seemed unquenchable. And apparently, from how quickly he got...revived, our absence had affected him the same way.

"Okay," I had to ask after catching our breath between *research.* "How did you find me?"

He only smiled but that wasn't going to be enough so

I pinched his nipple. "Ouch! Okay, okay. Baby, you do remember I'm a cop? There are ways of finding anyone, especially those who aren't trying to hide."

I guess that made sense. He had found me and I was so grateful he had.

Between acting like honeymooners, the only other things we talked about was how we felt for each other and what future we wanted. In our paradise, we didn't permit anything or anyone to intrude. We were too very opinionated people who never lacked for words or subjects to share our opinions about, and yet we also spent hours of quiet time in each other's arms.

My Danny was amazing in bed and, after dreaming about this for weeks, I was voracious. It wasn't just the great sex that made me scream into my pillow, but the oneness I felt with him deep inside me with my arms and legs wrapped tightly around him. Oh, and this was funny. One time, I had wrapped him so tightly in my arms and legs, he couldn't move in me, and, for a few minutes, I didn't care, as I tried to squeeze this wonderful man even tighter.

The poor guy realized nothing was going to happen and allowed me to lose myself around him. He lost none of his enthusiasm.

We fell asleep that night out on the balcony after watching the sunset with a bottle of wine. And, of course, the honeymooners gave the bright morning sun something to watch out on that same balcony.

"Honey, we have got to get out of this room and enjoy this beautiful island."

"I agree, Danny," I said, while drying my head with a towel after my shower. He was lying on the bed in a robe after his. I walked over and sat on the bed with him. "But first I want to tell you something I've been thinking about the last week." Looking in those brown eyes, I took a deep breath. "Danny, I want to settle down and have kids."

That made him sit up and stare at me. I loved the surprised look on his face.

"Ah…who is going to be the father of those kids you want?"

"Well, I was thinking about putting an ad in—" was all I was able to say when he grabbed me by my robe.

I was only able to escape with the towel around my head. The look in his eyes signaled his intentions, and I almost made it to the safety of the bathroom before he jumped off the bed, grabbed me up in his arms, carried me back to bed, and tried to make those kids—now.

"You look amazing in all white with your tan, Gabby," he said an hour later after I took another quick shower and was getting dressed.

"Thank you, sir," I replied as I ran a comb through my hair.

I had seen this outfit on a skinny model type, parading in the lobby—who looked like she could have been one of my sisters—on my first day in the hotel. I later saw it on a manikin in one of the local stores and only got up the nerve to go out and purchase it when I saw that skinny model checking out of my hotel yesterday.

He was right. My white shorts and white silk low cut sleeveless blouse did highlight my tanned skin. And of course I agreed with him, that the shorts fit my ass perfectly, and my white pumps highlighted my legs. I thought it a little dressy for the lunch he wanted to take me out for, but I wanted to look good for Danny.

He was wearing white slacks with a yellow T-shirt under a white shirt. He looked sexy and handsome with that natural tan.

"Why did you want to get dressed just for lunch, honey?" I had to ask as I finished applying my makeup.

We were wearing swim suits earlier as we had breakfast out at the pool.

"Casual is okay for lunch here at the hotel, but there is this exclusive beach-front restaurant I heard about and I want to show off the pretty swan I'm with."

I stopped applying my lip gloss and looked at him. He had scratched every itch I'd had and some I didn't know I had but, at that moment, I was willing to jump his bones again if he wanted.

"Come on, girl," he complained, ignoring that do-you-want-to-do-it-again? look I was giving him—for the first time today, I might add. He was looking at his watch. "Lunch is waiting, and I'm starving."

"Hey, be patient. There might be a potential father for my kids out there, and I need to impress him."

"Trust me, with your body in those little shorts, that won't be a problem. Now after he gets to know you…well?"

I threw my lip gloss at him.

We walked out of the hotel, and he held the door open as I got into a cab. Danny gave him an address and our exciting day was underway. I was so busy looking at the island scenery, I didn't realize when we arrived. I was expecting one of the more upscale restaurants at a resort like Sandals, but this was more of a local hang out, and I was cool with that. I had spent a month here and loved being around the locals and partaking of what this beautiful island had to offer.

"We're a little early. Would you mind walking down to the beach with me?"

He seemed nervous or anxious about something, but I was up for anything—or so I thought. I allowed him to lead me around behind the restaurant, took off my heels, and walked barefoot down toward the beach. I thought he wanted to go farther, but he stopped in an open area.

"Gabby, almost from the first time we met, you have become very close to me. After what has happened to both of us, I can't risk losing you again."

I placed my hand on his cheek and was about to tell him I felt the same way, when he did the unexpected. This handsome man dropped to one knee and looked up at me. I was stunned.

Suddenly, I couldn't breathe. "Danny?"

"Ms. Gabriel Joy Sumpter," he said nervously, pulled a small black box from his pocket, and opened it. "Will you marry me? Would you be my wife for life?"

As I looked down at him, his image became blurry. Never had anyone convinced me they loved me like the man kneeling in the sand awaiting an answer. I was speechless, and not because I didn't have an answer for him. He was the answer to my dreams.

"Gabby?"

"Yes, Danny, I would be privileged to be your wife for life."

When he stood up, I again jumped into his arms and wrapped my legs around him. Thankfully, he was prepared this time, and we didn't tumble down in the sand.

"I promise to make you number one always, and to love you forever."

"I promise—" Then I started crying.

"Baby, you are going to mess up that pretty face."

I climbed down off him, took the hanky he offered, and dabbed my eyes.

"Hold on to that," he said when I thanked him and tried to return it. "You might need it later."

What? I thought, but before I could question what he meant, he took my hand and slid the ring on my finger. Of course, it was beautiful and looked amazing on my hand. Instead of a large diamond in the middle, it had equal sized diamonds completely around the ring.

"Do you like it? " he asked anxiously.

"No! I love it, baby," I told him. "It's perfect. I love you." Then I kissed him passionately on the mouth.

"Time for our reservation at that restaurant." he said after he returned my kiss and looked at his watch.

Needless to say, I was no longer hungry, but I allowed him to take my hand, lead me away from the restaurant I thought we were going to, and farther down the beach. *Okay, I'm game for whatever,* I was thinking as I carried my shoes in my hand. Again, I was wrong. He led me up a hill and, when we reached the top, what I saw had to be a mirage. I found myself unable to walk as I stumbled forward at his tugging. Finally, he realized my legs weren't working, stopped, and just held me up.

Standing there behind a beautiful white arbor trellis arch, adorned with red roses, and in rows of white chairs, was a group of people I dearly loved. Included in that group were four people who meant the world to me. Now, I understood why he said to keep the hanky. "Danny." Sobbing, I turned and placed my head on his chest.

"Honey, don't cry. This is a happy occasion."

I looked up at him, watery-eyed. "Danny, how did you—"

"Not me, honey, your dad. I went to his house and asked him where you were, and he asked me why? I told him because I loved you with all my heart and wanted to ask you to marry me. I thought he would be upset, but he just stared at me for a moment, smiled, and then took me to meet your family. Your mom and sisters welcomed me. I couldn't get a word out. The Sumpter women really are…something else."

"Yeah." I nodded. "Tell me about it."

"Anyway, he was the one who helped me set all this up."

I looked from the man I loved to the man I loved

first. He was standing with my mother, gleaming with pride. I wasn't surprised that he would do this for me. "Why is everyone else here, Danny?"

"For our wedding," he said calmly and started leading me toward my family.

"What?" I asked, wondering if I heard him right.

"It won't be legal of course." He held me by my shoulders "But since we've already had the honeymoon," he whispered shyly, as if someone might hear, "it's time for the ceremony. I did have to promise your mom and your sisters that we'll make it legal when we return home, before they would agree to come."

I looked at this man who had stolen my heart. A heart, by the way, that was pounding in my chest, and I was sure I couldn't take any more surprises. But if he'd asked me to jump off a cliff, I would. What else could I give a man who had captured my heart, soul, and body? I had found with him something far greater than the Sumpter curse. "I love you, Danny."

"I know."

I looked over at my waiting family, waved to my sisters who were dancing excitedly in the aisles, and then had to ask—*it's who I am, I guess, needing to reason out everything.* "But what if I had told you no down on the beach?"

My handsome man looked at me as if that thought never crossed his sweet mind. "I would have taken you back to the hotel and, when we didn't show up here, the plan was for them to leave, and I would call them later at their hotel with the bad news. It was your sister's idea for them to stay the weekend. She explained that would give me some time to change your mind if you chickened out. But your other sister secretly told me on the plane ride that I had inflicted what she called the Sumpter curse on you and there was no way you could say no."

"Lea, right?"

He just smiled at me. "She wouldn't tell me what the curse was—"

"Later," I said, putting my fingers to his lips.

"Okay, then, shall we go?" Danny pointed to the group. "Your—our—family is waiting."

He stood back and allowed his bride-to-be to dance, skip, and run to my family, and I was enveloped by them.

"Surprised!" a laughing Lea said as she hugged me.

"Yes, I was. You guys are amazing."

"Hey, you're a beautiful Sumpter woman." Shay hugged both her sisters. "Nothing is too good for us."

My mom stood apart, watching her daughters. I walked over and hugged her. "Thank you, Mom."

"You look so happy, honey."

"I am, Mom. I've found the love of my life like you did with Daddy."

When her eyes watered up, I was surprised. This woman could always handle the toughest situation without flinching. She was the Sumpter rock.

"He's a lucky boy."

"No, Mom, I'm the lucky one."

I came here to get away and better understand myself. It took missing the man, my sisters were now flirting with, to realize I was only complete with him. This duckling wasn't a swan, like the three other Sumpter women, but I'd learned that, in the eyes of the man being forced to pose for pictures with my bossy sisters, I was the most beautiful woman here. From the looks my parents gave him when he walked up and joined us, I realized he knew that he'd been accepted into my family.

In the middle of the hug-a-thon, I looked around and spotted someone sitting in a chair in the back of the group with this look of joy on her sweet face. Tearfully, I walked over to her. She stood up and we hugged.

"Momma Washington, I'm so glad you could come."

"Baby, I wouldn't miss this wonderful moment for anything."

"Thank you." I kissed her on the cheek and, arm-in-arm, we looked around for Danny. I found him talking with my mom and looking past her at the two most important women in his life.

"I think," the elegant older woman hugging me whispered in my ear, "in that man grinning at us, you have found the only man you will ever love."

Looking in those wise eyes, I nodded. "Momma Washington, I sure hope so."

"Okay everyone, take your places," my daddy ordered.

When he motioned to me, I hurried over and hugged him. "Yes, Daddy?"

"You're with me, baby. I get to walk my favorite daughter down the aisle."

"I want to thank you for—" I tried to say as we walked away from the wedding party.

"Not now, baby." He kissed my cheek. "We have a wedding to perform."

My family had come in force—aunts, uncles, and most of the kids. They set up a small outdoor chapel with rows of white chairs. The trellis was the altar with the blue ocean as a backdrop. It was like something right out of a movie.

Walking down the aisle, I noticed everyone had tears in their eyes. Including the handsome brown man standing under the white trellis awaiting his bride.

Walking down that aisle with my dad was the most wonderful moment of my life. He seemed as happy as I was.

"Thank you for everything, Daddy," I finally had the chance to say just before the ceremony started.

"You're welcome, baby. How does that saying go? The third time is the best."

I knew he meant that. It was no slight against my sisters. He was always trying to build my confidence. But he no longer had to.

Walking with him, my eyes were fixed on the man standing there at the end of the aisle, waiting on me. I loved him with everything that was within me.

When my dad placed my hand in his, my love was sealed—forever.

The end

About the Author

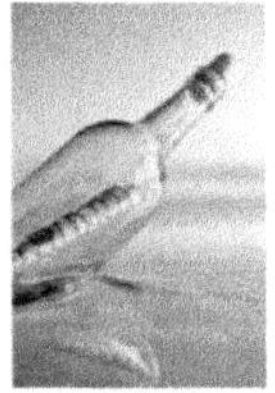

According to author, E. Lessly Taylor, "Looking into the mind of a writer can be a scary place depending on what he or she has to say." He started writing as a hobby, putting to paper the characters he saw in his mind. A place where he could take his vivid imagination, all the while presenting a calm face the people around him could be comfortable with.

Working twelve-to-fourteen-hours shifts, sometimes every day for three weeks at a clip, when an inspiration strikes, he would scribble notes on any piece of paper he could find. Riding the bus, he would get an idea and, afraid he might later miss the true meaning, scribbled notes on the inside of gum wrappers or on bus schedules.

His over a dozen novels cover a variety of subjects. "It's said great writers steal ideas from other writers," he claims. "My inspirations came from every day people. The words I've put to paper are meant to reach a variety of intellects and place them in situations they can relate to and with sensitive characters that energize their emotions."

Taylor's wish is that, when reading his novels, readers are taken to a place where the weight of life is lifted for a time, and, once again, that naughty you hiding inside can breathe.

www.ingramcontent.com/pod-product-compliance
Lightning Source LLC
Chambersburg PA
CBHW070428120726
47910CB00003B/693